shearwater

Andrea Mayes was born in the north of England in 1955 and emigrated to Melbourne in 1976. She has written stories and poetry since she was a child. Her writing has won awards and commendations and has been published in literary magazines, anthologies, newspapers, and broadcast by the ABC. Her first novel, *The Rose Notes*, was published by Penguin in May 2005. *Shearwater* is her second book.

For more information about Andrea visit www.andreamayes.com

Praise for *The Rose Notes*

'Andrea Mayes creates her characters with a crusty tenderness that is hard to resist.'
SYDNEY MORNING HERALD

'Part battle of wits, part romance, part mystery, this story has lots of heart, great characters and is charming in an odd, off-centre way that is deeply Australian and very familiar.'
AUSTRALIAN WOMEN'S WEEKLY

'. . . impressive first novel by an Australian writer . . . this story of a family secret has great charm, with its deft and subtle plot, memorably rounded characters and convincing dialogue. There's a deliciously quirky flavour in this parade of edgy characters and the way their lives echo across the years.'
SUNDAY CANBERRA TIMES

'Here is the amiable moral in this lively and sociable tale: none of the characters has the central role they give themselves . . . The story begins long before that...'
THE AGE

'The book is polished, wry and acutely observed . . . its author skilfully weaves subject matter and style, shifting her reader's sympathies with deft portrayals of complex people who all deserve our attention.'
CATE KENNEDY, AUTHOR

'A beautifully written story . . . Combining strong and quirky characters with the natural Australian landscape, *The Rose Notes* is a haunting exploration of the themes of isolation and ageing, and the truth behind a family's buried secrets.'
UNWIND MAGAZINE

'*The Rose Notes* is a novel rich in poetry and a deep understanding of the intimate connection between the human and the natural world . . . the story is satisfying and fast moving . . .'
THE COMPULSIVE READER

Praise for *Shearwater*

'Like judging a book by its cover, making an assessment on the basis of a blurb is a sin and sometimes too hard to resist. In the case of Andrea Mayes's *Shearwater* – "A delicious story of self-discovery that will make you laugh and cry" – you would be bang on the money.'
THE WEEKEND AUSTRALIAN, REVIEW

'. . . the disintegration and gradual recovery of Cassie's self-respect and the atmosphere of a small Australian seaside town - is very well done indeed.'
SYDNEY MORNING HERALD

'Mayes has a witty, engrossing style that pulls you into the fictional world of Cassie, hook, line and sinker. This book will have you experiencing the full gamut of human emotion from sorrowful tears to cheeky laughter.'
LET'SSHOP.COM/NINEMSN

'Most of all, it was the mystery of the strange Biddle family that kept me staying up at night saying "just one more chapter" . . . If you have some time on your hands this weekend and are not sure how to fill it, I recommend picking up a copy of *Shearwater*.'
MORNING BULLETIN, QUEENSLAND

'The descriptions of the uniquely Australian scenery, landscapes and coastal surroundings are vivid and imaginative. *Shearwater* is witty and engaging and entertaining enough to keep you reading right through to the end . . . '
THE WEEKLY TIMES

*For Margie Borden, dearest friend,
and for Barrie, who gave me Ben*

Andrea Mayes

shearwater

PENGUIN BOOKS

PENGUIN BOOKS

Published by the Penguin Group
Penguin Group (Australia)
250 Camberwell Road, Camberwell, Victoria 3124, Australia
(a division of Pearson Australia Group Pty Ltd)
Penguin Group (USA) Inc.
375 Hudson Street, New York, New York 10014, USA
Penguin Group (Canada)
10 Alcorn Avenue, Toronto, Ontario, Canada M4V 3B2
(a division of Pearson Penguin Canada Inc.)
Penguin Books Ltd
80 Strand, London WC2R 0RL, England
Penguin Ireland
25 St Stephen's Green, Dublin 2, Ireland
(a division of Penguin Books Ltd)
Penguin Books India Pvt Ltd
11 Community Centre, Panchsheel Park, New Delhi – 110 017, India
Penguin Group (NZ)
Cnr Airborne and Rosedale Roads, Albany, Auckland, New Zealand
(a division of Pearson New Zealand Ltd)
Penguin Books (South Africa) (Pty) Ltd
24 Sturdee Avenue, Rosebank, Johannesburg 2196, South Africa

Penguin Books Ltd, Registered Offices: 80 Strand, London, WC2R 0RL, England

First published by Penguin Group (Australia), 2007
This edition published by Penguin Group (Australia), 2008

1 3 5 7 9 10 8 6 4 2

Text copyright © Andrea Mayes 2007

The moral right of the author has been asserted

All rights reserved. Without limiting the rights under copyright reserved above,
no part of this publication may be reproduced, stored in or introduced into
a retrieval system, or transmitted, in any form or by any means (electronic,
mechanical, photocopying, recording or otherwise), without the prior written
permission of both the copyright owner and the above publisher of this book.

Cover design by Gaynor Murphy © Penguin Group (Australia)
Front cover photographs: flying gulls by Felbert & Eickenberg/Getty Images;
young woman by Soren Hald/Getty Images
Author photograph by Patrick Byrne
Typeset in 12/19pt Fairlight Light by Post Pre-press group, Brisbane, Queensland
Printed and bound in Australia by McPherson's Printing Group, Maryborough, Victoria

National Library of Australia
Cataloguing-in-Publication data:

Author: Mayes, Andrea.
Title: Shearwater / author, Andrea Mayes.
Publisher: Camberwell, Vic. : Penguin, 2008.
ISBN: 9780143005957 (pbk.)
A823.4

penguin.com.au

'Now, in general, STICK TO THE BOAT, is your true motto in whaling; but cases will sometimes happen when LEAP FROM THE BOAT, is still better.'
HERMAN MELVILLE, *Moby Dick*

'. . . none of us are anywhere near scraping the surface of what we should be crying over.'
CATE KENNEDY, *Sing, and Don't Cry*

'A man who is not afraid of the sea will soon be drowned, he said, for he will be going out on a day he shouldn't. But we do be afraid of the sea and we do only be drowned now and again.'
JOHN MILLINGTON SYNGE, *The Aran Islands*

Author Note

The town of Shearwater is a creation of the mind alone. All of the characters in the book are entirely fictional and bear no relation to any person, living or dead.

I

OBJECT OF ENDEARMENT

In that place, the birds come and go in great clouds, and the season turns at the rush of grey wings. Through spring and summer, dusk falls to their rhythm, and in winter the land is bereft, hushed and waiting for their return. These are the shearwaters, mutton-birds, of which the early settlers were so fond. Drab little birds, with spirits of tenacity and endurance, and other characteristics that some have found endearing.

They fly halfway round the earth to reach their coastal breeding grounds, returning to the same burrow every year. They mate at sea, mate for life, and lay only one precious egg each season. They cover hundreds of kilometres each day searching for fish. In sight of land they call loudly and frequently but at sea they are silent. Why? The human mind hungers for explanations even as the stomach yearns for diversity. Shearwaters were once hunted to the point of extinction when settlers discovered that the meat, arriving so promptly each September, was a pleasant change from their staple diet of mutton. Being an object of endearment isn't always what it's cut out to be.

She packs. Emptying drawers, stuffing clothes into bags, loading up the car. A part of her mind thinking of these things. A sharp little voice. She listens. It seems to know what it's doing. Take this, for comfort. And this. Better grab those too; you don't know how long it will take. She checks the credit cards in her wallet, stuffs the chequebook into her pocket, finds her passport. Identity. You might need to prove who you are. What a strange and skittering thought that is. She looks inside at the photograph. Cassandra Callinan. Yes.

I'm fifty-four years old. Where can I go? What am I good for? I am expert at dinners that keep without spoiling. *Sorry, Cassie, it's this damned Oreka business. Don't wait up for me.* Or it was the South Australian deal, or the Minne Brothers, or Cassek, Reicher and Hardy versus . . . Sometimes he didn't come home at all.

I am addicted to crime shows and the solace of a whisky or two, but I still draw the line at reality TV. You have to have standards. How else to define yourself?

Did they go to a hotel, or to her place? Is their bed anonymous, or familiar and warm, retaining the scent of their bodies between meetings? How often do they . . . ? She closes her eyes. I'm in the wrong story. I have been so careful. This was never, ever meant to happen to me.

She remembers to fill the petrol tank and stocks up on cash.

Then she's heading south on the highway. Driving fast. Anywhere. Away. Soon the city looms on her right and she's soaring up over the docks on the wide span of the bridge, driving, driving, and nothing makes sense. Flying along a curving cliff-top road, unmoved by immaculate vistas of sun-flecked waves, she is provoked by yellow warning signs of a 25 kph speed limit. Feels the engine roar in her blood, sees the car shoot across the road, dissolving barriers, soaring silver into wide blue sky.

'It wouldn't be like that,' she mutters desperately. Wonders how much blood and splattered gore, how prolonged the pain, and what certainty of death?

'One potato, two potato, three potato, four,' she chants, and bites her lip to stop it. Fear keeps her in the lane, as it always has. She drives for hours, the world a blur until by chance she sees the sign for Shearwater. Flickers of childhood. Summers long ago, travelling this south-west coast road on camping holidays with her parents and younger brother, Stuart. Damp canvas and spitting bacon, salt winds and seaweed and sunburn lotion. She swings the wheel at the last minute, earning a blast of disapproval from a huge Mack truck, and takes the turn-off. She's taken Richard's Mercedes Benz too, gathering up, more from habit than from any hope of a future, whatever scraps of solace come her way.

She cruises down the main street, looking for signs of anything familiar. I don't remember this. It's all so different. My hands are trembling. I ought to find something to eat. When did I last eat? Was it lunch at school, before . . . Before.

She parks. Walks over to the Post Office & General Store and sees a card taped to the glass. 'Peaceful, secluded furnished cottage for rent.' It might as well have had her name on it. She catches sight of herself in the shop window. A plump, motherly woman with a frizzy halo and a worried face. A well-cut brown jacket. Expensive leather bag hanging from one shoulder, the strap too long, the bag too full and bulging.

A bell rings as she pushes open the door and a voice descends from the ceiling.

'Hello? Won't be a tick. Martin! Martin! Can you mind the shop? I'm up the stepladder. Martin? Oh! He's never around when you need him, that man.'

A short round woman negotiates the rungs of a ladder with tiny slippered feet. Safe on the ground, she gazes upwards, one hand on her chest as though to calm the effects of altitude.

'Is it straight, do you think?' Her face is flushed. Little black eyes framed in a triangle of nose, brow and cheek, like a melancholy puffin.

Together they stare at a pyramid of baked beans on a high shelf. Cassie makes a mental note not to slam the door on her way out.

'It will have to do,' the woman says. 'You only just caught us. We're finishing up for the day. But here I am, keeping you waiting. Pity the weather's turned poor, isn't it? Never known such a wind, not even here, and we're used to gales. What can I help you with?'

'The cottage. I'd like to rent the cottage, please.'

'Want to have a look at it? I'll get Martin to take you out there.'

'No. No need for that. Is it clean? If it's clean and comfortable, that's all I want. Somewhere to stay for a while.'

'It's clean all right. I keep an eye on the place myself. How long will you want it for? Short term or long term?'

Good question.

Cassie remembers her father, Leonard, telling her mother how to make decisions. 'Shona, for god's sake. You make a list. See? Pros on one side, cons on the other.' *Simple, stupid.* Shona used to make lists diligently. Shopping, tasks, things to remember. She didn't list pros and cons though. Leonard made all the decisions. Richard made all the decisions too. No. Not true. We made them together. It's just that they always turned out to be what he had in mind.

Am I short term? Some lists, thinks Cassie, do not bear looking at. No doubt her mother knew that too.

She says, 'I don't know.'

The woman gives her a quick assessing look. Cassie has to quell an urge to run for the car and drive away. To where?

'You can pay a week in advance, or a month. Whatever you like. You'll find a front-door key on the inside window ledge of the outdoor toilet, but the door's probably open anyway.'

'Outdoor toilet?'

'An extra one. They had a full bathroom built inside. You'll see. If you decide to stay on for a while, you might like to pop up and see the owner, Elizabeth Savage. She'd like that. You can't miss her house. It's the big three-storey place up on the hill. Now then, I'm Myrtle. Myrtle Wilt. And that's Martin, my husband, out the back. Martin!' she bellows. There is no response. 'Daft old sea squirt,' she says. 'Two of you, are there? Any children with you? Friends joining you?'

'I . . . no.'

Myrtle waits with a cheerful smile to encourage an explanation. None is offered.

'Ah well, there's plenty of room if you change your mind. Two bedrooms, one of them all set up with bunks.'

Oh god, get me out of here, Cassie thinks, as the woman scribbles something on a piece of paper.

'I'll draw you a map, show you how to get there. You'll love it here, if you like the quiet. No one around much, once the summer's over. Low light over the water, lots of storms and rainbows. All the holidaymakers gone back to the city and only the real people left. You've picked a wonderful place to stay.' Glitter of unholy curiosity in her eyes.

Cassie sets down a loaf of bread, margarine and a jar of raspberry jam. Myrtle's gaze locks onto the pink gold of her wedding ring. Cassie slides her hand into her pocket furtively. I am oozing shame. Why? Why do I feel as though I could have prevented it? As though it's my fault? As though I've let everyone down?

'What about eggs?'

'Sorry?'

'Eggs. I have free range. Martin and I can't keep up with the chooks. There's only the two of us, you see. Even after all these years. Never blessed with children but it's fun trying, isn't it? We put the extras into the shop.'

Cassie is confused by these mixed revelations. Children? Don't ask about my children. Please don't ask about my children.

'First dozen free,' says Myrtle.

'Oh, I couldn't possibly . . .'

'Up to you. If you don't take them, someone else will soon enough.' She smiles, cocks her head. 'Won't it be lonely for you, out there in the cottage all on your own?'

Cassie, searching her purse for small change, doesn't answer.

'Anything you need, just pop in or give me a call. I've lived here all my life so there isn't much I don't know about this place. 'Course, sometimes you can know too much and that's a fact. But there's no way of unknowing, is there? Not that they've come up with yet. Plenty to see around here if you like the coast. Lots of things to do, even off-season. You'll see.'

Cassie allows the stream of words to pour over her and wash her right out the door. What an attractive proposition, she thinks. Unknowing. Halfway down the street, she discovers that Myrtle has put a carton of eggs into the bag with the bread, free of charge. She feels the colour rise in her cheeks. It is exactly these small acts of kindness that bring you undone. More of a threat to stability than any nightmare, or any fear. They creep in under your guard and weaken the walls, and no weapon can counter their attack. They come under the cover of a smile, and they go straight for the heart.

Nervously, she follows the directions to the cottage. It's on the far side of the river marshes outside the town. The only building on a straight dirt track running parallel to the dunes.

The front door is not locked. It opens onto the living-room. Cassie stands on the threshold, peering inside, assailed by scents, shapes and shadows that belong to someone else. In the air all around her and rising up from the earth at her feet come reverberations of the unseen surf, drumming on the skin of her loneliness.

Well, here I am.

No judgement, no explanations. No brave smiles. No pity. No whispers. Not yet.

It begins to rain as she unloads the car. By the time she's got everything inside, it is growing dark. She lies on the bed fully clothed, staring at the ceiling with exhausted eyes. Decisions can wait until tomorrow. It is enough that she is here. I haven't the heart, she thinks. I haven't the heart. In her arms is the pillow she has brought from home. She breathes in the scent of it, holding it close.

2

ALL THOSE YEARS

The first time Cassie Callinan ran away from home, she'd been nine years old, still spirited and rebellious, still believing that happiness lay out there somewhere, just over the next hill. There had been a row about homework. *You'll stay there until you get it right!* Her father. Left alone, she had scribbled Goodbye! across her schoolbook, slipped a tomato into her pocket and rushed away down the track that led into bushland adjoining a neighbour's property. Somewhere between the quiet click of the door and the tantalising scent of freedom amongst the blue gums, she began to realise that a tomato was no defence against falling temperatures and gathering shadows. She didn't want to be cold and hungry. She didn't want to be alone at night. She began to see how the fulfilment of dreams might require assiduous preparation. She crept home. Happiness would have to wait.

The second time she ran away, she was a grown woman, a wife and mother running from reality too sharp to breathe. It had been a mental absence only, merciful but brief. Too brief. An abrupt physical departure or gradual retreat had not been possible. She was needed. She came back. Mostly. It was obvious to her by now that happiness was forfeit for all time, for some wrong she had committed, somewhere, in one lifetime or another.

This time, her running away had been Richard's idea.

'You need to get away, Cass,' he said. 'You have to decide what you're going to do. You aren't tied to that school. Take some time out. I'll help you in any way I can. There won't be any difficulties over money. I'll see that you're all right. I don't want to cause you any more pain.'

Any more than I have to, to get what I want.

She was sitting at their kitchen table, twisting her worn wedding ring round and round on her finger. He stood beside her.

'Do you want some breakfast?' she asked, her voice ragged.

He didn't answer but she felt the sting of his exasperation and a small cry escaped her. She put a shaking hand to her lips to silence herself.

He said, 'Jenny Dalton's giving me a lift to the airport. She should be here any minute. I'll be back tomorrow night.'

She looked up at him in astonishment. He's going to work? Business as usual?

'Cassie, why don't you go and stay with a friend for a while?'

'A friend?'

'A girlfriend. What about Sheila what's-her-name? From school.'

Oh yes. That would be perfect. Then everyone would know.

He touched his fingers to the white gauze patch covering five stitches on his forehead.

'What will you tell them?' she asked.

'That I walked into a door,' he said, deliberately misunderstanding her. He hesitated. 'It might seem impossible, the way things are now, but I'd like to think we can come through this as friends. It isn't that I'm not fond of you, you know.'

When the front door closed behind him, she laid her head on her arms and contemplated the beechwood pepper grinder that was standing in exactly the same place as the day before.

All those years. A husband and children to look after, the house to run, the dinner parties for Richard's legal cronies and her own part-time teaching work. All that rushing about for everyone else. And more recently, she had begun to feel calmer. Becalmed. Stranded, actually. As though the house at Melaleuca Drive had become an island from which one might peer out at the living. But then, yesterday, Richard had come home early from work. In all those years, it had never happened before. One minute you are strolling along, basket over your arm, so to speak, looking in the wrong direction, listening for the wrong sound. A sudden rustle makes the hairs prickle on the back of your neck. You stop. What was that? A shadow takes on substance and there is no one to save you. No one can ever save you.

'We have to talk,' he'd said.

An earnest expression on his face, so she relaxed. Not a tragedy then. Not her daughter.

'What's wrong?' she asked.

He spoke. She heard the snap of bloody fangs in the undergrowth and stopped swinging her basket.

'An affair?' she said. Incredulous. 'What do you mean, an affair?'

'Come on, Cass. You've had your suspicions, haven't you? It's been five years, give or take a month.'

Five years?

He said, 'It's not an affair. It's a relationship. A serious relationship.'

He said, 'Look, we can do this the easy way or the hard way.'

Easy for whom? Pretend, she thought. Gain a little time. Do a little fast-talking, Cass, a little sweet-talking, a soft-shoe shuffle. Keep the audience engaged while you struggle to recall what you're doing here under a most unwelcome spotlight. What part is it, that you're meant to be playing? Why can't you remember your lines?

He said, 'Listen. It was never my intention for things to turn out like this. It was just a bit of fun when it started. To be honest, she's not the first. You have to admit that things haven't been great around here, have they? Not since . . . well, not since Tom died. You haven't been the same, Cass.'

Not since Tom? But that was a lifetime ago. Who have I been, then? All these years?

He pulled out a chair and sat down, elbow on the table, a hand shielding his eyes.

Sometimes, a last time occurs, and you have a real sense of its finality, a full awareness of the implications. But other times, you don't know. No one has warned you, and you would have it otherwise. Oh yes.

The sight of his hunched shoulders made her want to put her arms around him and press her cheek to his hair, to make it better, to make it go away. She held her breath until the impulse passed. What peculiar timing.

Is her marriage over? Is this it? She peered down at the outline of this preposterous idea. It didn't feel real at all. It felt like vertigo with a long way to fall. It felt like a farce. Who's that behind the curtain? In the wardrobe? Under the bed? Ta-dah!

Five years? Say something.

'Richard, please . . . we've been married for twenty-eight years. We care for each other. We talk, don't we? We enjoy each other's company. We . . . we still have regular sex, even after all this time together. We have Eleanor . . .'

And Tom . . .

'It's a good marriage. Too good to walk away from. No one on earth knows you as well as I do.'

'There's no point in this. It's not going to change anything. I've made my decision.'

Irritation in his voice. Obviously the time allotted for explanation had expired. And the time allotted for illusion. He was at the end of his patience and ready to strike. She could always tell. The averted eyes, that peeved narrowing of the lips. She lifted her chin to meet it.

'And sex?' he said. 'Sex? My god, Cass. Hate to break it to you so late in life, but good sex consists of more than lying there like a cabbage, however regularly.'

Cabbage? she thought, seriously surprised.

How to respond? Laughter would be good but has never been further beyond her resources. She reached for it and the sound emerged like the last gasp of a bird with a cat at its throat. It was a visceral betrayal. She felt the shadows of her own inadequacies huddle, point and gibber.

'I didn't hear you complaining!'

'Cass.'

'Evidently cabbage can be quite sustaining, as long as you have a little sauce on the side!'

He wasn't expecting sarcasm. She was breaking the rules of civilised encounter.

'It's beyond negotiation,' he said. 'It's gone too far for that. She's pregnant. She wants a home for her baby, a home with me in it. She's had a lot to put up with. I'm sorry, but that's how it is. There've been too many years of going through the motions, Cass. All the passion, all the fun in this marriage shrivelled up a long time ago, for both of us. I know it. You know it. Life's too short.'

The words seemed to float in the air around her. Pregnant . . . baby . . . home . . .

All except one word.

Cabbage? A domestic vegetable. Homely, with a hard, bitter heart.

You've gone and done it now, she thought. There's no going back on this. No hiding anymore.

'It hasn't been exactly easy for me,' he said, triggering an impulse in her that flashed, laser-like. She picked up a glass and threw it. Watched as it hit him. His head snapped back, eyes wide and astonished. The glass bounced once, rolled, and did not shatter.

Waterford crystal, she thought dully. It pays to buy the best.

In her mind she heard a song from her childhood. *One potato, two potato, three potato, four. Five potato, six potato, seven potato, more.* Saw a group of children, herself among them, small fists one on top of another, making a tower in time with the chanted words. She saw it vividly, remembered an accelerating rhythm, a scurry of excitement, but she couldn't for the life of her recall the object of the game, the point of it all.

'Jesus!' he said, holding his forehead. 'Jesus, Cassie. Look what you've done.'

3

AT THE EDGE OF FOCUS

There have always been Biddles in the town of Shearwater. Even back in the time when men hunted down the great whales with harpoons, and killed the barking seals, even then there were Biddles here, eating mutton-birds.

Jack Biddle has the look of a tramp. Wind-blown. Wind-tossed. Wind-chafed. Salt in his eyebrows. Sand in his beard. Layers of unmatched clothes and ravaged boots. Pockets bulging, stuffed with shells and seaweed pods, wave-worn feathers and secrets. He has rough brown skin, seafarer eyes shading from blue to grey when clouds gather behind them. Too much staring at the fine line between sea and sky. Too much staring and other things appear, out there at the edge of focus. At forty-eight he has faith in facts and something more, but not much. His philosophy is bleak but it's a bleak world, with no one to blame.

Once upon a time, Jack was a fisherman. Fished salmon, squid and crays off the south coast, prawns off the north, and in between he trawled a wife who loved him and warmed him and wanted to save him. They had a daughter, and lost her. Too many holes in the net, Jack. Tap, tap, tappity, the facts come knocking, crowding out memories, pushing away the dark horror of imaginings.

Jack lives alone in a flat over the newsagency owned by his father, Ralph, who lives downstairs behind the shop. Ralph Biddle has a soured and furtive face. Take what you want, said the god, and pay for it. Ralph has the look of someone who's paying for it. Resentments lurk in his ordinary eyes; grievances seep from his wrinkles. Father and son seldom speak, but it is good sometimes, lying in a bed that has space for one more, or sitting in a living-room that holds too many empty chairs, to hear the coming and going of another person.

Then there's Simon, Jack's younger brother. Some say the least said about him, the better. He's a fisherman and an amateur photographer, mainly seascapes. Reads a lot of books. Keeps to himself, mostly. Lives in a weatherboard shack by the jetty. On a shelf by his bed, a statue of the Virgin Mary with the babe in her arms. Every morning, first thing, he says a prayer to her for all that sustains hope in a man. In this man. He has an eccentric, ecclesiastical manner of dressing, favouring black clothes with a pristine rim of white – a high-necked cotton skivvy. A handsome face in a clean-cut, bland fashion. Hasn't ever married, and some know why.

Take a town, any town, small or large, and what do you have? Old houses, new houses. Old people, new people. Old loves, new loves. Old stories. The town of Shearwater is no different but, being small, its essence is concentrated. Its waters are littered with wrecks and its land with basalt boulders. Gales and geology have governed and restricted its growth.

High over the bay looms a mountain with no heart and ribs of black honeycomb basalt extending down into the sea where southern right whales come to give birth and rub off their barnacles. Orcas come here too, hungering for the newborn calves. What's yours is mine and what's mine's my own. Life goes on.

On the steep slopes, amongst ironbarks, acacias and casuarinas, lie dusky lava bombs with hidden cores of olivine from the deep mantle of the earth. This mountain once rose high into the sky. It sat quiet, simmering for thousands of years, building up pressure. When the boiling magma burst out, it took the heart of the mountain with it and left only half a crater behind. Long red tongues of lava ate up the land, hissing down the slopes, lapping their way into churning waves, sending up great clouds of steam into a sky grown so dark with ash and dust that it rained mud for weeks. Visible scars tell a tale and give fair warning. Careful where you set your foot. All is not as it seems.

On this foundation, the town grew. One hundred and fifty years ago, a muddle of huts around the succour of church and pub. Then came the squat, dark-grey buildings built to keep out the winds and the weather by men who knew all too well what weather could do. Later, there were timber and red-brick constructions raising salt-stained windows into the wind's teeth.

Anything for a view. And bright shop fronts with their banner advertising along the dark warp of the road.

It's peaceful enough now, looking down from the crater slopes at this small enclave, curled in upon itself, sealed and self-sufficient with its whorls of habitation and cultivation. By the time Cassie Callinan arrives, the town has achieved a more or less permanent population of 887 people. Most of the inhabitants live within a few square kilometres of the river mouth. Some of them still make a living from the sea, but only just. Some farm the sloping, grassy pastures of ancient dunes, with dairy cows and sheep. Others grow onions and potatoes in the rich volcanic soil.

Further down the coast road stand the regimented rows of the caravan park. Beyond it, the river winds through marshes, approaches the town in a diffident, leisurely way and is abruptly channelled by a concrete jetty in a straight line to the sea. Sturdy, paint-flecked bollards line the jetty. Down the middle, blue and yellow plastic crates are stacked and tied, wicker cray pots tiered and secured. Coils of rope. Pink and orange floats. The boats moored and pretty, bobbing and knocking fenders in the pale morning sunshine. *The Shirleen*, *She's Apples*, *Passing Wind*, *The Amy Peveril*, *Sagacious*, *Ma Cherie*, *Gunna Getcha*, *Dreamboat*, *The Gannet*. Busy figures, swabbing and swilling, cleaning away the remains of the night's work. Pelicans, patiently rising and falling with the ebb tide, waiting for scraps. A cloud of silver gulls, wheeling, swooping, squawking, coming back for more.

There's Hannah Oklow hanging out her washing at the back of the Sealers' Rest. Lines of coloured tea towels. Aprons and sheets. A great pair of billowing trousers. With a seam to join the legs, you could make a fine spinnaker from Fat Harry's trousers. She shakes out the creases. Take you right across to Werong in a fair breeze, they would. Hannah isn't going anywhere, except in her dreams.

Boards are out at the front of the newsagency but no point calling in for a paper because Ralph Biddle has found something better to do this morning.

The girl, Lily, cycling past, in a temper by the look of her. The pedal-power of rage. Body hunched over the handlebars, misshapen school bag clinging to her back. Her eyes a dull flash of olivine slitted against the morning light.

Beyond the river lies a chain of marshes, lagoons, sand-hills, and then the white lace scallops that mark the edge of the ocean, and then the dreaming deeps right out to the edge of the world.

Only one perfect crescent on this part of the coast, a sheltered bay on the far side of Shearwater Point. A sharp headland with a church of dark stone. An old cemetery – a waste of shifting sand and scoured gravestones, some that never marked a body's place. Drowned, you see.

Biddles there, too.

4

THE BATS

At some time during the night, Cassie had crawled beneath the quilt, still wearing her clothes. She wakes disoriented, limbs stiffened with the cold, and lies still, listening for clues.

'You can't stay here all day.' She speaks aloud, firmly. Firmness is required, and sustenance, to counter this miasma of unreality.

'Sustenance,' she insists and gets off the bed.

The kitchen overlooks a narrow back veranda where a brown vinyl armchair stands, cushioned with drifted sand. Through the window she can see the high ridge of the sand-hills, a louring horizon. The floor in here is grey flagstones, hard on the feet. A worn broom is propped in the corner by the door. Pine cupboards, orange bench tops with many cuts and scratches. A microwave. She flicks a light switch; the mains power is on. She turns on the small refrigerator and it judders noisily to life. A sealed carton of UHT milk, a tin of dry biscuits and a half-empty jar of peanut butter on a shelf.

Emergency supplies? Under the sink there are basic cleaning items, a neat pile of tea towels, a box of firelighters and matches.

Richard will be at a morning meeting already. Tonight he will fly home to Melaleuca Drive and find her gone. Will he be sorry? Five stitches to the cut on his head and not a word of remonstrance from him. A queer, shameful elation, when she thinks about hurling the glass. No comfort though. It puts her on the other side of something. Out with the wolves.

In the living-room, she sees a basket of sticks and pinecones next to the stone hearth, and six tiered logs. It is not even autumn but she lays the fire quickly and sets a match to it. The chimney draws well and flames roar up. She finds teabags, helps herself to the milk, and makes a cup of tea. One thing at a time. That's the way, Cass. One thing at a time till you can see where you're putting your feet. No home, no work, no Richard. The entire protective fabric of her life is gone. She has only memories to draw around herself, and a poor thin veil they make.

He always wanted a domestic wife, she thinks, slicing the bread, spreading a thick layer of jam. He wanted someone dependable, loyal and appreciative. Someone he could count on to keep everything running perfectly. And I served up gratitude for breakfast, lunch and dinner. Ate it on my own, too often. She looks thoughtfully at the peanut butter. I am a champion provider of food and ever-ready smiles. A try-hard (as her daughter, Eleanor, might have said with perfect scorn). But useful. Oh yes. I've been useful. I've made it all possible.

She slices more bread and takes it outside. Once upon a time, there had been more to life. Excitement, anticipation, hope. Way back in the mists of time lay the fragile beginnings of love. Were the seeds of this moment buried there? Was it something I did or didn't do? Is it something I am or am not? She walks around the cottage. It is not what she had in mind. She hasn't anything in mind beyond the vortex of the moment and the dizzying distance from familiar skies.

It will take her a good half hour to walk into town from here. The cottage is a long way from the flats and units built to accommodate holiday visitors. It faces the river marshes, its dark bluestone walls backing onto the high dunes and the ocean beyond them. There's a garage. Rickety grey boards with flaking green paint. An old bicycle propped against the wall inside. She eases Richard's Mercedes in next to it, grateful for a roof to keep the salt from the car. Richard would expect nothing less.

She finds the outdoor toilet in a bluestone hut in the backyard. There's a tap fixed to the outside wall. That will be useful, she thinks (just as if she is here on holiday), for rinsing sand from feet and cleaning tide-line trophies of doubtful provenance. She hears the laughter of her children, the murmur of waves, sees white salt-maps drying on little brown arms.

'Look, Mummy. Look what I can do.'

'Go and play, Ellie. I have to see to Tom right now. He's very tired.'

'Mummy, Mummy, I found a starfish!'

'Not now, Ellie.'

'But Mummy . . .'

She looks round, startled. There is no one here. Eleanor, her first-born, has flown so far away it seems unlikely she will ever find her way back. She now works in Boston, USA, with a team of management consultants. She rings home once a month or so, to see if there is anything she should be worrying about. She sends brief emails to her father's laptop, informing them of her progress and whereabouts. She flies to many places, but never home. Once, she had screamed, 'Get a life, Mother, and leave mine to me!'

The cottage will do. What does it matter? At least I won't have to worry about neighbours popping in, avid with curiosity.

Won't it be lonely for you, out there in the cottage all on your own?

Nothing on earth could make her feel lonelier than she already is. She pushes away the thought briskly and sets to, cleaning and organising, unpacking her clothes, setting out her few possessions, pausing occasionally to listen to the whispers.

Well, I for one am not surprised . . .

I never understood what he saw in her . . .

She was never really . . .

I always thought she was a bit, you know . . .

He will come, she thinks. He has to.

Two tiny mummified bats are lying in a corner by the bed, wings spread as if they'd just coasted down there to rest a moment, and forgotten they were ever supposed to move again. Leathery little bodies, perfect in every detail, except life.

Cassie picks them up, sees how they would have flung

themselves from wall to wall, corner to corner, ceiling to floor, until exhaustion and starvation brought them down. Blind terror. No miracles. They look so peaceful now. How had they got into the bedroom? The chimney? It's a small hearth. A bare, clean basket-grate. Green tiles with a cream flower. It's a lily. Very pretty, but formal, like a William Morris design. Someone lived here once. Someone chose those tiles. With what care and delight? Someone lit that fire to warm this home. She stoops and cranes upwards. No soot. I won't light it, she thinks. Too messy in a bedroom. All that smoke and ash.

An old mirror etched with a spray of wattle hangs above a narrow oak table. She puts out her Dior perfume, a sea-green glass vase that she bought in Paris on her honeymoon, the little flowered china jug that had belonged to her mother's mother, and a silver-framed photograph of herself with her two children. Eleanor, very young, blonde hair in pigtails, has a possessive arm around Tom, skinny and bright-eyed in his cherished Chicago Bulls basketball singlet.

She's trying to warm this home. Doing the best she can with what she has.

Next to the photograph, she sets down an unopened bottle of Valium and two boxes of sleeping tablets. She's had them for longer than she cares to remember but still doesn't think she's reached her use-by date.

The living-room has faded brown curtains pulled close against sunlight. She tries out the sagging sofa. It's so comfortable that she has to make a real effort to stand up again. A person might fall asleep forever lying there. It has a floral design of pink and green and possibly coffee stains. Can't live with that, she thinks. Not even short term. I'll buy a throw.

On the wooden mantelpiece is a black and white feather, a pair of binoculars, a scrap of shiny red fabric and a silver key that fits the cottage door. On the battered coffee table, a pair of sunglasses, a hardback book – Dakin's *Australian Seashores* – and a framed photograph of a young girl in a short red dress. The camera has caught her, hand raised to a strand of long brown hair that the wind has blown across her face, head dipped slightly so that she is looking up at you, and laughing.

Cassie gathers up these items and discovers that the scrap of fabric is a pair of knickers trimmed with lace. Lost property? She lays the book on the coffee table, aligning it with the right-hand corner, ten centimetres in, and puts the binoculars next to it. Everything else, she stores in a box under the sink.

The small bathroom has a deep, rust-stained green bath with more of the lily tiles, an old top-loading washing machine and a toilet. A second bedroom holds two sets of bunks. She cleans in there, checks the linen, and thinks, maybe Eleanor . . . without daring to complete the image in her mind. The future possible wavers and vanishes. Who would dare make plans?

She can't bring herself to throw the bats into the rubbish bin. She carries them carefully into the kitchen and props them on the windowsill, looking at them each time she passes. Upright, there is a smug complacency in their gnomic old-man faces and sightless eyes. *We know something you don't know.*

I need books, she thinks. I need something to occupy my mind till this is over. But all her books occupy a different space in another world. She has a vague idea that she saw a bookshop in the main street. It seems hardly likely in a town this size.

After the unpacking, she's aware of a brittle optimism. She walks around the cottage touching things, her photograph, the rough surface of the coffee table, the warmed and gleaming mantelpiece that now bears only an unnoticed smudge of fingerprints, not her own. I'll buy some new bedding. A rug for the kitchen perhaps. The flag floor will be cold when winter comes. And with that thought she is suddenly terrified and full of despair. Gradually, this too, ebbs. The fire comforts her. Life, she feels, is better than nothing, though occasionally, more often now, nothing beckons. Best wait and see, she thinks. Give him time to understand what he has lost.

At dusk, she carries the bats out to the river marshes. They are crisp and dry, as though one squeeze might reduce them to powder. Venus, the evening star, already shines in a luminous sky. Tomorrow, when she is sure that Richard won't be home, she will leave a message on the answering machine, telling him where she is. What will he do? He's always been one step ahead of her, understanding her impulses before she does, making light of her fears, manoeuvring her through tricky situations to achieve the best possible outcome with the least trouble. She struggles in a brief confusion of gratitude and compassion, knowing that rage would be far more appropriate. Oh Richard. How did you get us into this mess? How will you get us out of it?

A single swallow flies past purposefully, like a messenger in dark silhouette. Feeling somewhere between a fool and a witch, she raises her arms and flings the little bats into the air where they take flight, briefly, blindly, one last time.

5

HANNAH AND THE ROCK

Lily is fourteen and just about as bored, angry, fearful and hopeful as any fourteen-year-old can be. When she's sixteen and has some money saved, she's going to leave this shit-hole of a town and these people who never go anywhere and never do anything, and she won't be rushing back. She's got her dreams, Lily has, and she doesn't share them with anyone.

For the last few years, since her mother married Fat Harry and they came to live here in the Sealers' Rest, Lily's world has been full of strangers. Nights of sitting at the top of the stairs, secretly watching instead of doing her homework. There are men who come in so often that the pub is like a second home to them, and the others, the strangers who are just passing through but who come back again for the beer, the warmth, and the chance of a smile from Hannah. Any one of them might be somebody's father.

How they stare when her mother squeezes between the

tables. How they drool when she leans over to put down a tray of drinks, as if eyes alone might peel those clothes away. And poor daft Harry looking on, besotted, from behind the bar. Fifty-two years old! A whole twenty-two years older than her mother. All he can do, all he ever does, is to smile for the glory of her and he can't see the shame of it. Sometimes, thinking about Harry, Lily gets a pain in her chest that makes her savage.

Seeing the nudges and winks, sensing the hunger behind the smiles, she wonders how it must feel to have men look at you that way. Imagine the power of it! At night when she lies in bed, stroking and squeezing her own soft skin, it is Lily, waltzing between the tables, leaning low to put the beers down. It is Lily's body they gaze at, not Hannah's.

Fat Harry Oklow is a rock. He doesn't know it, or maybe he does. Maybe he feels the strain sometimes. But nevertheless he is a rock, a boulder, a fixed point about which you may, with total confidence, fling your rope, your grappling iron, your arms. Not too much is expected of a rock, except that it should hold true to its form and its place.

The rock is leaning against the table, meaty forearms flat to the surface and chin jutting forward. He is concentrating so hard that he doesn't hear his stepdaughter come in.

'God!' she says, spitting the word in his direction.

He jumps defensively. 'Hello, Lily.'

'What are you doing?'

'Nothing.'

He sits up and looks around, wondering what he should be doing, keeping an eye on the tomato-sauce drip as it moves slowly down the neck of the bottle. Will it reach the label before it solidifies? In front of him on the table are the crumbed remains of a vast cheese and pickle sandwich.

'How was school?' he asks, not expecting an answer and not getting one.

Lily spots her mother through the kitchen window. Hannah, battling sheets in a high wind, is trying to get the dry washing off the line. Harry hoists himself from the chair to have a look. The sight of Hannah is the only thing that can ever persuade Harry to move when he doesn't have to.

You can barely see the woman for sheets, wind-wrapped and flapping around her face and body. Lily gives a snort. Harry looks fondly on. It doesn't occur to either of them that Hannah could use some help.

'Getting wild out there,' she says, coming through the door with a piled basket under her arm, her face flushed and wisps of brown hair escaping from its top-knot. 'Be tossing the boats around tonight, that wind. They won't go out. There'll be no fish tomorrow.'

Harry, the luckiest man alive, sees her freckled arm stretched across the width of the basket, and just looking he can smell its secret soft places, taste the salty crook of her elbow and nuzzle the little cushion of fat where her arm meets the swell of her breast. She edges between him and the table with her back to him. He sticks out the low bulk of his belly to brush against her.

Hannah spies her daughter, hovering over food.

'If you want pie, cut yourself a piece, please, and don't pick at it like that.'

'Not hungry.'

'Looks like it. You're too thin. All arms and legs, isn't she, Harry?'

Hardly, thinks Harry, glancing at his stepdaughter's plump breasts before he can stop himself.

Lily, who hates being discussed even more than she hates her body, folds her arms across her chest and lets her long dark hair fall forward to veil her face as she glares at the floor.

'Give us a hand folding these sheets, Lily, will you?'

'Can't. I'm going out.'

'Lily–' The plea coincides with the slam of the door.

Without moving from the doorway, Lily turns up her collar against the wind and listens to their voices.

'She's impossible, Hal. Never lifts a finger to help. I can't even get into her room without having to put up with a week of screaming fits. I wish you'd have a word with her.'

Me? thinks Harry. Fat lot of good that will do. 'It's her age,' he murmurs. 'She'll grow out of it.'

'If she lives that long.'

Lily scowls. Fat Harry, bleating excuses for her. What a joke. The big tub of blubber, she thinks, and is suddenly ashamed. Harry loves her. But Harry loves Hannah more.

Hannah says, 'When I was her age, I was . . .' but she stops.

Lily wanders around the corner and sees a man in the

distance, cycling towards her. She waits to see if there's anything familiar about him. A silver Mercedes parks outside the newsagency. It's the woman that Myrtle was blathering about. The one who moved into River Marsh Cottage last week. The cyclist lifts his head as he rides by and gives Lily a smile, looking back over his shoulder as though he likes what he sees. Dirty old bugger! she thinks. A moment later, unaccountably cheerful, she pushes open the kitchen door. Hannah and Harry, caught in the middle of the sheet-folding dance, arms high and stately, stop and look at her in surprise.

'Thought you were going out?' says Hannah.

'Changed my mind. You seen that woman who's moved into River Marsh Cottage?'

Listen. Can you feel it? Gossip creates its own energy field, particles of possibility trembling invisibly in the air. The town sucks up your secrets, grows fat on your habits and hopes. Nothing is spared and nothing is free.

'River Marsh? Somebody's moved in?' says Hannah.

'Mrs Callinan. Drives a flash silver Merc. Going to be around for a while, I heard. Not just here for a holiday.'

An uneasy silence follows her words.

Hannah says, 'You're sure it's River Marsh, where she's staying?'

'Yup.'

'Who told you? Was it Simon? I've warned you, Lily. Stay away from him.'

'It was Myrtle, if you must know.'

'It's none of her business. And none of yours either.'

'Yeah, yeah, give it a rest.' Lily departs in a swirl of disdain.

They wait, still holding the sheets, until the house shakes from the slam of her bedroom door. Harry raises an eyebrow and Hannah, smiling now, smiling for Harry, in fair exchange for safety and serenity, advances on him with Tudor dignity, bearing the folds of fresh sea-scented cotton.

Emerging from the shop, eyes scanning the headlines, Cassie collides with someone hurrying past. She puts out a hand to steady herself, feels old bones, an alarming fragility.

'I'm so sorry,' she gasps, and meets a ducked head, a soft hat the colour of pond scum, pulled low over the eyes. On the brim, a scrap of torn green net and three blue feathers held in place with a pink nappy pin. Keeping her face averted, the woman darts between two buildings and disappears. Cassie stares after her in astonishment. No harm done, obviously.

6

SHAPE OF A WAVE

The great forward-moving swell on the open ocean is an illusion, created mainly by the gravitational pull of the moon. In exactly the same way that ripples will move forward along a cracked whip, but the whip itself does not move forward, so it is the shape of the wave that moves, not the water. Only the tiniest fraction of all the water in a deep-water wave makes any forward movement. It is a lunar triumph of *trompe-l'oeil*. Jack can occupy himself with this for hours. Sometimes, he'd like to explain it to someone else.

Facts entice and distract. Built one on top of another, they serve as conversation when simple words of interaction elude him. He can hide behind them. He can read a fact and sense the miracle. It is not enough.

When the swell moves into shallow waters, when the waves sense the sea floor at last, then the water itself rushes forward to topple and crash in a wild creaming of surf and spindrift. But far away, out where the waters meet the sky, there are different rules.

Illusion, he thinks. Try telling that to a squid boat caught in a squall.

From his nook in the dunes, he can command a wide sweep of the beach to the south. If he wants to see north, he'll have to stick his head out into the wind and let it rip the breath from his throat. He faces south, sees his brother Simon digging for bait and he ducks back further into the sandy hollow. Simon wouldn't be happy if he thought Jack was up there keeping an eye on him. A very private person, his brother is. With private pain.

Jack sees the albatross diving through spume trails torn from the backs of predatory waves. Watches a dark bobbing shape, noticing how it is not at the mercy of the ocean but at one with it. He imagines the sleek body twisting in muted turbulence under a swell, the bright glance offered up from intelligent, inhuman eyes. Seal.

He finds them sometimes, cast up past the high-tide line, not sleek and shining then but stuck all over with sand, matted with weed, eye sockets emptied of sight and flesh. Sometimes a mature seal, more often a pup. How do they come to be there? If the smell wasn't too bad, he'd stir them with his foot, looking for clues. Do they get caught by the waves? Do they misjudge the weight of water, hard as stone, tossing them up, then crashing down and breaking them? How is it that some are returned to land, and some are not? Where do the others go? Are they eaten? Does the flesh slowly break up into smaller and smaller fragments, dissolving into the ocean, becoming a part of the waves? Do they sink and become covered with fine silt, drifting sand on the ocean floor? Are there clean white bones lying amongst the nautilus and the wentle-trap, the green-striped warrener and the purple sea urchin, the scallop shells and cockles? A frilled white venerid lying reverently on an eye socket? A scattering of periwinkles, glowing like sapphires amongst the slender ivory branches of a ribcage?

She comes into his line of sight. Foreshortened, battling the wind, her scarf flying wildly, caught back and flapping loose again. It's the shape against the backdrop of water, the movements of the arms trying to control the scarf, that tell him this is a woman. Will she look up and see him? Probably not. Sunglasses filmed over with salt spray, eyes screwed tight against sand and wind. He's right. She pushes on past him, out of sight. Will she come back this way, or move inland over the dunes to where the river creeps through the marshes? His stomach is making lazy growls for food but he will wait and see. Waiting is something he is good at. Wait, and the world can tip you into action and save you the trouble of having to make up your mind.

The tide is on the turn now. The albatross skims the water. Pacific gulls hover and dive, and terns slice through the air on keen-edged wings. Two pied oystercatchers poke and dip their long beaks amongst the tangles of weed, shell and driftwood, dead man's fingers and Neptune's necklace, carcass and carapace and cuttlefish bones. One of the birds flies out over the water. Its mournful cry reaches him, a delicate vibration plucking at his loneliness long after the bird has disappeared.

This wind has sucked the last trace of summer from the air, he thinks. The shearwaters will fly out early this year.

Elizabeth Savage sits at her attic window, stitching a side seam with tiny, precise movements of her needle. She has two jobs on hand. There are trousers to let out for Myrtle and a hem to drop on Lily's jeans. She's growing so fast, that one. She has Hannah's looks too, god help her.

A dressmaker all her life, Elizabeth no longer seeks out these tasks but accepts them for the pleasurable habit of wielding a needle and because it has always been a principle of hers to be useful. People are less likely to forget your existence, if you are of use to them.

For all of her seventy-two years, she has lived in this town. Alone by her own insistence, she is nevertheless permanently within its embrace. The life of Shearwater surges and eddies around her home, built high on the basalt slopes overlooking the bay. The inhabitants roll close with their dreams and secrets, bedraggled bits of flotsam, but she is secure in her vantage point, safe on her perch.

The surf is rising. Seagulls hanging and wheeling strongly over the waves. Is that an albatross? She lays aside her sewing and picks up her binoculars. How do they negotiate the wind? How do they manage to be where they want to be, against the irresistible force of the air? Something miraculous in that. If I were out there on the beach, she thinks, I would hear the silver gulls calling their excitement to each other. It is one of the few sounds that ring out clearly through her growing deafness. Their shrieking squabbles on her roof often disturb her afternoon naps, the sound amplified by the chimney so that, lying there with her eyes shut, she imagines her room filled with birds, alighting gently on her shoulder, her outstretched arm, speaking to her in harsh tongues. Such a fondness for birds. She would have one here, for company, but cannot bear to see anything caged.

The day is growing darker as more clouds pile up on the horizon and wind raises the water to even greater heights. She moves the binoculars to the left and focuses on River Marsh Cottage. Beyond it, the high dunes prevent her from seeing the beach where Cassie Callinan struggles to keep her balance in a fractured world.

The phone rings. Elizabeth's heart knocks erratically. She's been expecting this call.

'It's me. How are you?'

'Fine, Hannah. Just the same as always.'

'I heard you let the cottage.'

'Yes. Only had the card up in Myrtle's window for two days. Amazing.'

'Is it a long-term arrangement?'

'It might be.'

'Was that wise?'

'Hannah, I . . .'

'You know what I mean. Is there any point going through all this again? You know what will happen. He can't help himself.

He can't let go.' Her voice holds more than a hint of accusation. 'I can't understand why you don't sell the place once and for all.'

Elizabeth does not answer, except to sigh.

Hannah puts down the phone.

'It's not for my sake,' Elizabeth says flatly. 'It's not a question of the money. I haven't done it for myself and I don't expect thanks.' She hears the absence on the line. 'I won't sell,' she whispers. 'I can't be sure what would happen if I did that.'

Sometimes the rut is deeper than they know, and darker. There's little enough that anyone can do to shock him out of it. She shivers, summoning the symptoms of a deep betrayal, an ingrown terror, but in truth, after all these years, she cannot feel anything anymore, except the little tides of daily fears and satisfactions, an underlying murmur of her closeted existence.

When darkness falls and the long spaced line of squid boats lights the horizon like small stationary moons, she will draw thick curtains from which not a chink of light escapes, and alone on the hill, away from the street lamps of the town, she will disappear from the world entirely.

Cassie, coming around the point, slams into a wall of wind, staggers and pushes determinedly into it. The wind resists her, exhausts her, tugs her lips into a grimace and whips saliva from her mouth. One step forward, two steps back. One step sideways. The long line of beach stretches before her. The town, hugging the basalt slopes, lies behind. The wind is everywhere. One step forward. You can lean into this force, Cass. You can let go. For one second, incredibly, the wind bears her weight, then dumps her sprawling on her knees.

Getting to her feet, brushing sand from her gloves, she hears Richard's shout of laughter in her mind. Twenty-eight years of marriage. How can she breathe without seeing him, hearing him, feeling him? What's the protocol? Till death do us part. Where are the guidelines? I'm not ready for this. I'm not at all prepared. There should have been a warning. A low growl from the bushes. The stale odour of old lies. How could I not have known?

She tightens her mind against the swift prickling of fear. He will come. There will be a resolution, a new understanding and, eventually, forgiveness. Don't give up on it, Cassie.

The swells come on, each one appearing first as a taut smooth line across water that rises as though sucked up by the sky until it towers, white-veined and dense with lifted sand. The curling crash begins at one side and runs down the length of the wave.

But all the lies, she thinks. Layers and layers of lies. And she has played her own role so well. As long as everything looks all right, it is all right.

The shining skin of the ocean creeps towards her, around her and away, sliding down the steep slope of sand again and again, gleaming briefly, erasing her footprints. She walks briskly to an outcrop of basalt, searching amongst the rock pools for a distraction from the single fact that her heart still refuses to acknowledge – that he will never come after her, that he will never again make it seem as though everything is all right. She has found space to breathe, but it is a space without boundaries, limitless as the ocean, and she trembles in the cool transparency of her solitude, in the rising swell of her fear. Reality goes rolling on, right through her, and she isn't getting any closer to the shore.

7

THE LOVERS

Gudrun and Grace have run the second-hand bookshop in Shearwater Road for twenty years, more for personal satisfaction than for profit, which is just as well.

Gudrun is Shearwater-born and bred but Grace Fiskett is a blow-in. Thirty years ago, she'd been passing through en route to Adelaide when she met Gudrun Wolonski and fell in love with her tiny, delicate features, olive skin and large dark eyes.

Grace is a monolith. A giant of a woman topped with curls that remain defiantly red as the years pass. She asks for little more from life than the ability to nurture and defend the partner of her choosing, and tells her so, rather frequently, and is forgiven for this and for everything, and loved excessively in return. She is never intimidated and rarely surprised. By the time you get to sixty, she says, there isn't much you haven't seen, one way or another. Nevertheless, on this particular afternoon, she puts down her coffee cup and misses the saucer altogether.

'Gudrun,' she says cautiously, 'there's a man in the garden with a blowtorch.'

'Mmm. It's Ralph Biddle. He called the other day while you were at yoga. Asked if there was any gardening he could do.'

With a blowtorch? Grace goes over to the window. 'Doesn't look like Ralph Biddle.'

'It is, darling. Here, put your glasses on. See? He's burning off the weeds. He's got the hose in his other hand.'

They watch him together. Torch – spray – torch – spray.

Grace's face takes on a mutinous expression. 'Tell him to stop, Gudrun. I can weed the garden. We don't need him.'

Waste of time. She can see it in Gudrun's eyes. Her heart's too big for this cruddy world.

'Oh, Grace, we've been talking about clearing it for ages. You know we have. He promised he'd have it done in an hour. It would have taken us days.'

'He gives me the creeps.' She shudders dramatically. 'He thinks we're godless women, you know. Abominations.'

'Grace.'

'They're a weird lot, the Biddles.'

'Not without cause.'

Ralph Biddle stoops to clear the earth of charred sodden debris with his bare hands, scraping it awkwardly into a garbage bag. He is aware of his watchers but he doesn't show it. He can see the judgement in the tall one's face as clearly as if she's yelling it at him. Always the same. But he can cope. After all this time, he's learned that much. A breakfast noggin of whisky and don't look at yourself in the mirror. Careful with the whisky, he told his sons. Straight path to the devil, too much whisky. Fires the madness in your heart and jump-starts your cock till everything's hunger and heat and a man doesn't know who he is anymore. Told his sons this, after the troubles, when everyone wanted answers, but that's the thing about the troubles. They all stopped listening to him. No excuses. He sees himself in other people's eyes. It isn't pretty. Still, he has a place in this town. A right to be here, where generations of Biddles have lived and loved and died. They can think what they like but they'll never know for sure. She's never said a word and she won't now. Bending to the bag, he catches the eye of the little bright one at the window and her kindness turns him to stone.

Grace groans when the shop bell rings for the second time.

'I'll go,' she says. 'You keep an eye on the fire-bug out there.'

Hauling her bulk onto the stool behind the shop counter, she glimpses Simon Biddle perched in his usual spot by the window, partly hidden by one of the big book shelves. They used to let him borrow the books until Grace found he'd been cutting out illustrations. Now he reads in the shop, occasionally buying something to forestall further protest. He always sits in exactly the same place, where light from the window falls onto the pages of the book he's chosen.

A woman with her back to Grace is studying the selection under 'Crime'. Tourist, thinks Grace, noting the smart heels. She won't get far wearing those around here. That dull frizzy hair might have been blonde once but it's closer to khaki now.

A good red rinse would brighten her up a bit. She stares at the soft cosseted skin, the dumpy little figure. Taken to middle age like a duck to water, evidently. Those thick pink-gold earrings must have set someone back a dollar or two.

'Want any help or are you happy to browse?' she calls suddenly.

The woman spins around, glasses in her hand. 'Oh! I didn't see you there.'

Pretty hard to miss. Smile for the customers, Grace.

Simon Biddle lowers his eyes to the book again.

The woman says, 'I'm . . . I'm just having a look, thanks.'

'Just passing through are you? On holiday?'

'No,' says Cassie calmly. 'I live here.' Her lips shaped the words. Her throat gave voice to them. Why? Why didn't you say you are here for a holiday? Having some time out?

Because it might be a very long holiday. Never-ending time out.

Cassie is growing to hate that cool practical voice in her head.

But now they'll ask questions. Where are you from? What brought you here? Where do you live? You haven't rehearsed this, Cassie. They'll all want to know. Listen to the whispers.

I live here, she thinks. It has the shape of a lie, but the awful resonance of a truth. Which is it?

'Oh!' She drops her shopping bag, glasses clattering to the floor. Blood on her hand. She puts it to her mouth.

'Look at that. You've broken your glasses.' Grace kneels and picks them up. A flimsy affair of gold wire and glass. 'The lens has come right out of that side. However did you manage to cut yourself?' She looks up into gentle grey eyes brimming with unshed tears. Oh dear.

'It's nothing. Really. I'm fine. Thank you. I have another pair.' Cassie sucks at the cut, feeling in her pocket for a tissue. There isn't one.

Grace takes hold of Cassie's arm and uncurls her fingers. The cut is a small one, straight-edged. Dark blood welling up from the cushion of flesh below the thumb. 'Rubbish,' she says. 'Come with me.' She doesn't relinquish her grip on the arm. Cassie can either struggle or comply. She complies. Years of practice.

'I'm Grace and this is Gudrun.' They are back amongst the coffee cups and chocolate biscuits.

'Cassie Callinan,' she says, holding out her hand to greet the small dark-haired woman and withdrawing it hastily as blood runs over her palm and drips from her wrist. Grace produces a wide plaster strip. Cassie holds out her hand like a child, waiting as the backing strips are peeled away. She smells smoke. Through the window she sees a sudden leap, a flickering of flame.

'Your garden's on fire!'

'Yes.' Grace, smoothing on the plaster, offers no explanation though her lips pucker in annoyance. 'Press down on that for a while and make sure it sticks.'

Cassie obeys and thanks them for the first aid. Makes a bid for freedom.

'What was it you came in for?' asks Grace, following her.

'I was just browsing for something to pass the time. I . . . I have to go now. I'll come back.'

'That's good.' But the tension vibrating in Cassie has Grace alert and wondering, *pass the time till what?* 'Take this one with you,' she says. 'It's a good read. You can bring it back when you've finished.'

'But . . .' Cassie protests.

'Take it.'

Cassie looks down at the book in her hand. *The Sunken Road*, she reads.

'It's excellent,' says Grace. 'Garry Disher.'

How do they know I'll return it? The offer seems to have a binding stickiness. She has an urge to push it away with both hands, but thanks Grace politely and puts the book into her bag.

'You'll be back,' says Grace, mind-reading.

On her way out, Cassie notices for the first time the man sitting in the corner by the window. From where she is, the book he's looking at is upside down but surely that's a print of a Caravaggio Madonna? He is very still, concentrating. Is he studying art? Religious art? The two women might be invisible for all the impression they seem to make. Thinking of him later, she recalls his short grizzled hair and black leather jacket and something else. A glimpse of a priest's collar. Outside, when the door swings shut behind her, she lifts her chin and walks purposefully down the street, just like any normal person with somewhere to go, something to do.

'It's worse than summertime,' says Grace to no one in

particular. 'Used to be the buggers would leave you alone when the season was over.' She sniffs in disgust. 'All these people wanting a sea change. I wonder if she's the woman who's moved into River Marsh Cottage? It's been empty for a long time.'

She looks at Simon Biddle out of the corner of her eye.

He carefully turns a page and makes no comment.

'Not exactly the chatty type, Miss Frizz,' she says to Gudrun in the kitchen. 'Very proper. Wonder what's bubbling away under all that frost? Something.'

'I thought she had the look of someone in shock. The expression in her eyes, you know. As though she's living in a different world. As though we're not quite real to her. Did you frighten her away?'

'Me?' says Grace indignantly. 'More likely that poor fool on the stool. He's enough to frighten anyone off.'

'Hush, dear, I think Ralph's at the door.'

He stands there, one grimy hand outstretched for the twenty dollars Gudrun has agreed to pay him. The garden is a blackened moonscape, stinking of the burn-off.

'Turn her over,' he says. 'And don't leave it too long. Just get a spade out there and turn her over. You'll be right as rain then.' He squares up to the expression in Grace's eyes. 'You've got a clean slate to work with now. Ought to get a bit of lavender in there, with that sandy soil. Cryin' shame to let a garden get into that state.'

'You've scorched the lemon tree,' Grace points out. 'We should be charging you for damage.'

'It's just a touch,' he says. 'No harm done. Best way to handle it when the weeds get to that stage. And there's no need for that tone. No need at all.'

'Why haven't you got the shop open this afternoon?' she asks, knowing the answer but wanting to distract him as Gudrun extracts a twenty-dollar note from her grandmother's brown teapot.

'No one around.'

Gudrun says, 'You've done a wonderful job. Thank you so much, Ralph.'

'Right.' He pockets the cash without a word of thanks.

Grace snorts but keeps it to herself.

In the bookshop, the fool on the stool listens and thinks about the woman who has moved into River Marsh Cottage.

Hours later, sitting alone in his shack by the jetty, he's still thinking about her, listening to the wind slamming into his walls. There'll be no fishing done tonight. A newspaper spread on the table but he's not reading it. A dusty, half-empty whisky bottle set before him – declaration of his powers of resistance. He has only one vice. Sins of omission and sins of potential but only one little vice that he puts into practice. A man of many faces. On her shelf, the Virgin Mary smiles demurely at the child in her arms. No room in that gaze for Simon but sometimes the light reflecting from a face full of love can warm a chilly soul that has forfeited the right to any.

He's seen the woman walking on the beach, taking her time, pausing to pick up shells and driftwood, gazing out at the sea. He was there, watching, when she walked to the edge of the waves and stopped. Saw how she looked back, first over one shoulder then the other, and began to walk backwards, awkwardly, trying to place her feet exactly in her own footprints and not succeeding. She uses the binoculars too, watching birds and the far container vessels that traverse the horizon. She doesn't have the air of someone on holiday. But she's brought little with her if she's intending to stay. He turns the clues over in his mind, gnawing at his fingernails. There is no need to panic. She's a nuisance, not a problem. *I live here*, she told Grace. Not there, you don't, he thinks. Not for long.

In the old rafters above his head, black rats and furry huntsmen spiders watch, awaiting the fall of complete darkness. Dusk is drawing in earlier now that the season is turning. Simon looks at his watch. At eight o'clock, muttering a prayer for the safety of those at sea, he will put out the light and go off to the Sealers' Rest where he will sit in a corner for the rest of the evening with his pint pot of lemonade, watching Hannah Oklow out of the corner of his eye, dreaming of her warm and pliant flesh, her wet lips at his throat, her hands stroking, unfastening, grasping, until he can bear it no longer and has to hurry home to pray for forgiveness, kneeling on the bare floorboards until the dawn lights his single window.

8

APRIL FOOL

In the soft glow between daylight and darkness, when the senses are bewitched and illusion reigns, the little shearwater has the remarkable ability to find the one burrow, amongst thousands of burrows, thousands of birds, thousands of chicks, that is home. How do these birds discern the familiar in a twilit world?

For Cassie, even the darkness here has the taint of the unfamiliar. In a life grown suddenly, terribly unpredictable, she conjures familiarity from meagre pickings. A half-glimpsed face in a passing car and she's turning, raising a hand in joyful greeting before realising, it couldn't be. Sitting in the cottage, a prolonged rumble of surf brings her to her feet. Richard's car! She'd know that sound anywhere. So many evenings sitting alone at Melaleuca Drive, anticipating the welcome flicker of his headlights on the curtains. Even when she remembers that his car is in her garage, still she strains to hear the sound of his approach, and the surf obliges. She gets up to peer through the curtains. The sight of her own anxious face looking back makes her feel physically sick. The burrow is lost, the chick is fledged and flown, but still she listens and watches.

There are many nights when sleep eludes her. She will not take one of the sleeping tablets, her last resort. Nor will she leave the relative safety of her bed for the strange cold kitchen where she might make a hot drink to soothe her fears.

Some nights, she is a little girl again, eyes screwed tight against the wash of nightmare. Some nights, she lies taut as a held breath, ears straining for the sound of someone else's breathing. When the wind blows from the north-east, there is no surf, and on those nights the silence is so dense you could break your heart listening for anything at all.

I am not very brave without him, she thinks.

In the mornings, she lies beneath the quilt for as long as possible with the whole day yawning before her. How defined her life has been. How gently regulated to Richard's requirements, Eleanor's needs. Now she has neither role nor duties. No energy and no use. What does it matter, Cass, how crazy you are, or where you are, or what stories you tell to protect and explain yourself?

'Who cares?' she asks the refrigerator.

It must have been tiring for Richard, dashing between two women, balancing that with the heavy demands of his work for five years. However had he managed it? But Richard always manages, always copes. Had he ever doubted that he was in control? Probably not. Sipping her tea, she looks at the casuarinas outside the living-room window and, picturing her other living-room, wonders if this one will ever grow familiar. The long curved needles press up against the glass like witchy talons, tap-tapping, and the grey tangle of twisting branches is an apt accompaniment to despair.

What if there was no one? No one to think about her at all. She plays with the image. Splinter beneath a fingernail. But if Richard isn't thinking of her right at this moment, he will. In the next hour or twenty-four, she will enter his mind, however briefly, and he will frown. And Eleanor is only a phone call away. *Leave your name and number and I'll get back to you.* Eleanor thinks of me from time to time. I know she does.

She looks at the walls again. At the furniture that is not hers. At the window and the world beyond, that is not her world. What if there was no one? What if I was really alone?

She has been trying to build a sense of routine into her days, even braving the inquisition of the main street. Excursions to the bookshop, the newsagent's, the post office and general store. Each one of these can comfortably take up the best part of an afternoon, if she walks instead of driving. When the weather is rough, she drives. It is her third week here in Shearwater and tomorrow is April Fool's Day.

'How are you finding the cottage?' Myrtle asks.

'It's fine. Cosy.'

'Let me see if we've got any mail for you.' She hands over what looks like a bundle of advertising brochures held together with an elastic band. 'I gave your cheque to Elizabeth. You'll pop up and see her sometime, will you?'

'Yes, I will.' Sometime.

'It's good that you're settling in.'

Cassie turns her face from Myrtle's inquiring glance. Look what he's done to me, she thinks. I could have made it difficult for him. I could have fought him every step of the way. But what would that achieve? Revenge? I don't want revenge. I want only what I had, and the chance to make it better. I want familiar walls around me.

She tries to walk on the beach every day. Healthy mind in a healthy body. Even when the sun is low and the shadows are long, hers are still the only human footprints she sees.

Today, in the valleys of the dunes, there are spaces of respite from the wind, invisible calm spots into which she falls, gasping for breath, only to be almost blown off her feet again without warning. It doesn't let up for long, this wind. It sings in the sand-hills, an eerie whistling rising to a wail. It creeps under the skin and scours the soul, exposing the old wounds of her insignificance. Low matt grey clouds obscure the sun but there is still some warmth in the air. She ploughs on, staggering through soft sand.

What if I was alone? Would it be enough, to see the sun come up and listen to the birds? To walk on the beach and cry into the wind? To greet strangers in a shop, or colleagues at work? To be, here? Would it be enough?

As she fights her way over the top of the last dune, an involuntary moan escapes her at the sight of the massive green walls of water. The noise is astonishing. Waves roar, crash and boil up onto the beach. Birds, swooping low and diving. There must be fish close to shore. Unable to keep her balance, she sinks to her knees in the sand and remains there, pinned at the centre of a maelstrom, blue scarf flapping at her back like a broken wing.

The following afternoon, Cassie remembers the bundle of brochures that Myrtle handed to her. She searches the house but can't find them.

How odd. Did I throw them away? I don't think I did.

She looks in the waste bin. No brochures.

I only walked from the post office to the car. I put it in the bag with the bread. How could I have dropped it?

'It was just a pile of rubbish,' she tells the kitchen table. 'Nothing to worry about.' But it niggles. The more unsuccessful her search, the more anxious she becomes. The eye can see what the mind won't accept, and the mind may register what the eye doesn't see. She has a bad feeling.

She finds the bundle, with a cry of triumph, down the side of the passenger seat in the car. It must have slipped from the bag when she drove around the corner.

'Knew I hadn't thrown it out.' Knew I wasn't going mad.

She takes it indoors, and doesn't notice that the old bicycle is missing from its spot beside the car.

In amongst the advertising paraphernalia is the jutting edge of a white envelope. Richard's handwriting. The knocking of her heart makes her giddy. She puts out a hand, grasping the arm of the sofa. Has he come to his senses? Is the pregnant one going to receive her just deserts at last? (But the baby, the baby . . .) Is he missing me and the home comforts I provide? (But the cabbage, the cabbage . . .)

'It's more likely to be something legal,' she tells the kindling basket, sternly.

Or a letter from someone else that he's sending on? She feels the outline of the paper inside. Not much there. One sheet maybe. She turns the envelope over in her hands. I can read it. How can he hurt me any more than he has?

But sealed, it seems to her that it might, just might, contain all the potential for her future happiness.

Fool!

Sauerkraut!

Her breathing becomes a tearless sob. The letter falls from her hand. How dare he? How dare he do this to her, of all people. How dare he make her hope? After everything I've been through. Why isn't he here?

She rushes into the bathroom, convinced she's going to be sick.

'Stay calm,' she tells herself, holding a wet cloth to her forehead. 'You must stay calm.'

Her voice is thick with fear, croaking. In the speckled mirror on the front of the bathroom cabinet, her reflection appears lopsided and pock-marked. She has to stoop slightly for an image of her whole face and even then it bears little resemblance to the face she remembers from the gleaming bathroom mirror at home. You are not the same, Cass . . .

'You tired old thing,' she whispers, smoothing her cheek. Look at those sags and bags. Look at this body. Gone to seed. Head like a dandelion puff. I'm all sadness and cellulite and varicosities now. Why would he want me? Why would anyone? I'm too tired. I don't care what's in the letter. I don't care if he's confused and upset and wants to be friends. I don't care what he wants. I'm not going back. Not yet. Not until he finds me and begs me to.

She opens the letter.

Cassie, your backpacking English nephew, Kit, has turned up here. I've put him in the guest room for now but it's not an ideal situation for us, given the circumstances. I have tried to call you several times but your mobile seems to be turned off. Call me, please.

Richard

Kit? Kit here in Australia? Stuart's son. She hasn't seen him since he was five years old. He must be, what, eighteen, nineteen now? I'll have to call Stuart, she thinks, and knows she won't. She won't call Richard either.

. . . it's not an ideal situation for us, given the circumstances . . .

For us? she thinks. For us?

And suddenly she knows, as clearly as if the admission is written there in black ink, that the woman with whom he'd betrayed her, the woman who does not, presumably, make love like a cabbage, has moved into her home.

She screws up the letter, flings it into the fire. It flares briefly, curls like a black rose, holding its shape despite the flickering creep of flame, the delicate glowing fracture lines between form and oblivion. And then, in an instant, all is ash.

9

CUTTING THE CORD

Jack Biddle is dreaming his dream.

Mid-morning. The sun is high. The heat still has a bite in it but summer warmth has left the water. The wind gusts fitfully from the east, with long periods of calm. Out on the horizon, a low bank of cloud is building.

A girl, tall and thin with short blonde hair, is high-stepping through shallow waves, sliding her feet into them without splashing. She's wearing pale bathers, visible with certain movements of her body, but otherwise she looks naked, a sea nymph who has risen quietly from the water and is about to disappear into it forever.

Jack can see the sharp angles of shoulder-blades, elbows and knees. Her arms are crossed and hugging tiny breasts, her body hunched against the shock of the water. Sometimes she turns a laughing face towards him. Sometimes she looks back at the dunes, searching for him and not finding him. Sometimes she raises a long slender arm in farewell.

Before the waves are slapping at her thighs, before she braces herself to dive, Jack is racing down the slope, bawling hoarsely, feet anywhere, arms out for balance. He can't stop himself. Susie!

By the time he reaches the beach, she's gone. Melted into the sun dazzle, an impossibility, a prayer, a shimmer on the immensity of the ocean.

At River Marsh Cottage, Cassie is in free fall, tumbling through memories, pleas, justifications, protestations. Hey, presto! Here is Richard, pulling her favourite yellow roses from his sleeve, apologies tumbling from his lips. All a mistake, he cries. All a terrible mistake!

She goes time-travelling. Backwards, of course. She has no curiosity about the future. It is a void. Who would want to go there? But she discovers voids in the past too. Blurred times where memory cannot find a perch. And Eleanor. There are whole periods of her daughter's life for which Cassie can recall only the odd, still image. It's as though I wasn't there, she thinks, knowing that Ellie felt that way too. Reason enough for Ellie to spend her adolescence and young adulthood proving to her mother (and herself) that she didn't need mothering. Didn't need love. Didn't need Cassie.

But I was there. I was.

And now nobody needs Cassie.

Too wounded, she thinks. Too many regrets.

At least the waiting is over. At least now I know where I stand.

She falls asleep just before dawn and dreams a deep-sea diver in an old-fashioned, lead-weighted suit, panicking on the sea floor. Movements grotesque and balletic. A slow-motion clown. Head encased in a huge round helmet. Her own eyes peer anxiously from behind its small glass face plate. Her mouth is open, a round O.

Fear rises in perfect bubbles and breaks out in sunlight a long, long way above her head. A thick cable, fastened to her waist, snakes up through the water, towing her across the seabed at a faster pace than she can manage. She struggles on in graceless bounds with heavy limbs and a fast-beating heart. Broad fronds of kelp sway in the currents and large slow fish swim past. Far above her, always ahead of her, is the dark shape of the ship from which the tow-rope descends.

Mid-leap, in a moment of utter desolation, she understands. She will never catch up. She will never return to the ship. Better to cut the cord and be done with it. As her gloved fingers fumble for the knife at her belt, she wakes.

Later that morning, staring through the kitchen window with the dream still thick about her, she finds it difficult to loosen the grasp of her hands from the edge of the sink. Her head is pounding and her throat is tight with grief. I'll have to eat something, she thinks. It wouldn't do to be sick.

The wind sends gusts of rain skittering across the roof. The door of the outside toilet slams and slams again. The violence of the sound hurts her. Its random rhythms shrivel her nerves.

'Must take an aspirin,' she mutters, and gives a harsh laugh. Aspirin! I'll be rattling with tablets, soon enough.

The door bangs again. It won't do. She slings her red anorak around her shoulders.

The second she steps outside, the wind drops and the garden grows eerily still as if waiting, marking the moment. High above her, white clouds scud past. Life goes on. She fixes the note to the door, breaking her thumbnail as she struggles to drive the drawing pin into solid timber. The paper curls up once, twice, feebly flapping, then it lies still. I should have put it in a plastic bag, she thinks. If it gets wet, the ink will run. But areas of blue sky are opening up and sunlight spangles the grasses, making the dunes shine so brightly that her vision blurs with tears. Suddenly fever hot in her coat, she shrugs it off and leaves it lying on the path behind her. What does it matter? She is tired to death.

The path to the toilet, flat and sandy, has never seemed so long. The she-oaks glisten and dazzle, raindrops caught amongst their needles. A stray rill of moving air swings the door. Bang! She winces.

The old white toilet is dusted with sand that filters down from the roof and blows in through invisible cracks even when the wooden door is closed. Inside, it is shady, a kindly light. Might as well go, now I'm here, she thinks, brushing sand from the seat.

It is such a tiny hut. You can lean forward from where you sit, and lock the door, and that's just what she does. She doesn't consider the necessity of the action, miles from anywhere and quite alone. Sitting on a toilet, she locks the door. She leans forward and slides the bolt into place with the small round disk that comes off in her hand as the bolt disappears into its own mounting. She looks at the thing stupidly. What?

Now don't panic, she thinks, panicking.

The bolt has snapped clean. There is no thread or rim, no way of attaching the disk, even assuming she could find a way to get at the bolt. She stands up too quickly and has to steady herself, leaning back against the stone wall. Her head is aching so much she can barely see, let alone think.

There must be something I can do. I can't possibly be locked in a toilet in the middle of nowhere. How will anyone find me? I'm going to be sick. No, I'm not. I'm not. There will be a solution to this.

She scrabbles at the bolt, trying to edge it out with her fingernails but it is bedded in the housing and looks like it's staying put. Stay calm, she thinks, and holds her breath for as long as she can. It's supposed to be good for panic. Twice, she fights off an urge to giggle.

It's too ridiculous. I can't even get this right.

There must be something . . . Screws? But the fittings look as if they've been there for a hundred years and there is nothing to turn a screw with, no way to get any kind of a grip on it. No way to rattle the door, made of sturdy wooden planks and fitting snugly into its bluestone frame. No handle, no ledge. It might as well be another wall. No – don't think that!

She looks up at the little window on the back wall. Two panes of opaque glass with a greenish tinge. She climbs onto the toilet seat, waits a moment for the agony in her head to subside and then calls out, banging her fist against the glass. It hurts. Even if she could somehow push out the glass, there is no way she'd fit through the gap. She pulls the sleeve of her jumper down over her fist and bangs on the corrugated iron roof, gasping and blinking at the sudden shower of sand in her face. It made a good loud noise but the roof isn't loose.

Who am I kidding? I wouldn't be able to climb out of there anyway.

Tears come and her nose dribbles. She climbs down and blows it on toilet paper.

What a mess. Am I going to die in here? How long can a person exist with only water to drink? It will be so cold tonight.

She thinks of her anorak lying uselessly on the path outside. I'll freeze to death. They'll find me here, one day. White bones and a wedding ring. She feels another giggle rise, swallows it. Hysteria is not going to help. She bangs on the door. Kicks at it until her head aches so fiercely that she's dry-retching. She slides down the wall and sits crumpled on the floor.

I didn't want this. It wasn't meant to be this way. Not like this.

'Help!' she cries. 'Help!'

Someone might be passing. Someone might hear her. Someone has to.

10

A RIGHT TO-DO

The aquarium is a shed, an old and storm-worn structure of planks and galvanised iron. Inside, under fluorescent lights, tanks of assorted sizes stand on shelves around the walls. A faint humming noise is always present; bubbles rise in the water, and the air smells of seaweed, wet timber and fish-meal. Most of the tanks are empty. Lily is alone and singing to herself, rearranging a table of exhibits – a dried swim bladder from a porcupine fish, a piece of driftwood fringed with blue goose barnacles, the grey fanned wing of a shearwater.

The big octopus has begun to ignore the restrictions of his tank and sometimes, like today, she finds him waiting for her behind the door. Just as well I'm here, she tells him. Just as well somebody looks after you. Simon's probably messing about on his boat or off taking photographs. Next summer, he's promised, the aquarium will be ready for visitors. Lily has learned enough about promises to have her doubts. Besides, Simon doesn't like to have people around him. Sometimes he won't come in for days. She doesn't mind. She likes having the place to herself. It's good to have jobs to do, important jobs, without anyone telling her to do them, and she understands that he needs her. When they are working side by side, when he explains the characteristics of a fish he's caught, or slips in a story she remembers from her childhood, about the monster crayfish that ate his bait and got away again, she knows that he is happy, as far as he is capable of happiness.

But she refuses to speak to him when he turns up wearing the stupid white skivvy under his black jumper, looking peaceful and mysterious, as though he knows something ordinary people haven't a hope of understanding. She doesn't ask him why he does it. She can't explain, even to herself, why it makes her feel afraid for him. She walks away from him muttering 'wanker' angrily, but never loud enough for him to hear. She leaves him alone at those times, obeying her mother's much repeated instruction to stay away, but not because she agrees with Hannah. What right does she have to tell Lily not to see him? What reason? Lily prefers to work things out in her own way, in her own time. Mothers don't know everything.

When the creatures die, when she finds them floating and bloated in neglected tanks, she hates it. She screams at Simon then. 'If you're going to do this, you have to do it properly! You can't just shut them up and forget about them!' For a while, he pays more attention, helping to keep the tanks clean and changing the seawater. Doing what she tells him to do. You see? She makes a difference here.

She used to write out neat labels and stick them on the wall next to the tanks but the creatures changed so often she grew tired of that. A tank now containing a juvenile stingray has the label 'Black Bream – Estuary' and various empty, labelled tanks bear witness to the passing of earlier inhabitants. Most stays are brief; Lily's efforts not enough to convince them of a home from home. It's as if they don't want to play anymore, as if it's easier to die.

She spends hours watching the octopus, looking for acknowledgement in those lidless alien eyes, or in the random gesturing of a tentacle. She has rushes of guilt about keeping him captive but wants him to be happy here, with her. She is crooning to him, holding him in her arms, when the yelling starts on the jetty and all hell breaks loose.

In the clear water at the jetty's edge, a stingray moves slowly over rippled sand. Grey fish, needle-sharp, dart swiftly in and out of the shadows. The dark sleek shape of a fairy penguin flashes briefly and is gone.

Kit Giller had walked along the beach until he reached the jetty. Ahead of him is the town of Shearwater and, somewhere, his aunt, Cassie. Like Richard, he tried her mobile number but with no luck. All he has to go on is the name of a town and a post office.

Sounds of activity issue from the moored boats, a smell of fish hangs on the air. Men in overalls with beanies pulled low on their heads stoop and scrub and stack. Kit feels unusually shy about interrupting their work to ask for directions. Imagines how, if one of them stops to answer him, they will all stop, heads popping up from every boat to check him out. The jetty seems as exposed as a catwalk. He says nothing. The heads pop up anyway.

To his left, some distance away, two young boys and a girl slide bum-first down steep metal handrails to land in soft sand. He hears the girl's high squeal, half-fright, half-laughter, and wonders why they aren't at school. It must be Saturday, he realises. I've lost track of the days again. He watches them for a while. The landward edge of the small crescent of sand is backed with steeply piled blocks of honeycomb basalt to stop the encroachment of the tide. Beyond is a line of low buildings. The post office will be on the main street, he thinks. That shouldn't be hard to find. Will they tell him her street address? What if they aren't allowed to give out personal information? He isn't even sure what Cassie looks like. She'll want to talk about the split, he thinks. She'll go on and on about it all, and how unfair it is. She'll probably cry a lot, like Mum does. Not that his parents are separated. Not technically. Might be better if they were. He sighs, consciously dawdling, reluctant to taint a clean, fresh day with a sense of purpose and responsibility.

After the awkwardness of Richard's revelation, Kit's first reaction had been to move on, fast. Middle-aged trauma is not his idea of fun. He'd come twelve thousand miles to get away from a mid-life disaster zone and walked right into another one. He hardly knows his aunt and uncle. Call in on them, his father insisted. They'll put you up, introduce you to people.

Thanks, Dad.

'Cassie's having a little time to herself, to help her cope,' Richard explained. 'She's not here.'

Sharon was sweet. Blonde and heavily pregnant. Sharon slept with Richard in the main bedroom.

Where's my aunt? Kit thought, and waited for someone to tell him.

'The thing is, Kit,' said Richard, after checking that Sharon had left to see her obstetrician, 'I'm worried about Cassie.'

Bit late for that.

'I've tried to ring her to see how she is. She doesn't answer her phone. She won't return messages. She just took off. All I've had is a message telling me she's in Shearwater, wherever that is. I wrote, care of the post office, to tell her you're here but I haven't heard back. It's been a difficult time for all of us. I was wondering if you'd look her up, Kit? See if she's all right. I know it's a lot to ask,' he added hastily, as Kit took a step back, hands raised, palms outwards. Whoa!

'Why don't you go yourself?'

Richard shrugged, smiled, looked down at his hands.

Kit felt fourteen again and wrong-footed. 'Fine,' he said. 'I'll go and see her.'

His uncle said quietly, 'Things aren't always as simple as they look, you know.'

But Kit wasn't about to get into a morality debate with a lawyer. Cass was family, his father's sister. Somebody ought to be taking care of her.

'Thanks for the room, and the food,' he said. 'Say goodbye to, er . . .'

'Sharon,' said Richard dryly.

'Yes, Sharon. I'll call you.'

At the last minute he realised it would have been a good idea to have used their washing machine and dryer. Too late now. He gave his underarm a sniff. Could be worse. Backpack full of grot, too. His jeans were ready to walk off him, but what the hell. The front door closed quietly behind him. No one came to the gate to wave him off.

When I find Aunt Cass, I'll listen to her, he thinks. That's what she'll need, I expect. That's what they all seem to need. I'll let her talk it out. How long can it take?

Basking in the little rays of his own compassion, he imagines himself discussing it with his father later. He'll be glad I was here to help. He'll be proud of me. He'll be sorry he got me into the situation in the first place.

Sunlight is warm on his head and shoulders. Every breath he draws holds the tang of the ocean. There's no rush, he decides. I can stay here in Shearwater. A few days should do it. And if there's a problem, if she's having a nervous breakdown or something, Uncle Richard will have to sort it out. They can't expect me to handle that.

He has a mournful image of his mother in her dressing-gown of quilted lilac, the day he left for Australia. Her hands like little birds swooping and flitting, touching his face, his arms, his neck. Eyes swollen and her naked face crumpled with grief. He couldn't get on the plane fast enough. Guilt is the price for freedom. He rings her every week and listens to how much she's missing him, how his father doesn't understand, how alone she is.

Sometimes, it seems to Kit that the older generation is falling apart. Thousands, millions of middle-aged people chasing dreams at any cost, or watching them dissolve. It's like they're staring the last chance right in the face, terrified of missing something or convinced they already have. And they are the adults. They're supposed to know what they're doing. It's seriously stuffed, in his opinion.

He sits on the edge of the jetty, legs dangling over the water, rolls himself a fat spliff and smokes it. Later, he takes a sandwich from his pack and eats most of it. He rubs small pieces of bread and chicken between his finger and thumb to make a pellet, then he takes out a hand line and drops the bait into the water. That's better. He's part of the scene now. He props his back against a bollard and pulls his cap low over his eyes.

When the hand line jerks, he's disoriented, shocked. Flicks it sharply out of the water on a reflex. Turns his head to watch as the fish – looks like a sweet little bream – sails over his head in slow motion, taking the line with it, wrapping the line around the neck of an immense red-haired woman.

Kit's mouth falls open. There is a second of stunned silence. Then all hell breaks loose.

Lily rushes out of the aquarium to see Grace roaring and trying to disentangle herself while the fish flaps frantically on the vast shelf of her breasts. All down the jetty, heads emerge from boats in time to see Kit let the hand line fall from his fingers as he slides spluttering, laughing helplessly, off the edge and into the water.

It is, as Myrtle observes to Hannah later that day, a right to-do.

They haul him out. Someone hands him an old towel that stinks of fish and worse.

'It's okay,' he mumbles. 'I've got everything I need in the pack. Thanks, mate. Thanks. Sorry about that,' he says to Grace, but can't meet her eye. They all watch, bemused, as he sets off down the jetty, dripping wet.

Lily steps forward. 'You can change in here, if you like,' she says, with a nod in the direction of the aquarium.

Grace yells, 'You've forgotten your hand line, you menace!'

He turns when he hears this, fully intending to reinforce his apology, but words fail him at the sight of her. She still has the fish round her neck.

'Bloody idiot,' says Grace, storming past them all.

The fishermen call after her.

'Hey, Grace! You taking your lunch with you?'

'Aw, Grace, throw him back. He's not big enough to eat.'

'He means the fish, Grace, not the boy.'

Lily watches in amazement as Kit drops his rucksack and collapses beside it, wrapping both arms around it and hiding his face as his body shakes in spasms of silent laughter.

'You want to get changed, or what?' she asks eventually.

He looks up at Lily. Well, hello Shearwater! But he keeps a

wary eye on the jetty. The redhead has gone. Work has resumed on the fishing boats.

'Any camp-sites round here?'

'Yeah, over at the caravan park.' She points. 'It's not far. Take you about ten minutes to walk there.'

'Guess I'll do that then. Thanks.'

She watches him squelch away. 'See you round?' she calls.

He waves one hand in the air without turning. She thinks she sees another shudder of laughter shake him before he disappears around the corner.

11

TIDYING UP

Had Cass been able to communicate telepathically with Kit right now, she would doubtless have agreed with his assessment of mid-life management skills. The toilet door is firmly stuck, the lock firmly locked and she is still on the wrong side of it.

Richard will not be pleased that I died in a toilet. A vision somewhat lacking in elegance. She would have preferred a wooden boat borne along on a calm river, a fragrant breeze, tasselled silk cushions, and the song of birds as the last sound she would ever hear. But where can you find that kind of peace, without someone interrupting, interfering, wanting to save you? You have to be practical, if you want to be sure. Sure, she thinks, looking at the walls and weeping.

She doesn't have the energy to panic anymore. Somewhere out there, people are eating, drinking, laughing, talking, quarrelling, making love, working to deadlines, running for trains, leaving phone messages, planning tomorrows. It is still daylight. It is still the same day.

I am dying from an excess of absurdity, she thinks. Even the universe is laughing at me. Is there no pity? This will be a truly ridiculous death. I do not want to die. It surprises her, this fervour for breath. The timing could not be more inappropriate or more excruciating. She drowses and wakes shivering, drowses again.

I didn't ring Eleanor, she realises. I didn't explain about Richard. I didn't explain about anything at all. Some mother I am. What if she rings home and the pregnant one answers the telephone? I didn't say goodbye. She will grieve. She will blame herself. She will try to convince Richard that it wasn't his fault but that won't work. Who will comfort her? Who can comfort me? Who was ever able to comfort me?

She sees herself standing at the far end of the garden, at the house where she'd grown up. There's the peach tree, her mother, Shona, on her knees beneath it, hands busy in the dirt. What is she doing?

'Hi, Mum.'

Shona looks up at her daughter. 'You took your time,' she says.

'I know. I'm sorry. I've been really busy the last few months. It's the school hols now. I thought I'd come and see how you both are.'

Her mother has returned to her earlier preoccupation. Cassie watches, curious.

Shona is picking up leaves, one by one, and arranging them

on top of each other in neat little stacks around the base of the tree. They look like offerings.

'What are you doing, Mum?'

'I'm tidying up,' says Shona, getting to her feet and brushing off her knees. 'No one else is going to do it, are they?'

'But . . .'

Cassie's father, Leonard, comes out of the house and calls to her. 'If you want lunch, I hope you've brought it with you. You won't find anything to eat here. She does nothing around this place. Nothing!'

Cassie half-turns to him and turning back is in time to see her mother's right leg move out and across, as her arms go up into the air and she flows into a slow pirouette before falling heavily, flat on the ground. By the time her daughter reaches her, Shona is dead.

Leonard looks from his daughter's face to his wife's body. His eyes, behind their round spectacles, reflect nothing but astonishment.

'That's it then,' he says. 'If I had my way again, I'd never have married her.'

His own decline had been rapid. Cassie and Stuart managed to find him a place in a home that had, they agreed, a comforting atmosphere with its large gardens and pleasant staff. Leonard kept trying to escape, slipping through doors, beyond gates, walking purposefully in any direction. When they found him and asked him where he was going, he'd tell them in a tone of gentle admonition that he was going to find Shona, of course.

Staff had to lock the doors because he became such a nuisance, missing at all hours of the day and night, wandering the streets, sometimes in his pyjamas. He always remembered to put on his hat – Shona liked to see him in his hat – but he didn't always remember his socks or his shoes, or his trousers. Shortly after they'd begun to lock him in, they found him one day, in raincoat and boots, kneeling behind the front door, calmly unscrewing the hinges. Nurse Morrissey lost patience and raised her voice.

'You aren't going to find Shona, Mr Giller. She's dead. Dead. Do you understand? You aren't ever going to find her, so you might as well give me that screwdriver.'

He pushed her roughly out of the way and ran around the hall uttering little cries of distress, the raincoat flapping around his scrawny calves. From then on, it was a matter of steadily increasing sedation until the end came.

The stone wall behind her shoulder-blades is cold and hard. She draws up her knees and leans her head on them. *If I had my way again, I'd never have married her*. She didn't blame her father for feeling that way; she blamed him for telling her. For the dead weight of lost time, lost hopes, that he dropped on her shoulders. For the sadness that was his to carry, not hers. There are some things your children do not need to know, and that's a fact.

Shona had married for love. It didn't last. Metamorphosed into martyrdom, and nobody cared.

You're on your own.

Please, please, somebody, come and set me free.

12

THE WAVING OF PRAWNS

Once he's got his camp-site organised and tent set up, Kit takes a long hot shower to wash the brine from his skin and the ganja from his head. Every time he thinks about the giant woman with the fish around her neck, he yelps. Can't help himself. That girl was cute. Keen too. Might wander back there, he thinks, pulling on his one dry pair of jeans and least filthy T-shirt. She probably thinks he's a total dickhead, after pulling that stunt. They all will. What a way to introduce himself.

I wish Sara and Annie could have seen it, he thinks. The two girls had travelled with him for three months from Cape York, where the three had met up, all the way down to the south coast. They left him in Melbourne to go on to Thailand, beseeching him to come with them, but Kit had had enough partying for a while, and it was getting to be an issue, who slept in which tent. The girls had declared it made sense to share one – his – instead of putting up their own, and that usually resulted in nobody getting much rest unless they were stoned. It's too easy to get stuck with people. He'll miss them, but not enough to want to go along. It's not hard to pick up a woman, he thinks. Trick is to find one who doesn't cramp your style.

He drapes his wet gear over the tent. If it hasn't blown away when he gets back, it will be dry. Washed too. Sort of. His mother would have a fit. But what she doesn't know can't hurt her. Sometimes he wants to go home, but mostly, thinking about the pressure of being the person his parents want him to be, well, it's enough to keep him walking.

He's grinning to himself as he swaggers up to the shed at the end of the jetty. No sign of the girl but someone's in there. He can hear hammering. Above his head, rough blue lettering with a crude fish design on driftwood: Aquarium. He raps at the door. No one answers but the banging stops. He pushes the door open a little way.

'Shit!' screams a voice. 'Stay where you are! Don't touch the door.'

Kit freezes.

The girl comes, peers at him, bends down and scoops something off the concrete floor. Eyes not yet adjusted to the shade inside, Kit can't make out what it is.

'Sorry,' he says. 'I had no idea . . .'

'Shouldn't go pushing open doors if you don't know what's behind them,' Lily says crossly, but she softens this with a smile when she realises who it is. 'Hi.'

'Hiya.'

'You look better dry,' she says.

You look good enough to eat, he thinks. 'Thought I ought to find the woman who . . . you know. And apologise or something.'

'Oh, Grace. She'll be all right. Funny as, wasn't it?'

'Yeah.'

'You're English.'

'How can you tell?'

She misses the sarcasm. 'The way you talk.'

'Ah.'

'Did you find the caravan park?'

'Yes, thanks. I'm Kit, by the way.'

'Kit?'

'Short for Christopher.'

'I'm Lily.' She pauses, searching for something else to say. 'Where've you come from?'

'Down that way,' he gestures vaguely in the direction of the sea. 'I walked up the beach from Lawes River.'

'That's a fair walk.'

'I've come a lot further than that. I've been backpacking around Australia for months.'

Her eyes are so green.

'On your own? Backpacking?' she asks.

'On my own,' he lies. He's never seen green eyes before.

'Don't you get lonely?'

'Yeah,' he says, holding her gaze meaningfully.

Lily looks away. 'I'd like that,' she says. 'Leaving everybody. Leaving here. Why don't you come in? I have to put this one back in the tank before he gets the idea he can stay out for good.'

As if in protest, the bundle in her arms begins to stir. Brown tentacles writhe slowly towards her neck, flushing from brown to rosy orange as they move across her tight scarlet cardigan.

'Bloody hell!' says Kit, awestruck. It's an octopus.

'I look after the aquarium,' she tells him proudly. She tilts her head to the octopus. 'This one gets out and waits for me by the door. I was just fixing an extra bit of netting to the frame across the top of his tank. It's for his own good. You nearly flattened him.'

'Sorry.' Kit's attention is now divided between the creature that Lily holds so firmly and the line of pale plump flesh exposed between the edge of her cardigan and the top of her jeans.

Lily detaches a tentacle from her neck and pushes at one that is trying to explore her mouth. It curls and tightens around her waving finger.

'Feel the suckers,' she says. 'They're really weird.'

He brushes a tentacle gingerly with one finger. 'Where d'you find them?'

'Simon found this one at low tide under a ledge in one of the rock pools.'

'I thought they were the grand masters of camouflage.'

'They are, until you wave a prawn at them.'

Her wry delivery of this remark surprises him. His interest in her sharpens.

'Have you seen it done?'

'Heaps of times. Done it myself.'

'And you keep them in these tanks?'

'Sometimes. Simon catches them for bait too.'

'Bait? Ugh.'

'Easy to see you're not a fisherman.'

'Don't know about that,' he says, smirking. 'Caught a woman with a hand line not so long ago.'

'She must have liked the look of your bait. It takes all sorts,' says Lily smartly. 'But you're a clever one, aren't you?' She's talking to the octopus. 'Sometimes he climbs out, raids the crab tanks and then climbs back into his own.'

'How do you know?'

'Vanishing crabs and an octopus with a big smile on his face.'

'How long can he live out of water?'

'I don't know.' She frowns. 'At any rate, he's not dead yet. I guess he's bright enough not to stay out too long.'

'The tanks look a bit on the small side.'

'Simon's only just started the aquarium. By the summer he'll have huge tanks all along that wall,' she says, improvising defensively. 'Anyway, the octopus is happy here.'

Kit doubts that. Imagines the creature behind the door, day after day, patiently awaiting its chance for a mad slither to freedom, only to find Lily's arms. Poor thing, blending with these surroundings, confined and defined by them.

He reads one of the notes taped to the wall.

'Fact: If an octopus goes blind, it loses its ability to change colour because it can no longer tell what colour is needed because it doesn't know the colours that surround it anymore.'

'Is that true?'

'It says "fact", doesn't it?'

'How do you know?'

'Simon told me. He knows lots of things,' she says, unwilling to admit that she'd learned this from her own reading.

'Who's the photographer?' he asks, indicating the seascapes that almost cover one wall. They have been shot at various times of the day in different light and weather conditions. All of them depict sea and sky, nothing else. Not even a bird. Every living thing is below the water, behind the clouds, out of the frame.

'They're Simon's. It's a hobby of his, taking photos. That one's my favourite.' It's a large photograph. A layering of white and pale-grey cloud that appears to feather vertically upwards, plumes of white bursting into the sky, and fringing prisms of rain falling into the sea.

'It's good. He knows what he's doing,' says Kit, casually assuming an expertise he doesn't have. 'Does he sell them?'

'No.'

She untwines the octopus and puts him onto the rock in his tank, refastening the netting.

'I'll be back in a minute,' she says, hurrying through another door. 'Just keep an eye on him.'

He watches nervously as the octopus slips down into the water, a dull apricot colour now, its body wrinkled as a scrotum, or old soft fruit. It squashes up against the glass of the tank, flattened like the nose of a child pressed to a window. Long tentacles moving independently of each other, questing, touching, curling and uncurling in a slow, sensual dance with the water.

'You want to go home, don't you?' Kit murmurs.

Lily comes up close behind him and says softly, 'I think he likes you.'

Shaken by a sudden rush of pheromones, Kit turns to her. She has put some lipstuff on, pink and shiny. It makes her look older. Her long dark hair is pulled back smoothly from her face and tied at the back of her neck. Her forehead is high and clear and slightly flushed. On the side of her nose, just above the flare of her nostril, there is a small, creamy-white pimple. Her skin is so flawless otherwise that at first he thinks it's a jewel. She has dark eyebrows and serious beautiful eyes. He wants to bring a smile to them, and flirt a little. Or maybe a lot. But is she old enough?

He recalls his mission. 'You don't happen to know a woman called Cassie Callinan, do you? She lives somewhere around here.'

'Why do you want to know?'

'She's my aunt. I'm on my way to see her.'

'And you don't know where she lives?'

'It's a bit complicated.'

'I know where she is. I'll walk you part of the way.'

'That'd be great, if you're sure it's no trouble.'

Lily locks up the aquarium. 'No trouble.' She picks up her small backpack, slinging it off one shoulder, and pushes her bicycle beside him.

'You in a rush to get there?'

'Er, not really.'

'Got some sandwiches with me. We could eat them on the beach.'

'Oh, I can buy some lunch—'

'I've got plenty.'

She looks up at him sideways from under her lashes and oh! lunch on the beach becomes a very attractive idea. It's like an itch, his need to know how it will feel to trace the line of her cheekbone with a fingertip, down her throat, down to those breasts. His hand curls unconsciously.

'You going to be staying round here long?' she asks.

'Mmm. I might. Not sure.'

She hands him a cheese and pickle sandwich and watches him devour it, amusement in her eyes. She says, 'Your aunt lives at River Marsh Cottage on Dale Road.'

'Do you know her?' He's eager for a few clues about Cassie, nervous, now that their meeting is imminent, and angry again with Richard for landing him with this.

'No, I've never met her. I've seen her around. It's a small town. Anyone new stands out like a sore thumb. Specially now it's getting quiet. Shitheap of a place,' she adds and takes a bite of her sandwich.

'Doesn't look so bad to me.'

'You don't have to live here. It's dead. Nothing ever happens. Bet it's not like that where you come from. Bet you've got lots of people and cafes and shops and clubs and things, haven't you?'

'S'pose so.'

'You take them for granted,' she says, sagely. 'Me, I'd just love to live somewhere like that. People everywhere. Always something new to do. One day, I'm going to live in America.'

You'd think it was Paradise, the way she said it.

Kit says, 'My cousin Eleanor lives in America. In Boston.'

'Yeah? Hey, maybe I could look her up? Say hi from you?' She laughs at her own fantasy.

They stroll down the main street.

'Keep on this road till you come to a dirt track on your right,' she says. 'It's a fair way out. Take the track all the way out to the dunes and then follow it around to the left and keep going till you see the cottage. You can't miss it. It's the only one there. I have to go now. See you.'

She settles the bag on her back, swings a leg over the bicycle and pedals away.

Kit calls after her, 'Hey! Thanks for the lunch.' But he's distracted by the sight of a large red-haired woman emerging from a bookshop across the road. She's glaring at him. Shit! It's her. The fish woman. Kit can feel himself blushing.

Grace puts her hands on her hips. Who is it, hanging around young Lily? Is it that idiot with the hand line? Is it? Grace knows trouble when she sees it. Problem is, she can't quite see it. She squints, wishes she had her glasses on.

Kit feels adrenalin surge. Is she going to have a go at him? An indistinct voice sounds from inside the shop.

'Won't be a minute, sweetness,' says the redhead, not moving.

But the feeling of menace dissipates.

Kit says, 'G'day,' with his best Australian accent. 'Er, I'm really sorry about the fish.' He gives her a cheeky grin. It doesn't in any way sway Grace's opinion that all men are up to no good.

Hurrying away, Kit realises he's not far from the caravan park. His tent beckons, the warm folds of his sleeping bag. Surely enough has happened for one day? I could kip for a while, he thinks, and then cook up some grub. I ought to see if my clothes are drying. I know where Aunt Cassie is; it's not like the sky's going to fall if I don't see her till tomorrow. One more day can't hurt.

13

PROMISES, PROMISES

The wind blows hot and cold, hot and cold. Cassie dreams a man. Broad shoulders and a warm bare chest with fair curling hairs. Long solid thighs. She presses herself close, feels the warmth coming off him, and the scent of clean, male flesh like the breath of life. Richard?

Not Richard.

Who, then? Is that his heart beating, or her head? There are voices in the vibration of the wind. A low incoherent muttering that sounds like an unceasing drone of complaint. Go away, she thinks. I've got enough problems. Where are the heavenly choirs?

She dreams Tom, her baby. She tries to stroke his face but he flinches, can't bear to have anyone touching his skin.

'Don't be frightened,' she tells him. 'It will be all right. I promise.'

Promises, promises.

Tom's face becomes her brother Stuart's, sticking out his tongue then grinning evilly as he locks her in the toilet.

'Stuart! Stuart! Let me out. Open this door now. I'll tell Mum . . . Stuart!'

'Hello? You all right in there?'

What just happened? Something is different.

Cassie lies still, listening through the thud of her headache.

It happens again.

'Hello? You okay?'

'Oh!' She scrabbles at the floor, at the wall, trying to get to her feet. 'Please! I'm locked in. I've been here for hours. Please help me.' Her voice strays between croaks and shrieks but someone is listening. Someone is here.

'All right. You'd better stay as close to the back wall as you can. I'll go and get some tools and take the hinges off.'

'You're going away?' Oh please, don't go away. Don't leave me here.

'There's tools hanging on the wall in your garage.'

There are?

'I'm going to need them to get this door open. You hold on in there. I'll have you out very soon.'

She crouches by the back wall, listens. Silence, for the longest time, and then he is back again. She hears him begin to work on the hinge.

'Watch out now,' he calls. His fingers appear in the space he has managed to lever at the top of the door. He wrenches it from the top down, splintering the bolt from its housing. Daylight shatters her.

'Coming out?' he asks.

She emerges unsteadily, legs stiff, eyes blinking and watering. 'I've got a terrible headache,' she says. 'I can't . . .'

Her legs give way.

'Steady. Steady now. I've got you. You're all right. There. Do you think you can stand?'

His arm is around her back, supporting most of her weight. She leans into him, inhales deeply. A scent of fish and cold mornings, damp wool. There is the cottage, the river marsh beyond it, slipping in and out of focus as if in a heat haze. Together, they move slowly along the path.

'How did you find me?'

He swoops to pick up her jacket without letting go of her and drapes it around her shoulders. 'Let's just concentrate on getting you inside,' he says.

He has a biblical look about him. Long grey hair blown back in a crest like spindrift. A straggly grey beard and a bleak storm in his eyes. Loose robes and a staff would not be out of place. Ought to be called Ezekiel, she thinks. Something like that. The ground swims away from her lead-weighted shoes, then floods back, her feet going down and down, or hitting the earth too soon and driving a sledgehammer blow through her body. She stumbles but he catches her, guiding her through the house straight to the bedroom. When she sits on the bed, he crouches at her feet and gently slips off her shoes.

'Lie down,' he says.

She closes her eyes, feels him pull the quilt up over her.

'Can I get you anything?'

'Tea,' she pleads. 'Hot and sweet. And aspirin,' she murmurs, sinking down into warmth and safety at last.

'No problem.'

He comes back carrying a mug of tea and two white tablets.

'I was up on the dunes and I saw your red coat on the path. Thought it was you at first, lying there. I came down. Saw your note on the door. Stuck my head inside and called out. I had a look around. Given what you said in the note, I thought I'd better.'

He waits for a response but she doesn't say anything.

'When I went back outside I heard you shouting, "Stuart! Stuart!"'

She tries to rouse herself. 'I think I was dreaming. Calling out in my sleep.' Thank god.

Leaning close, he holds her left eye wide open with thumb and forefinger.

'Have you taken anything? Should I get a doctor?'

'It's just a headache. Haven't even had an aspirin yet. Such a stupid thing to happen. The door was banging, you see.'

'The note?' he asks anxiously.

'It's all right. I'm fine. So good of you.'

He can see that she's almost asleep. 'If you're sure then? I'll be off. I'll come back to fix up the door for you sometime.'

'Oh, thank you, but I'll ring my landlady about it. Elizabeth Savage. She'll take care of it.'

'Save yourself a call. She won't have anyone but me touch it.

Do you want me to call someone? Want somebody to look in on you?'

'No, no really. There isn't anyone. I just need to sleep. Thank you, Mr . . .'

'Biddle. Jack Biddle.'

'Thank you.'

Ezekiel, she thinks.

Some time later, Jack Biddle looks at the note he'd removed from the back door and shakes his head.

To whoever finds me:

I am sorry for the inconvenience. There is nothing anyone could have said or done that would have made any difference. It is no longer possible for me to pretend I want to be here. I would like to tell Richard Callinan that I forgive him, but I don't, not really. Not that it matters now. The responsibility for this decision is mine alone. No one else should carry the blame for it. Please tell my daughter Eleanor that I love her. That I have always loved her. More than life.

Cassie Callinan

The broken lock must have spoiled her plans. Jack screws the paper into a ball, tosses it into the wind and strolls down to the water's edge. Even without the note he'd have known there was something. The woman is so full of sadness there's no room for anything else. By her eyes, the lines of her face, she's been that way for a long time. He thinks about sadness, its hollow grasp, the dead-penny weight of it on your eyelids. Thinks that his own wife's face no doubt bears those same shadows. Fiona, who tried so hard to save him from his wildness and his wandering and himself. To anchor him, she gave him Susie who, overnight it seemed, became his sole concern in life.

Jack knows that images of incredulous joy and harrowing darkness burn with equal intensity. The three of them together, catching deep-sea trevally off the continental shelf on the way to Tasmania, Susie only three weeks old and already miraculous. Susie, a leggy eight-year-old, curled on his lap, her sleeping head heavy on his chest. His heart bursting with the scent of her hair. A fragrance he no longer remembers.

Day after day, he plots the chart of his daughter's life, searching for a point at which he might have steered them all through the shoals to safety. Fiona left him because of this. Because Susie is still his sole concern in life. Because after Susie went, he didn't want to be saved anymore.

He turns his pocket inside out and shakes from the lining the pills he has taken from Cassie's bedroom. He stirs them into the water with the toe of his boot. Valium and sleeping tablets. He'd left the containers exactly as he'd found them, but empty. She won't notice. Not till she needs them again. There are other ways, of course. Plenty of them, if you've a mind to do it. Despair will suck the marrow from your bones, turn a sharp mind into a black swamp, but it won't kill you. Jack knows this for a fact. You have to be determined, watch for your moment, keep your focus, and even then, life will keep on lifting you up, sending you distractions. Why? A single bird, one of those shearwaters, say, or a plover, or even one little duck, can raise so many questions. You gather facts, heap fact upon fact, but the mysteries accumulate and the bitter ache of life is not assuaged.

14

THE GIFT

Towards lunch-time the following day, Cassie wakes feeling safe, thinking life, tasting life. If it hadn't been for the door, I could have taken those pills. I wouldn't be here. Life! It's not over. There's more to come. She feels no curiosity at the thought but there's no pit opening at her feet either. She lifts an arm from the bedclothes, holds it out, considering the sensitivity of warm soft skin. How fragile is a wrist. How tender the submissive weight of a breast. I am unregarded, she thinks. And will probably remain so. Disregarded, in fact. She feels compassion for this body, a hopeful organism. It has lost all trace of youth but is not yet so very old.

'Life,' she decides. Might stay under the doona for a bit longer. It's Sunday morning, after all. She yawns, bunches a pillow under her head.

'Oh no!'

The note.

She leaps out of bed in a tangle of sheets, hopping and stumbling to the back door. The note has gone. Only the drawing pin remains, a tiny scrap of paper caught there. Did it blow away? No. Wait. Think. Concentrate, Cassie. What was it he'd said to her? Ezekiel? *Saw your note. Did you take anything?*

I'll have to leave here. I'll have to go. It will be all around town by now. What a story I've given . . . what's-his-name. Sure to be a hit down the pub tonight. Why oh why had she stuck that thing on the door?

Because you knew it would be a while before anyone found you. Because even a stranger deserves some kind of a warning before walking in on a decomposing corpse.

Her skin crawls. How close she had come to it.

Is there even the faintest possibility he'll keep it to himself?

'Not a hope,' she decides, slamming the back door.

A pink oval casserole dish is standing on her kitchen table. Cassie stares at it. What? The back door hadn't been locked. Her rescuer had left her sleeping.

And popped back with a casserole?

A greeting card is propped beside the dish. *Get Well Soon* it says, in gilt letters over pink rosebuds.

'For Christ's sake!' she mutters, picking it up.

Chicken and mushrooms, she reads. *My own recipe. I'm getting Martin to drop it off for you. It will have you on your feet in no time. Chin up.*

Myrtle (General Store)

Martin? Who is Martin? Ah. Myrtle's daft sea squirt.

A complete stranger walks into my house and drops off a casserole? I could have been murdered in my bed. Chin up? What does she mean, chin up? Has that man told everyone already? Has he told them about my note, or about finding me hallucinating in a toilet? What a mess this is. A perfectly simple desire for personal annihilation turned into a pantomime.

She lifts the lid and sniffs. A wonderful aroma. How annoying. Now she has to be grateful to someone else. She'll have to go and thank them for it and endure another bloody inquisition. As she showers and dresses, her sense of outrage grows. To think there was someone wandering around her house while she slept! Have these people no sense of privacy?

When she hears knocking at the door, she can't believe it.

'What now?' she cries. Is it Myrtle, come to see if I've Got Well Soon? Perhaps she's sent Martin with dessert. Or is it Jack Biddle, come to see if I've tried again?

I could hide.

They'll come and look for you.

She pictures herself crouched in the wardrobe while they roam the house, calling out her name. *Come out, come out wherever you are. Wanted, dead or alive.*

More knocking. Louder this time.

Furious, Cassie swings open the door. She squints up at a young man standing with the sun behind him.

'Yes? What do you want? I'm on my feet. Still alive, as you can see. Nothing to worry about. You can go and report back to them all. Lunatic survives intact. Right?'

'Right,' says Kit, with a quick nervous glance over his shoulder.

'Well?'

'Er, Auntie Cassie . . .'

Auntie Cassie?

Stuart's features emerging from the young face. Kit! Here?

'Oh, Kit, I'm so . . . Oh my god . . .'

It is quite beyond her to explain. She wraps her arms around him, hides her face in his chest.

'People keep coming round. To see how I am,' she mutters into his shirt. 'It's driving me crazy.'

You haven't seen the boy since he was a toddler and you're lying to him already? Stop it.

Well, look at him. He's terrified.

She stands back, looks him up and down. Thank god, she's thinking. Thank god the bolt broke off. Thank god she hadn't . . . It would have been Kit who found her.

'How you've grown!'

'That was a safe bet.'

He has an attractive grin. Cassie begins to feel better, slips into mother-mode.

'Come in, come in. I'll put some coffee on. Have you had lunch? Did you get the train down? You should have called me from the station. Richard said you were in Australia. Haven't you got any luggage? Good thing I made a casserole this morning. Chicken and mushroom. I hope you like chicken. Do you like chicken?'

Behind her back, she slides the greeting card across the table and sticks it in the pocket of her jeans. Wonders how long Richard's letter had been waiting at the post office. How long had she been gone before someone slid into her bed?

'Coffee would be great,' Kit says. 'My stuff's at the caravan park. I wasn't sure how much room you'd have. Didn't want to impose. Anyway, I'm used to the tent.'

'Oh.' She fights the urge to insist that he stay with her. 'How's your father?'

'He's fine. I haven't seen him for a while. I've been travelling for months. But we talk regularly.'

'And your mother?'

'Yes, she's fine too.'

Long pause.

Kit blushes and laughs. 'I'm not a great one for talking.'

'You get that from Stuart,' she says. 'I expect Richard told you what happened?'

'I got the picture. He's worried about you.'

'Ha!'

He watches her as she makes the coffee. At least she isn't weeping and wailing. And she's certainly not wasting away. Not as old as he thought she'd be. Old enough for a hot-shot lawyer to trade her in though. What a tosser he is. And what was all that stuff about a lunatic surviving? She's really wired. And that voice! It pins him behind a school desk, squirming in short pants. *Miss? Miss?* She might be desolate. She might be heartbroken. You never know with women. Like Mum. Pretending everything's all right when it's not. And just when you think it's sweet – bam! – out it comes like a whack on the head and you're the one left spinning and wondering why.

Cassie pours coffee. 'Did you say you'd had lunch or not? I'm starving. You must be hungry. Boys your age are always hungry. Let's heat this stuff up. We can go for a wander on the beach afterwards, if you like. It's wild. Lovely.'

'Sounds good.'

She's thinking, I'll bet Richard asked him to check up on me. I wouldn't put it past him. The poor boy's probably wishing himself a million miles away. Oh! That face is exactly like Stuart's. She can hardly take her eyes off him. I'll manage, she thinks. There's nothing around here to keep a boy of his age interested for more than a few days. I'll make sure he's able to give them all a good report on me. Cassie is applying herself well . . . Cassie tries hard. Cassie has worked consistently this year and . . .

And what?

And look where it gets you.

After their walk, she shows him the garage. The old bicycle is there, propped against the wall.

'Take it if you like,' she says. 'Might as well use it while you're here.'

His face betrays a yearning to get behind the wheel of the Mercedes. Cassie, amused, pretends not to notice. I'll let him have a spin in it before he goes, she thinks. Why not? Richard would be horrified.

Kit rides away on the bike after arranging to cook dinner for her on Tuesday.

'I'll bring the ingredients,' he says.

'But there's food here.'

'I want to do something special for you.'

She bites her lip, to hide laughter that isn't anything to do with Kit and isn't kind.

15

THE BRIBE

Next morning, Kit rings Richard. Dutiful nephew, seriously pissed off. Even more uncomfortable with his role as Richard's spy, after meeting Cassie.

'I'm in Shearwater,' he says. 'I've found her. She's living in a cottage.'

'How is she? How does she seem to you? Is she handling things?'

This isn't my problem, Kit thinks. He's dumped it on me. He just wants to know everything's fine so he can ease his conscience, that's all.

'She seems okay,' he says, deliberately allowing doubt to creep into his voice.

'But?'

'She's a bit . . . er . . . excitable.'

'Excitable?'

'Unstable.'

'Oh god. That'd be right. Unstable. That's all I need. Christ! Listen, Kit. I need you to stay around there for a while.'

'Not a chance. This isn't my idea of a good time, you know. It's nothing to do with me. I'm supposed to be on holiday.'

'Three weeks, that's all I'm asking. Four, tops. I'll make it worth your while. I'll give you . . . let me see . . . how about three hundred dollars a week? Twelve hundred all up? That's got to be better than washing pots in a greasy kitchen or pulling beers. Kit? What do you think? Will you do this for me? For Cassie? Just to keep an eye on her?'

Kit hesitates. He could really stretch out the holiday with that kind of money. Hmmm. He thinks about a pair of smoky green eyes.

'What do you say, Kit?'

'Three weeks?'

'Four.'

'I guess I could do that.'

'Great, Kit. That's really great. And if she happens to mention coming back here, you'll be sure to call me right away, won't you?'

Ah. That's what he's worried about. A surprise visit from Cassie with the pregnant blonde already installed. That would seriously cramp his style.

'Cassie won't have to know about the money, will she?' Kit asks.

'It will be our secret.'

Kit has a bad taste in his mouth, but it's not as though he's being asked to do anything wrong. Not really. A job is a job, isn't it? And twelve hundred dollars is twelve hundred dollars, when all is said and done.

16

LONG-RANGE FOCUS

On a boat, you can be sure of who is coming and going. A boat on the water is a kingdom unto itself, afloat in a dangerous universe. On deck, amongst the crates and ropes, nets, floats and tackle, you can lose sight of who you are, what you've done, and what you yearn for. Sometimes, as a man works, all this is lifted from him, and he can give thanks, and it is possible, against all the odds, to maintain some kind of balance. But not always.

There are sixteen boats tied up at the jetty. Five yachts, two tinnies and the fishing boats. The wind is freshening. Halyards clink and tinkle. Simon's boat, *The Gannet*, rocks gently in the quiet chuckle and plop of the water. Simon is standing motionless next to a coil of blue rope, holding the camera to his eyes, zoom lens focused on something only he can see. Here it comes, itching, itching, creeping over him, till his face flushes and his breathing is short, and he can barely keep his hands steady.

Through his viewfinder, a man on the jetty is teaching a girl to fish. He's standing very close behind her, his arms coming around her at either side, his hands holding her hands on the rod, flexing it lightly. He can feel her awareness of the whole hard length of his body against hers, his chin resting on her brown hair. She is enfolded by him, as in an embrace. Her laughter reaches Simon, past the pied cormorant holding its wings out to dry, and the breakwater where sunlight fractures gold on the boulders, past the rocky nooks where fairy penguins sleep, and the bobbing flock of crested terns, past the sun-bleached, empty jetty, on and on through all the wasted years.

Simon blinks away quick tears and lowers the camera.

Swallows squeak and skim the water, swooping unafraid from the dark places into sunlight. Beneath the graceful arcs of their flight, the outline of a sunken rowboat glimmers, a bellyful of sand in a fathom of clear water, long strands of green weed hanging from the twisted rope still attached to the bollard. It looks as though it's been lying there for a century, as though Cook himself might have stood in the bow, telescope raised. But only a week ago it was afloat, a useful part of things. One storm wave, that's all it takes. And then with each slap of the water, the boat rides a little lower, accomplice to its own destruction. It is years ago, and it is here and now and always.

'Excuse me? Hello?'

He shudders visibly at the woman's raised voice. Turns to face her.

'What?'

'I said, have you any fish for sale? Any salmon, perhaps?'

'Salmon aren't running yet.'

'Oh. You're the man from the bookshop, aren't you? I've seen you there. With the art books.' If Cassie is hoping to strike up a conversation, she couldn't have picked a worse moment.

'Haven't got any fish. I've got work to do.'

'I'm so sorry I interrupted you,' she says shakily. It is the same man, she's sure of it, but there's no white collar. Must have been mistaken about that. So much for the delightful idea of buying fish for dinner, straight from the boat. Nothing turns out the way you want it to. The way you imagine it will.

She walks away quickly, her colour high, her bottom lip trembling. Hears him call after her.

'I'm sorry,' he shouts. Upsetting people. Alienating people. He's good at that. Best if they keep away. Specially that one. Coming here, confronting him. On the boat! It's enough to make him crazy. Bad enough that she's been in the cottage for nearly a month. But he doesn't want her complaining about him. 'Sorry about that,' he shouts again. She doesn't turn around.

'I'll get you a fish,' he calls.

I'll get you a bloody fish all right.

17

THE CHINA-WALKERS

Kit asks Cassie, 'Why here? Why Shearwater?'

'When I left, I just drove. I had no idea where I was going. I think I just needed to get far enough away to think. And then I saw the sign for Shearwater. Your dad and I used to come here as children on family camping holidays. I thought, why not? It seemed as good a place as any. It's still as good a place as any. I don't know if I'll stay or not.'

'My dad used to come here? That's so weird. Me being here too, I mean. You seem to be settling in.'

'No. It's only been a few weeks.' Incredible. The shift in time and circumstance still so utterly incomprehensible that she turns her mind from it, walks over to the window. 'I mean, look at the garden. If I'd been making a home, I'd have done some work on that by now. It's disgraceful. I used to like gardening. No. I'm just perching, till I decide. I could go tomorrow.'

Go where? Oh shit. Is she thinking of going home?

'Probably better to stay put for a while,' he advises. 'There's a lot of uncertainty, a lot of stress involved in moving around. Take it from me.'

She changes the subject, says, 'Do you fish? My father liked the fishing here. Used to sneak off for hours on his own. Mum complained that a camping holiday was twice as much work as staying at home, but Mum was always complaining. Nobody took any notice.'

'My mum's like that.'

'Is she?' says Cassie, surprised, thinking of Annette. The distance between herself and Stuart's elegant, high-maintenance English bride had always been more than geographic. There'd been no need to bridge it, living as they did on opposite sides of the earth. Christmas cards sufficed, with the annual letter and photograph slipped inside.

She moves around the room, straightening objects, picking things up and putting them away. His boots, drying by the fire, are placed neatly at the back door. A pile of his beach pebbles, ochre, brown and pink, are shedding grains of sand on the mantelpiece. There are too many and they are too big. She moves them all to one side, dusts them individually and puts them back, regarding them with a dissatisfied expression. Perhaps if she moved the large brown one to the back . . .

'Relax, Aunt Cassie. Take the weight off your feet.'

And then what?

'Call me Cass,' she begs. 'I feel old enough these days, without all this "aunt" business.'

She offers him a beer, pours wine for herself. He's going to stay tonight. His big red rucksack leans, bulging, against the wall. She drags it through the door of the guest room. A thick notebook slides from under the top flap. Kit is on his feet to retrieve it immediately. He replaces the book and takes the pack from her hands.

'I was just . . .'

'. . . I know, tidying up. Relax. Sit down.'

She sits and looks at the pebbles. She looks away. The order she creates in these small ways is the only certainty she has, and she craves it.

He thinks I'm crazy. He'll tell Stuart, who will call Richard, who will tell Eleanor. So what? Eleanor said I should have been committed years ago. Eleanor always knew. Daughters can see these things. And Eleanor is quite severely sane. Like her father.

'What's the book?' she asks.

'Just notes and things.'

'A journal? What a good idea. I thought they'd gone out of fashion. What do you put in it?'

'Oh, you know. Stuff. Things I hear. Things I see.'

'Why?'

'I write a bit. Stories. They're not very good,' he adds, afraid that she'll want to read them.

Cassie has more sense than to ask. What could anyone have to write about at nineteen, she wonders? What could they possibly understand about life? I am fifty-four and I don't understand anything at all.

'Are you going to write a book?'

'Maybe.'

'Don't let anyone tell you that you can't,' she says, despite her misgivings.

'I won't.'

She has an image of him then, striding through scrub with his pack on his back, all alone under a wide blue sky, not a track in sight, and quite sure that he will find his way. Dear Kit. He has a good heart. How has he survived out here without somebody eating him?

'Is that why you're travelling?' she asks. 'For the writing?'

'Adventure,' he says, grinning.

I'd give my right arm, she thinks, for an ordinary day. An unadventurous day. He ought to understand that adventure isn't always a bright and shining thing. Adventure can be exhausting, a lonely struggle in a dark place.

'Your adventure has home at the end of it,' she says. Not the kind of adventure where children get eaten by trolls and witches, or dance away over the hills, following the Pied Piper for ever and ever. He ought to be more wary. 'It puts me in mind of the China-walkers,' she says.

'The what? Didn't they play support for the Chilli Peppers?' he jokes.

She raises her eyebrows, waits till she has his attention. 'In the early eighteen hundreds, there were Irish convicts at Sydney Cove. Others too. Ex-convicts and settlers, hating the land they'd come to, longing for something familiar. A group of them gathered. Like minds. They thought if they left the colony, they could reach the Orient and eventually get back to their native land. They thought, no matter how far it was, they'd be able to walk home.'

'You can get a long way, on foot. As long as you're not in a hurry.'

'Sydney Cove to Dublin? But they were desperate. Australia was as alien to them as Mars. Imagine being marooned on Mars and longing for sweet mist and green fields and dairy cows. You'd forget all the bad things that happened. You'd forget all the things you couldn't wait to be rid of. They had nothing, you see. Nothing but the belief that they could do this, and in doing it, find some kind of fulfilment, some meaning. So they left. More than fifty of them. People called them the China-walkers.'

She thinks of the ones who would have packed what little food they could spare, to give it to the walkers. Those who would have filled the water bags and said, 'Godspeed' and 'Farewell'. Those who wept. And prayed. There would have been people, as always, who spat in the dust and said, 'They'll never make it.' People who laughed and shook their heads. And the ones who wished they were going and pretended not to care. The ones who said, 'Maybe next year.'

'Bunch of dreamers,' says Kit but he's thinking about the octopus escaping from his tank, making his way through a hostile environment, waiting for the door to open.

'Did they make it?' he asks.

Does he understand? She can't decide. 'No,' she says. 'They were never seen or heard from again.'

'You think they should have stayed put?'

'I think we do what we have to, and dream what we need.'

'How about doing what you dream?' he asks.

'See? You're a China-walker,' she says, shaking her head in mock dismay.

But he tells her, 'You don't know for certain that nobody made it home.'

He's right.

Later, she's amazed, watching him chopping chicken, dicing chilli and onions. 'Where did you learn to cook?'

He laughs. 'I can't really. Just have a few tricks up my sleeve. Useful for impressing the ladies.'

'It impresses the hell out of me.'

'Kit?' she says, when they sit down to eat. 'Isn't it a bit quiet round here, for someone your age?'

'Someone my age is supposed to need clubs and parties and flashing lights all the time, are they?'

Well, yes, she thinks. Or at least a peer group. But what do I know? Eleanor wouldn't have stayed two days in a place like this when she was nineteen.

'You trying to get rid of me already?' he says cheerfully, confident of his welcome.

The next day he buys two fresh fish and cycles back with them balanced on the handlebars. He wants to please her, and ease the discomfort of taking Richard's guilt money.

'I got them from a fisherman on the jetty,' he says. 'I told him they were for my aunt who lives here, and he refused to take any money for them. Have you got an admirer already?'

'Shearwater people seem to have an odd predilection for giving things away.'

No doubt there'll be a price to pay, she thinks, but keeps it to herself. Was it the man who'd been rude to her? Is he trying to make amends? What do I care about any of them? Men. She washes and scales the fish, bakes them in the oven with lemon and bay leaves.

A few days later, Kit presents her with a tiny fossil. A heart urchin he'd found on a beach below yellow limestone cliffs a morning's ride from the cottage.

'Probably millions of years old,' he tells her. 'See the markings? Beautiful.'

She should have heard the warning bells. A thoughtful boy, bestowing gifts, bringing her beach trophies, taking the time to make her laugh, make her feel special. Look at her, doing his washing, ironing his T-shirts to a state of perfection that clearly horrifies him. She bakes muffins for him, cooks a roast. Neither makes any reference to his moving on.

He's just put half a planet between himself and his own mother, she tells herself. He doesn't need your mothering, Cass.

Lucky Annette, with a son like this. Is she missing him? Does she lie awake at nights, worrying if her boy is safe, seeing him victim, seeing vehicles smashed and ambulances flying, thin knives flashing silver on dark street corners? Does she? Lucky, lucky woman.

18

ANOTHER GIFT

It's been almost two weeks since Cassie's rescue but the toilet door still hasn't been fixed. No word from Mr Jack Biddle. In the garage, she sees tools hanging on the wall, just as he'd said. A wrench, a hammer, some screwdrivers, a large pair of pliers. Garden tools as well. He'd seemed to know his way around the cottage. Helping her into the bedroom, finding aspirin in the bathroom, making her a cup of tea.

The door ought to be put back on, she thinks, driven to distraction by the sight of blown sand and leaves, but quite unable to step inside to clean them up. He said he'd come. Promises, promises. He's probably forgotten all about it. Or is he avoiding the crazy woman who wrote a suicide note? No one in town appears to be treating her differently, or looking at her more closely. Hard to say though.

I'd just like to ask him. I'd just like to know if he's told anybody about it.

She decides it is time to visit her landlady.

Elizabeth Savage watches the silver car cruise up the hill. She knows who it is. There's only one Mercedes in Shearwater. She switches the kettle on and goes downstairs to meet Cassie Callinan at the front door.

'That's a fair slope,' says Cassie, when introductions are out of the way.

'One in three gradient. That's volcanoes for you. Would you mind bringing the basket up with you?'

The basket is full of large pieces of wood for the fire. Elizabeth collects a packet of biscuits and a carton of UHT milk from the shelves at the back of the room. Cassie can see tins of beans, tuna fish, sweetcorn, bags of sugar and dried pasta. It looks like the storeroom of a grocery shop. Is she expecting a nuclear attack?

Elizabeth sees the question in her face. 'The back room is just as bad. Enough detergent, soaps and toilet paper for a hundred years, I expect.'

She is a tall, spare woman with cropped silver hair and pale eyes under bristling dark-grey eyebrows. An upright carriage, vulnerability in the sharpness of the shoulder-blades and the ageing, wattled neck. Cassie picks up the wood basket and follows her landlady up the narrow stairs. By the time they reach the third storey, her arms and shoulders are aching.

'It's very peaceful here,' she pants. The only thing she can hear is her own breathing.

Elizabeth stands back to allow Cassie to precede her into the long, bright room. Setting down the basket with relief, Cassie makes straight for the enormous picture window overlooking the town, the ocean, the river and beyond.

'Oh! Is that my cottage?'

'It is. There isn't much you can't see, from up here.'

'It's wonderful.'

'It's my world. I never leave the house.'

'What? Not at all?'

'Not anymore. Never.'

'But how do you . . . ?'

'Manage? Very well. I've had lots of practice. This town supports eccentrics, if they belong.'

'But you aren't a recluse. I mean, I'm here.'

'A recluse is someone who shuns the world. I simply stay at home and the world comes to me. It's actually very difficult to shun the world. Might be easier in a city where people mind their own business. No hope here.'

'I know what you mean,' says Cassie. She tells Elizabeth about Kit's arrival because he's spent a couple of nights in the guest room and a landlady might want to know these things.

'Do you have children of your own?' Elizabeth asks.

'Yes. I have a daughter. Eleanor.' And my son.

'I have no time for children,' says the older woman. 'Nothing but trouble and heartache. And what do you get for it?'

'Oh, but . . .' Cassie bites off her protest. 'Well, anyway, Eleanor is a grown woman now. She lives in America.'

'America? At least that's far enough away for her problems to be her own affair.'

'That's a worry in itself,' says Cassie, but she keeps her voice light, aware of an undercurrent to the civilities.

'Would you like some tea?' asks Elizabeth.

'Yes, please. If you're having one.'

'I usually do, around this time. You speak very clearly. I'm having no trouble hearing you and I have to admit I'm a little deaf.'

In the kitchen, Cassie looks down from the window onto scarlet bottle-brush flowers, stringybark trees and the rusty needles of she-oaks. A drift of pale pink ironbark blossom on the windowsill, the line of their dark scarred trunks stretching away up the slope behind the house.

'I like to have the trees close,' Elizabeth says. 'They bring the birds.'

The benches and table, of plain design, are Tasmanian oak, the colour of dark honey. Underfoot, polished boards and a worn, intricately patterned rug in reds, blues and cream.

Cassie says, 'If I could design a place that was perfect for me, I think it would look something like this. There's a strong feeling of harmony here. It's very relaxing.'

'I find it so. It's safe.' She has a curious way of smiling, lifting the top lip from her front teeth. It's a moment or two before Cassie realises it is a smile. It hovers, inviting complicity perhaps, but not offering cheer.

With a sudden shiver, Cassie sees the ghost of her own ageing self in a beautifully appointed kitchen, safe and alone. She banishes the vision by telling Elizabeth about the toilet door and her gallant rescuer, Jack Biddle.

'I was very lucky,' she says. 'If he hadn't happened to be passing, who knows what might have happened.'

'He wasn't passing. He haunts those dunes.'

Studying the old face to see how much is known about her own situation, Cassie sees a shadow of pain. She says, 'He said he'd be back to fix the door.'

'No doubt he will, one day. Is it a problem for you?'

'Not really, I suppose.' But I'd like it fixed.

'He'll turn up, when he's ready. Jack tends not to measure time the way other people do. He's more a seasonal sort of person. Lightly tethered.'

'You know him well, do you?'

'Me? What do I know? I'm only his mother. The last to know everything.'

Oh!

'I'm sorry you had that experience with the lock. I hope it hasn't spoilt your enjoyment of the cottage?'

'Not at all. The cottage is lovely.'

'Anything else you've had trouble with? At the cottage?'

'Everything's fine, thank you. The people here are very nice. Very . . . helpful.'

'They have their moments. You don't need to worry about Jack,' she says, as if Cassie has betrayed anxiety. 'He might look wild but he's a good man. He's the eldest. You're supposed to be able to rely on your eldest, aren't you?'

Cassie reflects that it's probably best learning early in life to rely on no one but yourself. Eleanor did.

'You'll be staying on, will you?' Elizabeth asks.

'For a while, yes. The cottage suits me. I love being close to the beach.' Better get out of here, she thinks, before the queries lead elsewhere. She thanks her hostess. 'I'll let myself out, save you the trouble of those stairs again.'

At the front door, she pauses before a row of coat hooks on the wall and wonders why a woman who never leaves her house would have need of a raincoat. You're becoming very suspicious, she chides herself. It might have been there for years. Perhaps hanging there, it suggests a possibility of departure, one day. Raincoat as symbol of potential. Why not? She is pleased with this fancy.

'I keep it there for visitors,' says Elizabeth, who has followed her silently down the stairs.

Ooooh! Jumpy, Cass. Very jumpy.

At home, as soon as she parks the car, she can see that the door to the outside toilet is no longer propped against the wall. The job is done. Jack Biddle has been and gone. Cassie is none the wiser as to what he's said to people about her note. The day turns flat and cold. She is suddenly weary. It's this business of having Kit around, she thinks. Having someone to care for and worry about. It's weakening her.

Inside the house, one of the kitchen chairs has been moved back, as though someone has just left the table. There's an odd, disgusting smell in the air that she can't place. She leaves the door wide open.

'Kit?' she calls.

No answer. Kit, it appears, has also been and gone. She straightens the chair. Sees a half-dozen carton of eggs on the table. Kit's contribution to the larder? She picks them up and feels moist cardboard as the stench of sulphur rises, hits her full in the face. Dry-retching, she rushes outside and drops them in the bin. Whether they're from Kit or another gift from Chin-up Myrtle, they've been out in the sun too long. She airs the kitchen thoroughly, and forgets about them.

19

GREAT WHITE HUNTER

Cassie cooked a leg of lamb last night and Kit provided a surprisingly good bottle of cabernet merlot. Afterwards they watched the Friday night film on television and Kit slept in one of the bunk beds again. He's stayed several nights since he arrived a fortnight ago, but only those nights when they dine together.

Cassie, frying bacon and tomatoes for their breakfast, experiences a thrill of precarious contentment that stills her hands for a moment and brings up her head. What is it? Demons under lock-up today? Relax. Enjoy it. She tops up their coffee, senses on alert, but as usual, she's looking in the wrong direction, listening for the wrong sound.

'Want some more toast, Tom?' she says.

Kit swallows his coffee. 'Tom?' he says. 'Who's Tom?'

It all happened so long ago, she thinks. Everything is forgotten.

Kit is bewildered by the sudden onset of emotion in the room.

She can't help him. Can't explain. She gets up to put bread in the toaster. With her back to him, it is easier.

'Tom was my son. He died when he was seven. Seven years and three months old. It was leukaemia. You would have been too young to know about it. It was a long time ago. He'd have been twenty-four this year. Not so different from you maybe. Being around someone else's son . . . it just slipped out. It's always there, you see.'

How could he see, Cassie? He's just a boy. He isn't supposed to understand what it feels like to lose a child. No one is.

'Oh, Auntie Cassie.' He's stricken. Embarrassed.

You're the grown-up, Cass. Sort it out.

'It's all right, Kit. Really. I'm sorry.'

'Life's a bitch sometimes,' he says and stands beside her.

Is he going to hug me? Please don't hug me.

But he simply slides an arm around her and presses his cheek to the top of her head. Sweet and stiffly self-conscious.

'I'm sorry,' she says again.

He shushes her. Just like Richard would have done, she thinks, vaguely amused. But she's given herself away. It won't be possible now, to pretend.

Kit goes out, returning later with a load of driftwood in his arms. He throws it down by the back door and catching sight of her face at the window gives her a wave and mimes that he is going into town. Does she want anything? She smiles for him and shakes her head. She's going in later on, herself. He wheels out the bicycle. Nineteen years old. Beard stubble. The charm of his dark wavy hair and those silky eyelashes. The ready, appeasing smile. She looks up at the sky to the west, where the weather comes in. He's going to get wet, she thinks, quelling the urge to run after him with a raincoat.

Tramping the beach alone, taking the long way into town, she counts twenty-three dead birds, blown ashore and dumped on the high-tide line amongst masses of kelp and spars of driftwood. Shearwaters, all of them. She hates to think of their little bodies battling the wind to make it home. Great hearts set against elemental forces. How is it decided, who gets to live happily ever after and who doesn't?

I can't do this, she thinks. Not alone. I can't. She faces the heaving grey water and wishes she knew how to let go enough to scream.

Grace, seeing Cassie standing disconsolately outside the closed newsagent's shop, darts across the road to her.

'You're too late,' she says. 'Ralph's already been and gone.'

'But I want a paper.'

'You'll get used to it,' Grace says, in a kindly fashion, for Gudrun has taken a liking to their new customer, Miss Frizz, as Grace refers to her. It is Gudrun's opinion that, given time, Cassie will fit in very well here. As long as she isn't frightened off by the locals, she added, with a meaningful look at Grace.

'You don't know a thing about her,' Grace countered. 'You've only seen her a few times.'

But Gudrun had smiled. 'I know what her face tells me. I know what her eyes say. You wait and see.'

Cassie is still fretting about her newspaper. 'But how does he make a living if the shop is never open?'

'Doesn't need the money – none of the Biddles do. Land and subdivision. Lots of the new construction around this town is built on what was once Biddle land.'

'Were they big landowners?'

'Not at all. Ralph's parents had a few acres that went to the developers after the old folks died. That's where the Blue Ridge townhouses went up. Seen 'em? Bloody monstrosities, they are. Complete eyesore. There was money to be had from crays, too, once. They bought up a bit here and there, over the years. Turned out to be good bits. Hasn't done any of them much good, far as I can see.'

'Isn't there a law about opening times, if you sell newspapers? Aren't they supposed to be available?'

Grace snorts with laughter. 'Fat lot of difference it would make, telling Ralph Biddle what to do. Sell 'em yourself, is what he'd say, and then he'd go off fishing, or shooting. Course they can't shoot mutton-birds anymore.' She nods towards a large photograph pinned to a board behind the window. 'That's Ralph, there. Years ago.'

Ralph Biddle? Jack Biddle's father? Cassie doesn't ask. The faded black and white photograph shows a wiry, swarthy man, late thirties, in a check shirt and braces, dark loose trousers. Across his back is a pole that extends beyond the length of his outstretched arms. Dead birds dangle from the pole. Fifty, sixty of them, tied in clumps. Ralph Biddle's gun rests casually against his leg. His face is expressionless; the eyes, staring into the camera lens, give nothing away. A black dog lolls at his feet, tongue hanging out.

Cassie is aghast. 'Some sport! Why would he shoot so many birds?'

'Because he could. There were millions of shearwaters. Even an idiot like Ralph Biddle couldn't miss. Look at him. The great white hunter. Gudrun's mother was famous for her mutton-bird pies. You roast the birds first, then put them in a white sauce with a layer of puff pastry on top. It was years ago,' she adds hastily, catching the look on Cassie's face.

'Thank god for that.'

'You seen them come in, have you? Same every night at dusk, between September and April. Thousands and thousands of them. Beautiful sight. The sky all dark with birds.'

'What do you mean?'

'You haven't seen the birds come in? What have you been doing with yourself? You ought to get down to the Point one night. Just on sunset. Don't leave it too long though. They take off soon and they won't be back till spring. Bet you've never seen anything like it in your life.'

In the distance, Cassie sees a tall thin figure come around the corner and hesitate. She recognises the shape of a hat, a scrap of green veil, and something about the bearing of the woman makes her ask, 'Isn't that Elizabeth Savage?'

Grace doesn't turn round to look. 'Shouldn't think so. Remember to wear a raincoat with a hood when you go, even if it's fine.'

'A raincoat?' The woman has ducked back, out of sight.

'With a hood.'

'Why?'

'There'll be birdshit flying everywhere.' Grace's eyes go back to the photograph. 'To think his great-grandfather used to hunt whales from a longboat with nothing but a harpoon in his hand and the strength of his right arm. How are the mighty fallen.'

A girl across the road waves, calls out to Grace.

'Lily! Why aren't you in school?'

'Finished early. Mum wants to know are you doing a run up to town anytime soon? She wants you to pick up a couple of things for her.'

'Tell her I'll be going up next week, if she can let me know before then. Okay?'

'Sure. See you.'

Cassie asks Grace, 'Who is she?' Something familiar about that young face.

'That's Lily. Hannah's girl. Hannah, from the pub. Haven't you met them? You ought to get down there for a meal sometime, meet a few of the locals. Hannah's cooking is worth stirring yourself for.'

'Lovely looking girl, isn't she? How old is she?'

'Must be fourteen now. Yes, fourteen. How's that boy of yours?'

'Kit. My nephew. He's fine.'

'Been fishing lately, has he?'

'I don't know,' says Cassie, puzzled. No one has told her he caught Grace with a hand line.

'Must be nice for you, having him around. English, isn't he?'

'Yes, we have family there.'

Grace waits, just in case, but Cassie doesn't volunteer any more information. 'Come and have a cuppa some time,' she says. 'Gudrun wants to know how you're getting on.'

It feels like a summons to see the headmistress.

'And don't forget the birds. There's only a day or two left.'

20

GIRL IN THE PICTURE

The old pub is empty. Not a soul in sight. No sounds of activity. Dull green curtains at the long windows and a green-flecked carpet give the main bar a shifting sub-aqueous light. Kit hesitates, breathing the odours of stale beer and furniture polish, sensing the voiceless muttering of a century of thirsty jostling ghosts.

'Hello?' he calls. 'Anybody here?'

A disembodied voice floats down to him. 'Hi.'

She's sitting at the top of the stairs, in the shadows beyond the windows. He peers through the banister. Her dark hair is unbound and hanging forward, half-veiling her face.

'Hey! Octopus girl. How're things?'

'Boring. You want a drink or something?'

'No thanks. Thought I'd see if there's anything to do around here.'

It's not that he needs the money, more the fact that he'll go out of his mind with boredom himself if he doesn't find a way to fill up his days. The remaining two weeks of his agreement with Richard have fiendishly extended themselves into a couple of doddering years. He *has* to find something to do.

'Work? This time of year?' Lily's voice is scornful. 'There's barely enough for us.'

'Ah.'

'How're things with your aunt?'

'Okay. She likes her own space.'

'My gran's like that. She says the hardest thing is getting people to believe it.'

'You don't know when to leave them alone and when they want company,' he says, more to himself than the girl.

'Want to come up?'

'Sure.'

'You should ask my step-dad, Fat Harry. He'll know if there's anything going, work-wise. He runs the pub with her.' She nods towards a bubble-glass door behind the bar.

'Who's that?' He's curious at the hostility in the girl's voice.

'Hannah. My mother,' she adds.

They've had a fight, he thinks. He knows what that's like. There's no winning in a fight with your mother. All you get is guilt. It sticks. It sits on your back, tapping your shoulder, whispering in your ear, and you run a little further, a little faster, but there's no running away from it.

Lily says, 'Come on, I'll show you round. There's nobody staying here right now. Summer's the time when things get crazy.'

She flings open a door. 'There are seven guest rooms but this is my favourite. You can see the boats from here.' She stays in the doorway so Kit has to edge past her.

A low ceiling and two small arched windows set deep into the bluestone. He doesn't notice the scuffed paintwork, faded bedspread and ill-matched furniture. The view is amazing. He can see himself sitting at the table, writing his masterpiece, light falling onto scribbled pages of terse insights and fascinating stories. *Surprising in one so young.*

Lily, watching his face, is satisfied.

'Not bad,' he says. 'Shearwater's okay. I like the beach and the river, all the fishing boats. You know?'

'Yeah, right.' Her tone would shrivel bull kelp. 'What sort of work are you after?'

'Anything. I don't mind. I've done a bit of bar work here and there. I can wash up, clean a fish, make a decent cup of coffee. Important life skills.' He grins.

Lily shrugs. 'There might be something. Ask Fat Harry. Tell him I told you to. Go down the stairs on the left, not the ones we came up. He'll be there, somewhere.'

'Doesn't he mind you calling him that?'

'It's what everyone calls him.' Lily sits on the bed and leans back on her elbows, showing off her legs in a short black skirt. He wonders again if she's old enough for the kind of trouble she's inviting.

'Wish me luck,' he says, not hiding his admiration.

At the bottom of the back stairs, he pushes through a door

into a large empty kitchen. He can hear a woman's voice, low and venomous, coming from the backyard.

'You can go piss up a rope for all I care, Simon. Just stay away from there. Understand? You've no right. It's a commercial property, not somewhere for your sick dreaming.'

Jeez! Kits ducks back into the hall as footsteps approach the back door. Perhaps this isn't a good time. He thinks about Lily, lying back on the bed waiting for him, and grins to himself. Hearing the clink of glasses, he pushes open the door again cautiously, and sees a woman stacking a dishwasher with her back to him.

'Excuse me?' he says, 'Lily told me I'd –'

She straightens and turns to face him, almost as tall as he is. Faded blue jeans skimming generous hips. Buttons straining at the front of her red shirt. Remembering her hissing anger with the invisible visitor in the yard, he tries – oh! how he tries! – not to stare at her breasts, but his gaze continues to drop there of its own accord and the effort involved robs him of speech.

She is the image of the octopus girl but older. No girl, this one. A sister? Single? Sweetheart, where have you been all my life? He finds his grin at last, but still no words.

'Hi,' she says. 'I'm Hannah. What can I do for you?'

Bloody hell. *This* is Lily's mother?

' . . . so you see,' Kit explains to Cassie, 'Hannah says I can have free bed and board at the pub if I help her out with the sanding and painting inside. It's years since they've done any redecorating. It needs a touch-up.'

'You're an expert on painting, are you?'

If he is surprised at the acerbity in her voice, so is she. What is the matter with me? I didn't want him to move in with me.

'I know enough about painting to be useful,' he says. 'We can still catch up, as often as you like.'

He's very light-hearted, she thinks, and wonders how much it has to do with the fact that young Lily lives at the pub too.

'Do you want your pebbles?' she asks, hopefully.

'No, it's okay. You can keep them. What about your key? Want it back?'

'No, no, keep the key. You never know. You might need it. Use the bicycle too, whenever you want to. I'm sure no one will mind.'

'Thanks. The pub food's pretty good, you know. You should come over and have dinner with me one night soon.'

He hugs her then, a brief hard hug. The expression on her face begins to waver. She bites her lip to stop herself from begging him to stay.

'See you soon,' he says, shrugs himself into his rucksack and leaves.

The kitchen grows unbearably still around her. She runs to the door but he's already far down the road, an enormous red rucksack with two legs. She imagines him whistling, carefree, on his way to Lily, and hopes someone mentions very soon that the girl is only fourteen. Suddenly, she remembers where she's seen Lily's face before. From the box of oddments stored under the sink, she takes out the photograph that she'd found on the coffee table. It's her. It's the girl, Lily. No doubt about it.

21

DIZZY COMETS

Larger raindrops explode on impact, water running down the window. People think that raindrops have the same shape as tears. It isn't true. Big raindrops can fall as fast as thirty kilometres an hour and then there's air pressure to take into account. The fact is, the shape of a good-sized raindrop is more like a mushroom top, or a hamburger bun. Tears have all the time in the world to fall. Jack knows.

He stands at the window until the sky lightens and the rain stops. There are glimpses of the sea beyond the green and russet droop of the casuarinas, between the tangle of coastal ti-trees. A white-sailed yacht makes its way slowly into the river mouth. It is nearly sunset. Time to go and see the birds.

Tomorrow, or soon after, thousands of shearwaters will begin their seasonal migration to Alaskan waters, to the Aleutian Islands and the Kamchatka Peninsula. It will take them two months to fly fifteen thousand kilometres. Jack pays homage to the birds because of this amazing feat, and because they remain steadfast in their habits and can always be counted on to come home.

Shearwater Point is lit peach and orange by the setting sun when he arrives. Other people turn up, alone or in pairs, until a small group has collected, rugged up against the evening chill, murmuring quiet greetings to each other, eyes on the sky. Jack stands some distance away from them.

The tide is out, water ruffled into a sharp chop by a cold breeze. As the sun sinks below the horizon, a woman's voice breathes, 'There!' and the first bird appears. A speck in a luminous sky. Another speck, and another. They come in their hundreds, in their thousands. Tiny dark flecks against the last flush of the day.

The birds circle, high and silent. Gradually the air is filled with the rushing whirr of their wings – so many wings! – and then they start to come in above the heads of the watchers, flying down to the ground, back to the burrows.

Cassie, standing with her head tipped back until her neck aches, dares not move for fear of standing on a bird in the shadows at her feet. A sudden splatter of white on her sleeve.

A woman laughs close by. 'Where there's muck, there's luck!'

Still the birds keep coming. How can there be so many birds in the whole world? Where have they been, and why do they all come back here?

'They feed out at sea all day.' Jack Biddle is beside her.

'Oh!'

'They bring fish back for their chicks in the burrows. They have to work harder now because the chicks are almost fully grown and hungry, and the parent birds will leave soon. The chicks fly out a couple of weeks later.'

'It's amazing,' she murmurs, her eyes on the birds. 'How are you? I haven't seen you since . . .'

'No.'

'I didn't get a chance to thank you properly.'

'No need.'

'I see you fixed the toilet door.'

'Didn't take long. I put a new slide bolt on there. You won't have that problem again.'

'Thank you,' she says, keeping to herself the thought that hell will freeze over before she steps through that door again. 'They look as if they are coming out of the sky itself, don't they? Like little black shooting stars, or tiny, dizzy comets.'

'Sir Isaac Newton believed that comets were a sign of God's wrath. Divine instruments of destruction. Hurled from the heavens to wreak vengeance on us all.'

'Really?' There is something oddly disconnected about his lines of thought. Not quite random. Not quite right.

'Do you agree with him?' she asks, carefully polite.

'Nah. Too many of them miss.'

Startled into laughter, she looks at him, searching his face in the twilight, but he is scanning the darkening sky and gives nothing away.

They watch in silence for a while, both standing a little apart from the group, both thinking about the same thing. She clears her throat, asks, 'Ah, the note . . . the note on the back door that day . . .'

'Note?' he says. 'What note? You know, those birds go out hundreds of kilometres from the burrow every day, hunting for fish, flying low over the waves.' He moves his hand to indicate their skimming flight. 'Short-tailed shearwaters.'

'Mutton-birds,' says Cassie, gratefully. 'How do they find their way home?'

'Winds and currents. Stars. Invisible magnetic highways in the air. There are theories. Some years ago, on one day in September, three hundred and fifty thousand were recorded crossing the south-east coast of New South Wales each hour.'

'Each hour? There must have been millions and millions.'

The sky specks are thinning out now. Safe to push back her hood.

She says, 'I've found them washed up on the beach sometimes.'

He nods. 'They'll fight the storm winds for hours to make landfall, but some of them become exhausted, sink down into the waves and drown. The tide delivers them.'

She thinks he makes it sound like a feather bed of a death, a soft descent into a longed-for embrace.

'That back fence of yours could do with another couple of props, to make sure it doesn't come down on you. It's the weight of the sand drifting up behind it that's the problem. No point clearing the sand away. It'd be back in a day. But I can prop the fence. So don't get a shock if you see me at the cottage sometime in the next week or two.'

'That's kind of you. Thank you.'

A mutton-bird, making a low pass over its territory, swoops close to her face. She gives a shocked cry and ducks her head to the right. Her face brushes the rough wool of his jumper and she breathes the odour of his tobacco. When she tries to straighten up, she finds that she has become entangled somewhere in the region of his chest.

'Ow! Oh, my earring . . . I can't . . .'

'Hold still. I think I can see what the problem is.' He tears the wool apart and frees her.

'You've made a hole in your jumper.'

'No problem.'

She's rubbing her ear. Would like to offer to mend his jumper but it seems an uncomfortably intimate suggestion. The soft gleam of the gold earring is a match to the ring on her wedding finger.

'Did you know the Aztecs called gold the excrement of the gods?' he says.

Cassie, distracted, can't decide how to respond.

He continues, 'Did you know that trees absorb gold particles spewed out during major volcanic eruptions? They've actually found gold in tree rings, corresponding to eruption dates. Did you know that?'

'I didn't,' she says. 'It's beautiful, to think of gold dust in trees.'

Jack, relieved, lights a cigarette. He doesn't usually smoke when he's watching the birds come in but he has to find some way of stopping himself from braying facts at her. Why the hell does he always have to do this? Because it's safer than interaction. Because it masquerades as interaction. Because it's all he can manage to do, most times.

She says, 'It wasn't a very good note, was it? I ought to be angry, but somehow, all I can feel is self-disgust. It wells up inside me.'

She's speaking as if he knows her. Knows what's happened to her. He says, 'Self-disgust?'

'That I allowed it to happen.'

He knows she isn't talking about getting locked in. And he understands what it feels like, to carry the burden of responsibility. He lives with it every day of his life.

'Write it down. Send it out on the wind,' he says. 'Best place for it.'

She pauses, wondering what he means. 'You'd think, with a note like that, you'd think you'd be able to produce something real. Something poignant and beautiful and clean. Something without bitterness. Something that will be remembered for a little while.'

They are still looking at the sky, in which the first stars are appearing.

'I think,' says Jack gently, 'a note under those circumstances is not something people would easily forget.'

'Everything is forgotten. Everything.'

'Sadness is heavy,' he says. 'It weighs you down and all you want to do is let go.' He hadn't known he was going to say that. See? That's what happens when you leave the safe lane. Never know what's going to come out of your mouth next. He sets his lips in a grim, tight line.

But Cassie thinks, yes, and wonders what his story is and how he knows. Remembers the dark dream-shape of the boat in the water above her head, sees the tow rope reaching down to her belt and feels again her own mute agony behind the round glass face plate.

People begin to leave, drifting towards the track and the car park. Cassie and Jack move with them. A couple of torch beams appear, thickening the darkness. Cassie catches her foot in a grass tussock, slips, puts out a hand and finds Jack's arm. He recoils from her unexpected touch.

'I'm sorry,' she says, surprised, and a little hurt.

'No, no. It's fine. I'd forgotten you were there, that's all.'

She's evidently made a big impression.

Later, driving the Merc into the garage, she notices moonlight shining bright on the cottage, throwing sharp-edged shadows. She looks up at the Milky Way stretching high over Shearwater, over the dark mystery of the dunes and the depths of a silver ocean, over Melaleuca Drive where Richard will sleep the night away with his pregnant lover. For a single moment, she feels the earth turn, the stars spin slowly above her. She thinks of the luminous sky flecked with millions of birds, and feels the beginning of belief, the cold touch of reality.

Approaching the house, still star-gazing, she stumbles on a plastic drink bottle. What? Rubbish is strewn all over the garden, her garbage bin toppled on its side.

22

DANGER SIGNS

'Possums,' says Kit, when she tells him about the rubbish.

'Possums? What do you know about possums? How can a possum tip a garbage bin over? Besides, if there were possums, I'd have heard them scrabbling on my roof.' And that awful old-man heavy breathing sound the males make, she thinks. I'd have heard that too. I'd know if there were possums here. Arch-enemy Number One when it came to Richard's camellia buds.

'What then?' asks Kit, reasonably.

'I don't know. And there's a book missing. Dakin's *Australian Seashores*. Sort of a dull orange colour with a gold sea-horse on the spine. Have you borrowed it? I don't mind if you have, I just wish you'd said something. I've looked everywhere for it.'

'I haven't got it. Haven't touched it. Honest.'

'Did you leave some eggs on the table for me last week?'

'Nope. What's all this about?'

'Just . . . I get the feeling sometimes . . .' Don't do it, Cass.

Don't put it into words. Don't make it real. 'It's nothing. Forget it,' she says. 'Do you feel like driving the Merc?'

'What! Really? Absolutely.'

So easily distracted, the male of the species.

'You can drop me off at the bookshop. I feel like a browse. I'll walk back.'

'Aw, Hannah, come on. Have you ever been for a ride in a Mercedes? No? Well then, what's keeping you?'

Kit is clowning around, teasing her. What price dreams? He's going to do his best to find out. She's batting him away but he knows she's pleased.

'It's just a car,' she says. He won't take no for an answer. They never do.

'It won't be any fun without you,' he wheedles. 'You don't have to do all the washing today. It'll still be there tomorrow. Come out with me. Please?' He gives her his best smile. The one that makes them melt.

'I can't today, Kit. Really. I've got someone coming this morning. Maybe another day.'

This time he hears what she means him to hear, under the words. *You're a nice boy but I'm busy, so run along and play.*

Does she think he's a child?

He tries once more, sulky now. 'What about Sunday?'

'Oh no, we'll be going to church and after that we have the Sunday lunch customers to take care of. Don't you go to church, Kit?'

She sounds concerned, but it's the body, not the soul, that Kit is worried about.

'Does Lily go to church?' He can't imagine that.

'Lily hasn't set foot inside church since she was old enough to argue about it. Some things can't be forced. She'll come to it in her own good time. Or she won't. Nothing I can do about that. Now, I'd better get on with things.'

She's not going to come with him. He turns from her abruptly. Manages, but only just, to say, 'See you then,' as he goes through the door.

Hannah hears him gunning the engine at the kerbside, accelerating out of town. She laughs to herself. Boys! He needs a lot of love, that one. Used to getting his own way, too. Somebody's spoiled him. She sets the coffee to brew for Jack whom she's finally persuaded to come in for a haircut.

She drinks the coffee by herself. Jack is half an hour late and arrives still protesting that there is nothing wrong with his hair or his beard. Hannah ignores this and sits him on a wooden chair, draping an old sheet around him to cover his clothes. As usual he is clean but shabby.

'Do I pass inspection?' he asks.

'You look like the wild man of Borneo, Jack.'

'Nobody's looking.'

'Nobody will if you get around looking like that.'

'Just do the hair, Hannah. Please?'

'How've you been? Haven't seen you in the pub for a while.'

'Autumn evenings. Lots of birds. I'll be in when the season

turns. That's the time for the pub. You get the big fire lit in there and put those lamb shanks of yours on the menu. I'll be in.'

'Looking after yourself, are you?'

'Right enough. How's the young one?'

'She's a bloody handful. Still hanging around Simon down at the aquarium. Doesn't seem to have any friends her own age. I don't know. I worry about her, Jack.'

'Natural.'

She sees his face tighten and touches his cheek briefly with her fingers. 'It won't always hurt, looking at Lily,' she says.

'I know.'

'Any problems at River Marsh Cottage yet?'

He twists his head round to look up at her but she twists it back.

'Keep still, please, unless you want to lose an ear.' She snips. Locks of hair drift to the floor.

'She had some trouble with a door. Hinges and lock needed fixing.'

'Nothing we need to worry about?'

'Don't think so.' He wonders if Cassie has decided that life is worth the trouble. Will she try again? 'We saw the birds come in.'

'You and that woman from the cottage? Together?'

'Her name is Cassie Callinan.'

'I know. Her nephew's got a room here. Do you like her?'

'Give it a miss, Hannah.'

'Think she'll stay around for long? At the cottage?'

'How would I know?' Don't know if she'll stay around anywhere for long.

'So there hasn't been any other trouble, Jack? Since she moved in there?'

He shrugs.

She finishes trimming his beard and then stands back to survey the results. He has a fine lean face when it's not hidden by all the hair. 'You'll do.'

He gets to his feet and rubs his beard as she takes the sheet from his shoulders. 'You've taken too much off again.'

'If you came by more often, I wouldn't have to. At least you'll look civilised for a while. There!' She gives his shoulders a brush and leans in to kiss him on the cheek.

He can see it in her eyes: *Poor Jack*, but he lets her kiss him anyway. Never turn away love. That's what Alexander the Great said.

'You'll keep an eye on things, Jack, will you?'

'I'm around.'

'Yes.'

Kit lies in a patch of coarse grass with his eyes closed. Sticky fingers and a hot sticky mind. Hannah leans over him, straddles him naked, teasing his face with her heavy breasts, stroking his mouth with her nipples, breathing his name in a sweet suffusion of desire. She wants him now. Oh yes. Oh yes. Oh yes.

He'll make her wait for it, pant for it, until she's moaning for him, pleading with him. Until she's desperate for it. And then . . . wham!

A bull ant crosses his arm, a tickling awareness. He flicks it off, sits up abruptly. This country is full of bugs! Can't even lie on the grass without some creature coming to see what you taste like. What you taste like . . .

Oh, Hannah.

He's off again.

Nineteen and hurtling into love.

You can't tell them, can you? You can see it coming, clear as the flat yellow light before a storm. Danger signs. You can throw all the lifebuoys you like. It won't make a shred of difference.

Sink or swim, Kit?

Sink or swim.

23

JACK'S STORY

Cassie, looking forward to a bookshop browse, has a pang of anxiety as Kit zooms off towards the pub in Richard's Mercedes. He seems a capable driver, but so young. All that testosterone fizzing in his veins. Will he be sensible, now he's got the car to himself?

There's no one in the bookshop. No rude fisherman lurking round the corner studying madonnas. No sign of Grace, either. Cassie spends a pleasant half hour totally absorbed in the books. She chooses three and raps on the counter. Calls out. Knocks on the door that separates their living quarters from the bookshop. Nothing. They won't mind if I take the books, she thinks. I could leave the money on the counter. But she can't find a price marked in them.

She pushes open the door, calling loudly as she goes through it, hoping she's not about to interrupt anything she shouldn't. 'Grace? Grace, are you there? It's Cassie Callinan. Gudrun? Anybody there?'

She finds Grace in the garden at the back of the house, planting lavender bushes. The odours of turned soil and crushed lavender leaves bring an image of her mother to mind.

'Sorry,' she says. 'I need to know how much you want for these books.'

Grace finishes thumping out the contents of a black plastic pot in a manner Cassie is sure no plant could survive. She surveys Cassie critically.

'You're looking a bit leaner. How long have you been with us now? Couple of months?'

'Not quite.' Cassie doesn't want to think about it. 'I'm leaner and meaner,' she smiles. 'It's all the beach walking. It's toughened me up.'

'Best thing for you.'

'I know. Although they do say weight-bearing exercise is important, too, at our age.'

Grace grunts, lobs the planter towards the back fence. 'Every damn step I take is a weight-bearing exercise.'

Cassie laughs. Gudrun comes round the side of the house.

'Ah,' she says, taking Cassie's arm. 'You're just in time for tea. Come on, Grace.'

There is between these two women the passionate tenderness of young lovers. It is in their eyes, in the way they regard each other and touch each other, so that an insignificant gesture becomes a declaration of affection. It opens a hollow beneath Cassie's heart.

'I like your boots,' says Gudrun. 'You're looking very rural, my dear. It suits you. I made scones this morning. Do you like scones? Grace, have we got any of that fig and ginger jam left? And some cream? We can have them with cream.' She sits at the table and Grace sets out teacups and plates and produces the scones.

Cassie recalls a line from a poem by Auden: *and bright the tiny world of lovers' arms*. It is here, that brightness, in this kitchen with its brown earthenware teapot, its biscuits and scones, its cosy enveloping air. It flows from Grace and Gudrun, bright enough to make anyone blink. Cassie pictures them, arms about each other, skin-intimate in the same bed every night. She considers them, not with prurience, not even with curiosity, but with the amused affection that lovers may sometimes instil in others. I will not grow old in the presence of such tenderness, she thinks.

'You're comfortable there at the cottage, are you?' asks Gudrun. 'No problems? Not worried about being there on your own at night?'

'I came here to be on my own,' Cassie points out. They all want to know why. Of course they do. Everyone likes a story. Not today, she thinks, and changes the subject.

'You don't happen to know a decent hairdresser around here, do you? I need a cut so badly I'm starting to look like an old English sheepdog.'

'Yes,' says Grace, agreeing with the comment.

'There's a young woman in Tullamurrin who isn't too bad, I've heard,' says Gudrun. 'We don't use her. We do each other's hair.'

'Yes,' says Cassie, staring deliberately at Grace's impossibly red curls.

Grace grins, unperturbed. 'I hear you went to see the birds,' she says, and presents Gudrun with the teapot, to pour.

'It was astonishing. Wonderful.'

'And you took your raincoat,' says Grace. A statement, not a question.

'And you saw Jack Biddle there,' says Gudrun, gently probing.

'Yes, I did. He told me all about the birds. He is very . . .'

'Barmy,' says Grace.

'Well-informed,' says Gudrun.

'I was going to say sad. He seems sad, to me.'

So they tell her a story. Jack's story. About his only daughter.

'Thirteen years old, Susie was. She would have turned twenty last month. Swam like a fish, didn't she, Gudrun? She used to surf out there. Rode the rips out past the breakers like a pro. Her dad taught her. Bit of a champion surfer, Jack was, in his day.'

In his day. It's a kindness, Cassie thinks, that you don't know when you're having your day, because all the days beyond it are a slick and slippery slope.

Gudrun says, 'Susie went in the water one day and never came out. There were odd cross currents and a strong easterly blowing. They never found her body. Just her backpack, a towel and her sneakers above the high-tide line. He won't talk about it. He's got it all locked up inside. You can't lock away a part of love without locking it all away, can you? Fiona couldn't bear it.

His wife. She was a good woman. She left him a year after it happened. Almost to the day, wasn't it, Grace?'

'It was. She went back to South Australia. Old fishing family. Can't have been easy living with a man who spends his days sitting in the dunes staring out to sea. Must have felt like she'd lost her husband as well as her daughter. We all have our limits.'

Cassie hears her own voice high and strained, words tumbling out rapidly. 'But why was the girl swimming on her own? It's terribly dangerous out there. A good swimmer would know that.'

'Oh, she knew it, but she was thirteen. Immortal. They never think it's going to happen to them. Besides, she'd had a blazing row with her mother,' Grace explains.

'How awful. She would never forgive herself.'

'No.'

They fall quiet, pensive. Cassie still shaken from this unexpected echo of her own tragedy. Lost child.

'I thought he was nice,' she says at last. A little odd maybe, but kind.

Grace sniffs. 'They're all nice till proven otherwise.'

'Hush now,' Gudrun chides her.

Cassie says, 'What's he doing, out there in the dunes?'

'He's waiting,' says Grace.

For life? For the thaw? For the seasons to turn?

'Waiting for what?' she asks.

Grace shrugs, looks down at her plate. It's Gudrun who explains.

'For his daughter to come back.'

Ah. Poor Jack.

Leaving the bookshop, Cassie sees the man again, sitting on a stool by the window. She pauses, pretends to check a title on a shelf so she can peep at what he's reading. Two glossy illustrations on facing pages. Mother and child paintings. Mary Cassatt? Yes. It strikes her that they are images of immense comfort. He looks up, straight at her, and she is disconcerted by his rueful expression and the sight of the white collar. Is he a priest, a fisherman, or both? I must ask Grace about him, she thinks, giving him a curt nod of acknowledgement before hurrying out.

Simon Biddle scratches softly beneath the white collar at his neck. He's wearing it more often, treading a fine line between what might be considered idiosyncratic and what is merely pathetic. On ordinary days, meeting strangers, seeing the look, the hesitation, the deferential smile, it's addictive. And on the other days, in those moments of supreme tension when he walks unseen amongst them, then he knows he is holy, and might walk on water without sinking, or turn back the waves, or track through sand and leave no footprints, and his only sin has been to love too much.

24

THE ISLAND

Despite the cold blast of autumn and mutterings of a dire season to come, winter sidles into Shearwater almost unnoticed, with a series of mild days and calm water.

'Make the most of it,' the locals warn each other. 'It won't last.'

'We could do with some decent rain,' Myrtle says, addressing the sky from her vegetable patch.

There is a sense of expectancy in the air, more usual in spring than winter. It draws Cassie out and fills her with a restless need to hoist a flag, to pinpoint her existence, to do something brave.

Jack feels it. An imbalance. Something out of kilter. Something to be resisted, like the sudden urge for company. He watches the big gulls. Pacific gulls. A pair over there, stalking the lip of the ocean. Three more, riding the swells. A youngster, same size as the others but a mottled brown instead of the clean lines of black and white. Head like a dodo. Huge down-curving beak, thick and cruel, with the red daub, like blood. The way they move through the air. The grace of it. Jack draws a stalk of marram grass through his teeth. Bites down on bitterness.

He hears the panting breath, feels the thud of feet transmitted through a billion grains of sand to his own still body, but too late to move. Kit comes over the top of the dune and down the slope, braking with his heels, skidding and twisting, with no chance of avoiding him. He slides, crashing into Jack. A fierce blow to the shoulder. Sand, cool and gritty, pours down Jack's collar. A tangle of arms and legs, yelps, curses and apologies. A blur of rolling sky and grass blades. Then Kit is lying breathless on the beach and Jack picks himself up and shakes off the sand. Must have had the wind in my ears, for someone to come up behind me like that.

'Sorry!' Kit calls up at him. 'You okay?'

'I'll be right enough when I get over the heart attack, thanks.'

Kit gauges the tone, decides it is safe to climb back up and shake hands.

'Kit Giller.'

'Jack Biddle. Where's the fire?'

Kit blushes. 'I was in a hurry to see the water.'

Jack looks at him, sits down again. 'Smoke?'

Kit sits, long arms loose on his knees, and accepts a cigarette gratefully. He stares out to sea. A patch of blue sky, dead centre, softens the waters.

Jack grunts, shifts his weight onto one hip. Pulls from his pocket the fragments of a sea urchin shell.

'That'll teach me to keep shells in my pocket.'

'Sorry.'

'You know about sea urchins?'

'I know you can eat them.'

'Sea eggs, they call them. You get some beauties here, blown into the grass. I wouldn't eat them though. Always wonder how they survive a battering like that.' Eyes on the waves again. Roaring and tumbling. 'I suppose they ride them, floating out of danger.'

He offers Kit the largest piece of shell, shakes the fragments from his palm and is reminded of the pills he'd thrown away for Cassie Callinan.

He tells Kit, 'They found a sea urchin off the west coast of America that lives for more than a hundred years. Lives forever, maybe, if nothing eats it or crushes it or poisons it. It doesn't grow old. Not physically. Still feeding, still reproducing, still living in the same way. Immortal sea urchins,' he says, and adds softly, 'Why sea urchins though?'

Kit holds up the fragment of shell, delicately purple on top, white and dimpled beneath. 'You an expert or something?'

'Something.' Jack is trying to swallow down the wave of facts that threatens to burst from him. 'I like to know about things.'

'Me too.'

'Now this here, this is the dune fan flower.' He indicates a flat spreading plant with lilac flowers. 'Your aunt all right, is she?'

Kit looks up, surprised. 'I was just there. She's not in.'

The bicycle wasn't there either, which is why he decided to head back to town along the beach. He is still puzzled about why the bicycle and the car are missing at the same time.

'You know her, do you? My aunt?'

'No. I met her. The fan flower is a member of the goodenia family.'

'I don't know much about Australian plants yet. I'm from England.'

'I'd never have guessed,' says Jack.

Kit laughs. 'You from round here?'

'Born here. Been away, too much. Always come back again. You get the hop goodenia a little further inland. Yellow flowers on that one.'

'I'm having enough trouble sorting out the gum trees,' Kit says. 'It's like, the more you learn about them, the less sure you are of knowing any one of them.'

'Like women.'

'Too right.'

They are quiet for a moment or two, contemplating the unknowable-ness of women.

'And yet . . .' says Kit, blowing out smoke, feeling his way.

'There is that,' Jack agrees.

They watch a big brown gull stab at a fish in the shallows. After a few attempts, it succeeds and flies away, shadowed by a hopeful squadron of smaller silver gulls.

Jack says, 'There's an island out there, you know.'

'I can't see an island.'

'No. You won't. Probably. Not many have. It's only ever been drawn on one map that I've heard of, back in the early 1800s.'

'What do you mean?'

'Just that. It doesn't appear on maps. And I've looked, believe me.' Jack stubs out his cigarette in the sand and puts the butt into his pocket.

'But isn't that a shipping route? If there was an island, it would have to be charted.'

'You'd think so, wouldn't you? Course the whalers knew how to avoid it, and the sealers knew how to find it, in the old days, so they say.'

'How do you know about it?'

'How do you know about anything? Stories.'

'But where is it?' Is he having his leg pulled? Is he looking in the wrong direction?

'Out there.'

They look out over the waves.

No island.

'Is it under the sea?'

'No. It's an island. A real island, with great black cliffs all around. Impossible to make a landing from a boat. A flat top. No trees. It's just not visible all the time. Conditions have to be perfect. The people who lived on this land before we came, the first people, well, they used to bury their dead right here on the mainland in a sitting position with the knees drawn up close to the body and their faces pointing towards the island. Bit like you're sitting now.'

Kit casually straightens his legs.

'They did it that way so the spirits would know where to go when they left the body. That island is where the spirits gather, to wait for reincarnation.'

'A sort of Erebus?' says Kit.

'A what?'

'Erebus. A faraway realm in the west where the souls of the dead go. We did *The Odyssey* at school.'

'Ah. Yes. A kind of Erebus, I suppose.'

'You believe in reincarnation?'

'Best not to believe anything you can't see with your own eyes,' says Jack. But there's nothing to stop you waiting.

'Have you seen it, then?' Kit asks.

'Me? Nope.' Jack studies the slip of sand grains as he moves his right foot.

'Who has? Anyone you know?'

'Well, that's the funny thing, you see. You try asking anyone about this island and they'll say they don't know what you're talking about. Never heard of an island, they'll say. Must be some other bit of the coast you're thinking of. Odd. People.'

Kit thinks about this, shoots a look at Jack's face for any sign of mischief.

'I've heard about the ship that appears and disappears,' he ventures.

'The Portuguese caravel buried in the sand-dunes. The Mahogany Ship.'

'Is it true?'

'Show me and I'll tell you.'

'But the island is true?'

'It was on a map. Just one old map.'

'Why tell me about it?'

'Because you're too young to believe me.'

Kit shakes his head, still suspecting a joke. 'Think I'll head into town. Want to come? I could shout you a coffee to make up for dropping in on you like that.'

'No, I'll stick around here. It's a good spot. Never know what you might see.'

'Well then, good to meet you. I'd better be off. I'm helping Hannah at the pub with some redecorating. Slapping a bit of paint on in the guest bedrooms.'

'Hannah, eh?'

Kit blushes again. I will grow out of this one day, he swears. I will not spend the rest of my life blushing like a girl.

'She needs a hand,' he says defensively. 'I can't imagine Fat Harry getting up a stepladder.'

'Can't imagine Fat Harry getting up Hannah but he's been managing that for a few years now. You never know, with people.'

Kit blinks.

'Watch yourself,' says Jack. 'And mind you don't go asking questions about that island.'

It's all a yarn, Kit thinks. A bit of fun at my expense. There's no island.

But it isn't a yarn. It's a way station. A halfway house. And when it appears, it will be Jack's time, and all the waiting will be over.

25

INDIANA

It is indeed possible to navigate by the stars, to orient yourself by the direction of wind currents and the myriad fragrances they carry, to follow invisible magnetic highways in the air. Some people get into a car and take off, trusting their directional instincts. Others trust road signs and street directories, still driving away with innate assurance. But others creep along familiar roads, have panic attacks at the thought of travelling anywhere new, pin detailed route notes to upside-down maps, and inevitably become lost, just as they knew they would. For them, it's a matter of destiny, and destiny rules over destination.

Richard had tolerated Cassie's inability to navigate as long as he wasn't personally inconvenienced by it. He found it reassuringly female.

She'd ring him – poor Richard, mid-conference: 'I don't know where I am! How do I get home?'

'Cassie, if you don't know where you are, how can I help you? Where's the river?'

'I don't know. What do you mean?'

'Think, Cassie. Wherever you are, is the river on your left or your right?'

'I don't know. I don't know which way I'm facing.'

Deep breaths all round.

Or he might say, 'Just head east, Cass.'

'East? Which way is east?'

'I don't do it on purpose!' she'd cry.

He believed her, but he didn't understand. Richard always knew where the sun would come up.

She has found Tullamurrin on the map. She has tracked down Miranda's phone number and made an appointment. She is doing something brave.

Grace said, 'Take the road out of town, turn right and then right again. They're both T-intersections, you can't miss them.'

Want to bet? thought Cassie miserably.

'And then you go left at the bridge and carry on along that road until you come to the town. Easy. It's only a tiny place. A few houses and a pub. Keep your eyes open or you'll be through it and out the other side before you know it.'

Great.

Looking at the street directory, Cassie can see that the place is only twenty-six kilometres from Shearwater, but somehow she still has the familiar feeling that's she's studying the wrong page, the wrong road, the wrong planet.

She follows the directions faithfully and finds herself driving along a road that becomes a cart track too narrow to allow the car to turn. She reverses, stomach churning, sweating hands slipping on the steering wheel. Is anyone watching her? Pretty hard to miss a silver Mercedes out in the middle of nowhere, going backwards. She imagines sniggers floating on the air with the scent of cow manure, though no one is in sight.

A dead cow looms at her window. She stops the car in amazement. The things you see. The things you don't see. The cow, black and white, with a splotch of green paint on its hindquarters, is lying on its side with all four legs sticking out stiffly like a wooden toy, as though it had been standing and someone had given it a push. You never know what life is going to serve up next, do you?

'Call me Indiana,' she says grimly, swinging the steering wheel with a grip that would have had Richard biting his lips.

The number is on the front of a green mailbox, just as Miranda said. The house is a worn weatherboard with a green water tank, on top of which a large marmalade cat is sunning himself. Cassie, who had expected a street, some kind of a salon, tells herself that she's got the wrong road. Right number, wrong road. This can't be a hairdresser's. She looks at her watch. She isn't late. She's never late. She's always either early or lost.

She decides to ask the inhabitants of the house for directions. A sensible move, and lucky too, because Miranda opens the door and introduces herself.

'I won't be long. I'm just finishing off Mrs Hartley. You make yourself comfortable in here and I'll be with you in a minute.'

The girl, who appears to be in her early twenties, casts a doubtful glance at Cassie's hair, and disappears into another room.

Cassie, startled by the revelation that she has in fact arrived, is further discomposed by the sight of her hairdresser's wild and greasy curls emerging from a red bandanna. Lurid orange streaks in dark-brown hair. Does she cut and colour it herself? Would it be rude to run away?

She waits anxiously for a glimpse of the current client but no one emerges. When her turn comes, she explains to Miranda how she usually has it trimmed and adds, 'There's a bit of a cowlick here, and the double crown can make things difficult.'

'Finding it might be difficult,' says Miranda, fingering the frizz. 'Been a while, hasn't it?'

The phone rings. Miranda answers it, takes a booking and returns with comb and scissors. She starts cutting, swears to herself and stops. Meets Cassie's eyes in the mirror with a rueful expression.

"Scuse me a minute. Nicked myself.'

Dear god.

The girl goes into a back room and emerges with a strip of sticking plaster and a bleeding finger. 'Damn sharp, those scissors.'

She licks her finger and sticks it out, handing the plaster to Cassie who binds it around the cut. The offered hand is smooth and brown and very young; the heavy eye make-up and wild hair have not completely disguised a face that has only recently left childhood behind. Cassie, contemplating departure before anymore damage is done (to either of them), finds herself quite unable to cause such disappointment.

As the cutting continues, she watches with horrified fascination what appears to be a random slashing of her hair. There is nothing she can do.

'So you live round here, do you?' asks Miranda.

'Mmm,' says Cassie, unwilling to provide any kind of distraction. 'Your hand is shaking,' she points out.

'My hands are always shaking. I think it's an adrenalin thing, you know?'

It seems impossible that Cassie will come out of this with anything presentable. Or even with her scalp intact. Great tufts of hair fall onto the black cape. She watches her own slowly changing image. Her face seems to be growing younger and less plump. Less maternal.

'There,' says Miranda. 'Run your hands through that and see what you think. How does it feel?'

Cassie obeys, sees her hair fall into place instead of standing out like a ruff around her head.

'It's good,' she says, amazed. Even Eleanor would approve of this. 'It's . . . it's modern.'

'Yes. It's much better.'

'Thank you,' she says fervently, fishing in her wallet for the ridiculously small amount of money required.

She wishes Richard could see her now.

Engine roaring, the Merc paws at the ground then rears up, backlit by glory. Cassie swings her hat in the air and gallops back to Shearwater. And does not get lost. Not once.

26

MAGIC

It's ten minutes to three in the morning. Cassie squints again at the tiny luminous bars on her wristwatch. Ten to three? Why am I awake? And wide awake, senses straining. For what?

For the sound that woke me up.

Here it is again. A metallic rattling. Click, click. Is that a key turning? She sits up. It can't be. Calm down. Listen!

Thud, thud. Click, rattle.

Is the noise coming from inside or outside the house? How do you know where to run if you can't tell where the noise is coming from?

She tiptoes to the bedroom door that she'd left ajar. Reaching a hand around the doorframe, she switches on the living-room light. Instantly, the sounds stop. Aha, she thinks.

Aha, what? All I've done is let the burglar know that I'm awake. But if he's outside the house, he might run away now.

And if he's inside? If he's standing silently, motionless, a few metres away, waiting for his chance?

For twenty, feet-freezing minutes, she doesn't move and there is no sound at all. Then, thud! A scuffling. Before thought or sense can interfere, she has marched out into the light. No one is there. Incredulity is still stronger than her apprehension. Is this really happening?

She goes into the kitchen. Nothing.

What would she have done if someone had been standing there, balaclava-clad and menacing?

'Fool,' she whispers, and stiffens as a sudden rattling raises goosebumps on her arms. The sound is coming from outside.

There's a switch by the door for the external light. She turns it on and opens the door in one movement, standing behind the flywire. The intruder turns to stare at her, caught in the sudden illumination.

A fox.

Garbage marauder. She's interrupted a raid. He's retreated a couple of metres, to the edge of the light. The flywire rattles in its frame, making her jump. A swift movement by her feet. Another fox, smaller. Vixen, she thinks. The female takes a few unhurried steps and pauses, turns her head to look up at Cassie. She is beautiful, with her russet pelt and thick brush held out behind. The bright eyes are wary but unafraid.

There's a lesson for you, Cassie thinks. There's a motto for life. A blazon for over your door. Wary but unafraid. An epitaph? Here lies Cassie Callinan. She was wary, but unafraid. No, perhaps not.

Cassie and the vixen stare at each other for a long moment until the dog fox lopes off into the darkness and his mate follows. Even then, Cassie is unable to draw herself away from the doorway, the circle of light on the garden, the utter stillness of the night, the sigh and scent of the sea.

The mild weather continues and with it, Cassie's restlessness. It was my choice to cut myself off, she thinks. I'm not ready to deal with the real world. I'm not ready to smile and pretend. I don't want to move forward, make contact, make plans. Not yet. But she feels adrift in a curious limbo. She feels less than real herself. Kit, still busy with his work at the pub, isn't calling round so often. Her forays into town serve to pass the time but have lost their challenge. No one has noticed her haircut.

Yesterday, the sea had been flat and featureless, a meek shorebreak and no discernible swell. She saw a plump fairy penguin, quite dead, head on one side, a dull gleam in the still intact eye. How blue the body! A rich royal blue on top and ruffled white beneath. Heartbreaking, the little webbed feet and ribbed flippers. She found a paper nautilus shell lying cushioned in a pile of bronze leathery bull kelp. A gift from the gods. She picked it up carefully, weeping without knowing why, and carried it home.

Today, the same cool breathless air hangs over Shearwater, and Cassie sits at the table and stirs up a squall of her own. *Dear Richard*, she writes. She avoids the promptings of self-pity. She refrains from pointing out everything she has done for him in the expectation of their future together. She does not speak of her own life, good or ill. She outlines his crimes, his deficiencies as a husband, as a human being. She writes those thoughts she hasn't been able to frame in words before now. A line of adjectives flows from her. Smug, wicked, cruel, selfish, lying, self-satisfied, callous. Come on, Cass. Is that the best you can do? She crosses them out. Writes them again. The exercise seems silly but faintly cathartic. She continues, hoping to summon anger, to feel the warming flare of a justifiable rage.

'Liar!' she writes, and chews the end of her pencil, waiting for further inspiration. By the end of the third page, she is getting the hang of it.

'She will leave you,' she predicts. 'You will know how it feels to be lonely. When your thinning hair has fallen out and your body has grown feeble from lack of use, when you are invisible because no one looks at you, then you (with your teeth still whiter than a two-year-old's) will know how it feels to be discarded!'

She signs it with a curse. 'May your penis wither away and your sad balls droop and knock between your knees!'

There! And all he could come up with was cabbage.

The exclamation marks help. She adds a couple more. Indignation is coursing through her veins. It's not rage, but it's a start. And as if she's stirred up the elements too, the wind is rising. The she-oaks are tapping at her window.

Invigorated, she climbs the dunes and tears the letter into tiny fragments, hurling them into the air. The wind hurls them right back. They cling to her hair, her skin, her clothes. She is frantic, contaminated by them, panicking as she tries to brush them off. They scurry over the sand, become impaled on twigs and tangled amongst leaves. It seems a terrible indictment. As though she deserves everything that's happened. As though she hasn't even the right to be indignant. Send it out on the wind, Jack told her. What had she expected? Magic?

Whenever she goes wandering, she looks out for Jack. Keeps an eye on the dunes. Notices the hollows that might accommodate a body, the shrubs that would give cover, the slopes where you'd have to brace your feet to stay perched in position. Walking alone, she wonders sometimes if he can see her. The thought brings its own tension to her movements, a self-conscious awareness of how she might appear to other eyes. Is there an audience up in the gallery of sand and shrub? Is there a watcher? Cassie stiffens her shoulders and lifts her head. Only the waves take a bow.

She'd like to talk to him. Here, in the dunes, it does seem possible that they might sit and talk of lost children. Of anything at all. She recognises the urge to comfort, to make it better, and reproaches herself. It's none of your business, Cassie. You've got enough problems of your own. You can't fix these things. You can't soothe or talk that kind of pain away. But she wonders how far grief has turned his mind, and will there be a turning back?

Another week passes slowly. Then one morning, she hears a hammering on wood. A drill bit drones and bites. More hammering. Jack has come to prop up the old fence.

Cassie, a little flustered, shouts hello from the back door. Asks if he wants coffee.

'Twenty minutes,' he says. 'Coffee will be good then.'

She goes back inside and watches him through the kitchen window as she brews up. How capable he seems, with his tools and his air of concentration. He's wearing a red and black wool shirt with the sleeves rolled up over strong brown forearms. When the breeze lifts his hair back, she can see the firm line of his jaw beneath a trim beard and fine cheekbones. He's not so old, she thinks, surprised. And not so biblical, either.

They sip their coffee by the fence, looking over tangled vegetation. She wants to apologise for the untidiness of it all, for the shameful neglect. Has an itch for secateurs.

The long lines of Jack's thoughts have curled and snarled into one impenetrable mass. Looking at the garden, he can feel the urgent softness of her eyes and the rugged beat of her loneliness. No way through this to small talk.

She feels reproached by his silence. It isn't my job, she thinks. The garden was like this when I got here. They can't expect me to –

'Brown stringybark,' he blurts.

'Sorry?'

'Brown stringybark.'

He balances his coffee mug on a fence post, points to a group of four squat spreading trees. He goes over to them and she follows him.

'What is it?'

'Wait.'

He tugs a thirty centimetre strip of grey bark from one of the trunks and begins to flex it and rub it, working it between the palms of his hands.

'What are you doing?'

'Wait.'

He rubs and kneads the strip until bark fragments begin to fly from it and he is standing in a cloud of reddish-gold dust particles. The sharp sweet scent tickles her nose, burns in her throat. When he's finished, he holds out his hand and presents her with a meshed ball of coarse fibre, the size of a duck egg.

'Great firelighters,' he says.

'Really?' She is thrilled at this evidence of bush craft.

'I'll show you,' he says. 'Got a match?'

'Oh no! Don't waste it. I'll put it in the kindling basket.' She has no intention of burning it. She carries it inside tenderly, as if she's holding a chick, a small living thing, a kindness.

When she returns, intending to thank him and ask him for another demonstration, he has disappeared. His coffee mug on the fence post: *Jack was here.*

Was it something I said, or didn't say? Something I am, or am not?

27

NOTHING TO DREAM ABOUT

June is blowing itself out on a mischievous wind, bewitching grasses into ripples and currents, swells and crests, turning the she-oaks inside out and exposing a shock of spindly limbs. It catches the white cockatoos, spinning them head over tailfeather, and lends to crows the grace of sea eagles so that they hover on up-draughts and swoop down on bewildered fish. It releases a fragment of paper from the underside of a leaf, dispersing faint and blurry words into the atmosphere, *penis wither*. Cassie's mood swings up one minute, down the next. Anything and everything is possible.

On three nights last week, her bin had been overturned and rubbish strewn over the front garden. She's put a heavy stone on the lid. It will be a nuisance, having to move the stone when she puts the rubbish out. At least the foxes solved that mystery. But she still hasn't found the Dakin book. How to explain its loss without acknowledging that someone has been inside here?

And wasn't there a rather disturbing precision about the distribution of her rubbish? Almost a pattern? But that's ridiculous. It's just the winter drawing in, she tells herself. Short days and less sunshine. It's the wind, robbing me of my wits. That's all it is. Nothing to worry about. But the book . . .

She has a bad day and then another. One night, after dinner, she opens a bottle of sticky wine and a box of iced Vovos. Extreme measures. The television is showing a James Bond movie, *Die Another Day*. Her weeping is intermittent and unrelated to the film. Wine releases, she thinks, keeping the tissues handy.

Halle Berry climbs on top of Pierce Brosnan and makes love to him. Cassie feels a jolt deep in her groin. Her breasts tingle, nipples erect. She looks down at herself in surprise, brushes off some flecks of coconut. 'That's enough of that,' she says sternly and pops another biscuit into her mouth.

'More wine?'

'Don't mind if I do.'

She thinks of Jack and the stringybark fire-egg. The boyish pleasure in his weathered face. The simplicity of his offering pleased her. It felt like an overture of friendship. He overstepped his own boundary, she guesses. He wanted to show me what he knew, wanted to share something with me. And then he ran away. He is drawn to the personal, and burned by it. So much in need of solace. Poor man. And what about me? Am I so lonely that I will turn to any smile to warm my hands?

She thinks about Kit and his travels with his love tent. Wonders how many young women have been enticed in there, and does he keep count? Love and all that, she thinks. It's been a long time since anything approaching fervour has quickened her pulse. The marital slide into calmer, compromised coupling occurred so long ago she'd almost forgotten it could be otherwise. But it had nothing to do with Tom. Richard had been wrong about that. After Tom died, she needed Richard more than ever. The hunger for his physical presence, for the reassurance of arms, kisses. I remember, she thinks. He hadn't felt the same way. He'd thought it strange, recommended tranquillisers, went interstate on business. He had dealt with the loss of their child in his own way, and sought his solace elsewhere.

Three men. Not much of a tally. Hardly a defining statement, either way. One, a brief discouraging fumble after a beach party. Another had been her boyfriend for four months until he went on holiday to Italy. She didn't see or hear from him again, and though he wasn't much of a loss, her confidence took a steep dive that she didn't pull out of till Richard began courting her. Three men. Might easily have been four, she thinks, recalling a moment of perfect astonishment.

Daniel Breeson. A confident, genial man, senior partner in Richard's firm, who'd always taken the trouble to draw her out and set her at ease when they met. If he'd been more handsome, or younger, she would have been intimidated by his attention, but he was short and fat with little eyes and shining greasy skin, so she relaxed and flattered him and was able to imagine herself equal to his social milieu for a while. If she'd been asked, she would have said she liked him.

She'd had a bath and was sitting curled on the sofa in her dressing-gown. She had no idea why he'd be knocking on her door with a bottle of wine at nine-thirty in the evening.

'Richard isn't here,' she told him, aghast at being caught without make-up.

'Oh? In that case, I might as well share this with you.'

He waved the bottle in the air and twinkled at her. He wasn't drunk. She thought he seemed a little . . . loose. It must be very serious news, to require home delivery. Was it the Asian transfer? Richard would hate that. She readied herself to behave as a good corporate wife should, regardless of dressing-gown.

'Mmm, you smell nice,' he said, when she returned from dressing hurriedly in jeans and linen shirt. She felt a slight recoil inside then, but ignored it.

She noticed how he relaxed into the sofa, stretching an arm along the back, easing out his legs. She perched on a chair. Smiled attentively. The wine was excellent, they agreed. Had he seen much of the tennis? Michelle had been looking at houses in Portugal. They already had the villa in Tuscany of course. Cassie listened and waited, doing her best to make intelligent small talk, for Richard's sake. Is Daniel going to retire? Is that it?

He said, 'Richard works long hours, doesn't he? We all do. How do you cope, Cassie?' He leaned forward, suddenly earnest. 'Really. How do you cope?'

Here it comes, she thought. How will I cope if he's transferred overseas? She said, 'I manage. As Michelle does, I imagine.'

He frowned. 'My wife barely has time to say good morning to me. She works longer hours than I do. Sometimes we don't see each other for days.'

Marital problems? Silence fell as she cast around in her mind for something to say. Children? What were the names of his children? Was the eldest Dominic? And there was a Lucy, wasn't there? The middle girl. 'How are –'

'I've always been fascinated by what it would be like to have sex with you, Cassie.'

Eh? Run that by me again, would you?

'I fantasise about you all the time.'

What?

He wouldn't meet her eyes. A slight quiver softened the line of his mouth, gently disarming her.

'I've fantasised about you for years,' he said.

'Me?'

'I've spent hours, wondering what it would be like to have you. Bet you come like a train, don't you, Cassie?'

'Me?' she said again and laughed nervously. 'Have you been drinking, Daniel?'

'Only this.' He held up the wine glass.

She wished she hadn't drunk the wine. She felt she'd be able to handle this sensibly, if the alcohol hadn't confused her. She needed to make the required sophisticated response. To utter the words that would put everything back into place with no harm done. Now, what were they?

'So how about it, Cassie? You and me? Right now.'

'Oh, I don't think . . .' But how to decline without hurting his feelings?

She allowed him to kiss her, with some idea of letting him down gently. It might still be possible to avoid an unpleasant scene, she thought. The kiss went on for longer than it should have done. The kiss was unexpectedly stirring. She broke away. He took it as a sign to unfasten his trousers. He had no doubt she would comply. An old hand, accustomed to guiding flustered women through their initial panic in order to get what he wanted. It would be very smooth, very practised. And if the kiss was anything to go by, very good. A mere adjunct to all those excellent dinner parties. Nothing to make a fuss about.

. . . and what did you do, after the cheese?

Oh, I did the rounds with Richard Callinan's wife.

I don't think so, thought Cassie.

She neatly zipped him up again and tried to push him away. He caught her in his arms.

'Come on, Cassie,' he mumbled into her neck. 'Shame to see a good woman go to waste.'

'Daniel!' Whatever did he mean? Go to waste?

'I can't have sex with you,' she said.

'That's all right. We'll just lie on your bed and have a cuddle.'

A cuddle didn't sound so bad. Perhaps if she . . . No, better not.

'I can't do that either. Richard will be home any minute,' she added desperately.

'No, he won't.'

He had moved away from her but he was unbuttoning his shirt.

'We'll just go to your bedroom and have a cuddle,' he said. 'No harm in that, is there? Just a kiss and a cuddle, Cassie. Through here, is it?'

'What about your wife?' she pleaded, following him.

'I love her. Don't get any ideas about that. It's just that we have different sexual requirements.'

Love. What a wonderfully elastic word it is.

He moved close again. 'I have this idea about what it will be like with you. How good it will be. Can't wait to find out.'

Curiosity, she reflected, didn't offer the best pick-up lines. No romance. 'You'd be disappointed,' she told him.

'Let's see.' He caught her arm, pulled her to him. Whispered in her ear what he would do to her. Startling, exciting, terrifying things. He was kissing her, both his hands on her breasts, when she burst into tears. The last defence?

'No. Please. Please, just . . . just do up your clothes and leave. Please.'

She was more horrified by her own body's response than by anything else. This is what people do, she thought. It's this easy. This is what married people do, everywhere. Not in *this* marriage, she vowed.

He was genuinely puzzled. 'But you're in my dreams, Cassie.' Alarmed enough by her distress to do as she asked.

Afterwards she thought, what a glorious thing to say. What a lovely, lovely lie. *You're in my dreams, Cassie.* Are there no limits to what a man will say to get a woman? Is it simply a question of what she can bring herself to believe? And how much she needs to believe it?

Fantasising about me, she thought. How likely was that? I expect he thought I'd be grateful. Middle-aged neglected corporate wife. Bound to be good for a quick one, isn't she? Bound to roll over with her paws in the air.

She almost had.

For some time after the event, whilst having sex with Richard, she had teased herself to orgasm with the memory of Daniel's whispers. It didn't seem wrong to do this. There was even a strange kind of justice about it, she thought, because over the years her orgasms had diminished to the point where she felt as though they were happening to somebody else.

She saw Daniel afterwards on several occasions, in the company of mutual acquaintances. His manner was exactly as it had always been. Easy, charming, attentive. You'd think he'd forgotten all about it. Cassie flushed whenever he was near, and refused to consider whether her rejection of him was due to loyalty to Richard, or her fear that Daniel would discover she was nothing to dream about, nothing at all.

28

TENTACLES

Kit is on his knees rubbing a wooden block covered in sandpaper along a broad skirting board. Ten weeks of sanding, filling, plastering, painting and odd jobs. Ten weeks of Hannah. Time flies when you're having fun. His plan is to spin out the decorating work and keep himself useful until the weather warms up. Fat Harry might need help behind the bar when the tourists return.

He gets free board and even a couple of beers now and again. The money Richard sent him is stretching out well because there's nothing to spend it on except when he goes up to town. Hitching and walking to get there, he stays at a backpacker motel on the outskirts, goes to pubs for the buzz and the music and the girls. Just to see if he can shake himself free. It hasn't worked. He's been away from Hannah three times and four days is the most he can manage.

In town, he prudently stocks up on ganja. A guy who lives behind the caravan park in Shearwater grows some (everybody knows), but Kit prefers to source it away from his own patch. That way, nobody talks, and nobody knows how much he's smoking. Too much. He's trying to cut back. Doesn't want the half-life that marijuana brings but it stops the aching and the burning for this woman. All these months of travelling and he's been so careful not to get caught, not to get stuck with people. Well, you're stuck now, Kit.

Too right.

Things could be worse, but oh god, they could be so much better.

He's stopped sanding. He's sitting propped against the wall, day-dreaming, when a knock on the door sends him into orbit.

'Kit? You there?' Lily sticks her head round the door. 'Fat Harry's boat's in. Want to come and have a look?'

Harry is part owner of *Half Your Luck*. The sleeping part. He'd bought his share from a local motel owner, a man of effortless charm and breathtaking insincerity, who had pursued Hannah for a couple of months before realising that his ego required more acknowledgement than she was ever likely to concede.

Why not? Kit thinks. Something to do. Lily's a great kid, sharp and funny and, yes, hot, but not, definitely not, in the running. The one thing Kit yearns for is the one thing he can't have. But he hasn't given up hope yet. And neither has Lily.

'Can we take the boat out?' he asks.

'Hell, no. Kev and Gill would have a fit. They're the other owners. But we can have a look.'

On the deck of the boat, she poses. Little Miss Nonchalance, radiating sensuality. Look at me, Kit, she commands silently. And Kit looks, can't help himself. She feels his eyes like fingers, running all over her, and she moves closer, leans next to him. He doesn't move away, small vanities appeased by her adoration.

'Grace said your aunt's on the run.'

'On the run?'

'From life, she says.'

'Ah.'

'Are you on the run from life, Kit?'

'Me? I'm running towards it, not away from it.' Time I saw Cassie again, he's thinking. He'd stopped suggesting that she dine at the pub with him. It's plain she doesn't want to, and he's worried anyway about what her sharp eyes might notice.

Lily says, 'You can't do one without the other.'

'You're not making much sense,' he points out.

It's true. The words coming out of her mouth have no connection with the images in her mind. She doesn't care how silly she sounds, as long as she is close to him. Her bright face is upturned to his. The sudden intensity of his stare disconcerts her; she drops her head. He can see the sun-glints in her dark hair, wants to fold his hands through it and gently pull her towards him. Hannah. Hannah with her hair coming loose from a topknot she'd fastened to keep it out of the way. Hannah reaching down with paint-splattered rubber gloves to load the roller. Short blue blouse buttoned to the plump crease of her breasts. Hannah, wasting herself on a man like Harry. Hannah, who told him, 'There, you see. All done. We make a good team, you and me.'

If only. She makes him feel the way he did as a small boy when he first smelled peanut butter in someone else's lunchbox. He had to have some.

Lily, feeling his attention waver, suggests they check on the octopus. They jump down onto the jetty. Sunshine and lack of wind make it a perfect winter day. Lily shrugs off her jacket and ties the arms loosely round her waist. She tosses her hair and moves ahead of him so he can watch her. He is aware of the deliberate display. He also knows how old she is. Fourteen. Hannah has made a point of telling him this several times. Warning him off. He wanted to protest. Why would I look at your daughter when you are here? But he looks. Who wouldn't?

Lily knows the line is running tight between herself and Kit. She can feel it. Just a few more tugs and anything might happen. *It* might happen. Just a few more tugs. See what your mother has to say about that.

She cautiously opens the door of the aquarium. No octopus lurking.

'He hasn't been wandering so much since I put the extra netting on the tank.'

He detects the note of regret in her voice. About to follow her through the door, he hesitates. This might not be the brightest idea you've had today, Kit.

As if he'd given her a sign, Lily reaches up. A hand on either side of his face, she brings his mouth down to hers. And he allows himself to kiss her, eyes closed, his right hand moving swiftly up her body from waist to breast.

Stop! Fourteen. Shit, shit, shit. Quick! Think about your mother. That always works.

Lily is clinging, moulded to his chest and thighs, arms like tentacles everywhere. He struggles to push her away.

'Don't be scared, Kit.' Her hand moves to his zip, grazing the outline of his erection. Kits gasps, catches her wrist tightly, hurting her.

'This is stupid,' he says, hoarsely.

'Why? You know you want to.' She is afraid but the taste of this fear is delicious, has her licking her lips to get every trace of it.

'Because you're a kid,' he says.

She jerks away from him, seared, and he escapes into the saving grace of daylight.

Lily lets him go. Smiling through tears, she takes the octopus from his tank, counting off the tentacles one by one. He loves me not; he loves me. He loves me not; he loves me. The image of Kit's face, so close to hers, fills her mind. His warm mouth and hungry eyes. He loves me not; he loves me . . . You've got to make it come out the way you want it to, haven't you?

I'm not a kid, she thinks. She runs her fingers over the breast that he'd held, circles the nipple with a dreamy look on her face. Kids don't have these, do they? He loves me not; he loves me . . .

He'll be back.

Simon Biddle, swilling down the deck of his cray boat, had seen Kit and Lily leave Harry's boat. Watched Lily prancing up the jetty. That girl! Now he sees the boy hurry out of the aquarium, pausing to adjust his jeans at the crotch. Knows what that means. Lily!

He shouts. 'Hey! You!'

And without forethought, but with a great blast of guilt and misery at his heels, Kit takes off, running fast as he can.

Simon, red-faced, pounding down the jetty, is too far away to have a hope of catching up. Lily steps out calmly in front of him, octopus over one arm. Simon stops, eyes her warily.

'You all right?' he asks.

'It's not what you think,' she says, disgusted at this turn of events. When is everyone going to leave her alone and let her get on with her life? 'Jesus! You must have frightened the hell out of him.'

'Don't swear, Lily,' he pleads. 'Don't carry on.'

'Don't swear? Don't swear?' Her voice is strident with scorn.

Simon takes a step backwards, looks around anxiously to see who might be watching.

'You listen to me,' Lily says, giving a fine imitation of Hannah. 'You've got to stop watching me. I can look after myself. You never used to be like this. It's creeping me out. It's like having a bloody guardian angel hanging around!'

He draws breath to remonstrate but she holds up an imperious finger.

'Stop it. Understand?'

He nods.

'Well, don't look so miserable about it. And you can stop worrying about Kit, too. Nothing happened in there.'

Not for want of trying, though.

When Kit stops running, he's on the far side of the headland and cursing himself. What a bloody stupid thing to do. It was Simon Biddle who called out. Now he's sure to think there's something going on. Panic grips him. What if he tells Hannah? Fuck! He collapses into the long grass, face in his hands, dangerously close to tears. But by the time his breathing steadies, he's realised there won't be any trouble. Lily will sort it out. Oh! He thinks of her hands on his body and groans. That girl would sort anybody out.

Before Kit left England, his father had wound up their man-to-man talk, straight-faced, with laughter in his eyes.

'Don't forget, son,' he said. 'Three rules for travelling in alien lands: Don't look the men directly in the eye – it may be taken as a threat. Don't look at the women at all. And never show fear.'

Sorry, Dad.

29

TRICKS

If anyone from that other world, from the separate universe containing Melaleuca Drive, cared to ask, she would tell them she is managing. Is, in fact, rather proud of the way she is managing. It's a pity there's no one here to notice. She might even sing to herself, or whistle now and again, while dusting or doing the washing up, but too often sees herself doing this and shies away from the pathos.

In the cottage, she has discovered little islands of comfort where she can relax her guard. In bed, with the curtains tightly closed. In the bathroom. At the sink looking out over the garden to dunes and sky. Other areas carry a hint of threat, set her insecurities jangling. It's largely a matter of shadows and proportions and unfamiliarity and . . . something else, she thinks. In the living-room, even when the fire is lit, she has a pervasive sense of unease. It's something to do with the fact that the front door opens right onto her sanctuary. She sets the sofa at an angle, so her back is to the door, but can't rid herself of the feeling that the eyes of the world are upon her.

She walks further than she has for weeks, thinking, focusing on anything except what she is going to do with the rest of her life. Her boots splash through the fine film of water that glides over the sand, blue and white clouds caught inside each shining curve.

The wind swings around bringing a sharp chill to the air. Sand grains sting her face. Seeking shelter, she takes a path that winds up steeply between sandstone cliffs of yellow ochre, pink and brown. A nankeen kestrel hangs high over her head, almost motionless, spying for the scurrying or scampering that signals food. The path is lined with a low tangle of scrub, glimpses of the dusky pink and green of correa bells, the golden brushes of dwarf banksias, a sudden blaze of red heath. Beside her is a deep scoured gully, dry now, but obviously prone to torrents of water. She reaches a series of wooden steps, shrubs massed to either side. The light is greener here and the scents are fresh and earthy, the air eerily hushed. She moves to the sound of her own hurrying footsteps, up towards the road where she turns left for the long walk back to the cottage.

A gleaming open-topped sports car approaches. A red Jaguar. Lovely, she thinks, and raises her head to smile a greeting. The car slows as it passes her. A man and woman in matching dark-blue baseball caps examine her as though she is an unattractive specimen of the local fauna.

How rude! If Richard had been with her, there would have

been a greeting. Like talks to like. *You're looking very rural, my dear.*

'It's going to rain on you and your leather seats!' she shouts after them. 'She'll play up on you with your senior partner!'

I'm behaving like a madwoman. Amazing, how good it feels. Grace would approve. The last tattered remnants of corporate wife sucked into the slipstream of a red Jaguar and gone forever. Grace would laugh.

Before returning to the cottage, Cassie climbs the nearest dune to get a signal on her phone. There is something she wants to ask Elizabeth Savage.

'Yes, I have a spare key,' Elizabeth tells her, 'hanging on the hook by the back door here. Is there a problem?'

'No. Not at all. It's just that, well, you know how it is. I am alone. I like to feel safe when I lock my door. Some rental houses have keys out all over the place. At the general store, for example. You don't keep one there? For emergencies?'

'Cassie, my dear, there are only three keys. I have one, and you have the other two.'

She is quite sure of that?

Quite sure.

But Cassie thinks she hears anxiety in her voice. Elizabeth can't have taken the Dakin book. She doesn't leave the house. She may have sent someone for it. But why wouldn't they simply knock and ask? There's some other explanation, Cassie decides. And it's probably best if her landlady doesn't get the idea that items are going missing from her house.

Elizabeth puts down the phone. Better keep an eye on the place, she thinks. Better have a word with Myrtle. Looks like it's happening again.

Back at the cottage, Cassie pauses at the gate, hearing a sound from the garage. The doors are ajar. A dim figure is moving about inside. Kit? Light from the back window briefly outlines a body. It's someone broader than Kit, a heavier build. Richard? Has Richard come for her at last? (It would be like him, to go looking for the car, to see what damage she's done to his pet.) But even as the thought frames itself, she knows it is born of need, not sense. This isn't Richard.

Fear bypasses the intellect, goes straight to the blood. Like love.

Heart thudding, blood feathering in her veins, she stands poised between battle and flight, one hand on the gate latch as the man emerges.

Oh! It's the fisherman who was rude to her. The Mary Cassatt man. She puts a hand to her chest, lets her breath go.

'Hello?' she says, with barely a trace of a squeak. What is he doing here?

He looks up, shock plain on his face. 'Mrs Callinan. You nearly gave me a heart attack.'

'Likewise.' *Does everyone know my name?*

'I was just putting the bicycle back. I noticed it a few days ago, lying in long grass down the road. When it was still there this morning, I thought I'd better bring it back for you. They don't last long out in the salt air, these old things.'

'How did you know it belonged here?'

Her tone is polite but he can feel her suspicion. She knows Jack too. He's seen her talking to Jack. He pulls at his white collar nervously, looks at the ground. 'I've seen the boy riding it,' he says. 'I'm Simon Biddle.' He advances, hand outstretched.

'Cassie,' she says, shaking his hand reluctantly. 'It's very kind of you to go to so much trouble.' Another Biddle? They're everywhere.

Whatever was Kit thinking of, leaving the bicycle outside? He probably wandered off to smoke a joint and forgot about it, she thinks, concerned. She's been careful not to comment on his marijuana habit but he seems to use it without caution, comfortably sliding out of life, in the way that a frightened child might suddenly fall asleep, unable to deal with a real or imagined terror. But what has Kit to be frightened of?

Her visitor is explaining, 'I thought you were out, with the car not being here.'

Oh yes?

'Otherwise I'd have knocked and introduced myself.'

His expression is gentle, sorrowful even, and his eyes skitter away from hers as though he's shy. He fingers the collar again, drawing her attention to it. It isn't an ecclesiastical collar at all. It's just the rim of a white skivvy beneath his black jumper. Does he realise the effect it creates? There is something instinctively disarming about a priest's collar, at least for someone of Cassie's generation and background. It inhibits discourtesy and predisposes you to a show of respect. Not one of you, it declares. Not playing by the same rules.

She says, 'My nephew has the car today. I've been out walking.'

They are both at the gate, one either side of it.

'Would you like to come in?' he asks, with grave courtesy.

She laughs, and the tension of the moment dissolves as they exchange places. Biddle, she thinks. 'Are you related to Jack Biddle?'

'Yes.'

'He . . . helped me. There was a problem with a lock. How is he?'

Simon pushes at a clump of dandelion leaves with the toe of his boot. Shut up. Shut up. Shut up. Saint bloody Jack. Always there. In your face. You couldn't do anything, couldn't even sit at the kitchen table chewing a bit of pork crackling, without somebody saying, 'Jack used to do it just like that'. And the chasm of difference between himself and the absent Jack would appear instantly before him and he would run from there, sick to the stomach, spitting the taste of Jack from his mouth. You could always count on Jack. Oh you could, could you? That right, is it? Well, where was Jack, when the shit hit the fan and the family blew apart? Where was he then? Tell me that.

'Jack's fine,' he says evenly.

Cassie is suddenly anxious, needs to feel walls around her. 'I'd better get in. Thanks again.'

He takes a step towards her. 'I could take you out one day, if you like? In the boat?' He produces a ghastly smile that makes her move back, out of reach.

'That's very kind of you, but I don't think so.'

'I've got all the safety gear. You've no need to be afraid. Not with me. It's really something, seeing the coast from out at sea. God's hand at work, you know? You can feel it.'

'I'm not a good sailor.'

'We can go out when it's calm. I could call you.'

They just don't listen, do they?

'I . . . I haven't got a landline connection here. And I can never remember my mobile number. The only thing that ever comes into my head is my home number.' She stops in confusion. 'My phone number at home. My other phone . . .'

My other home.

He doesn't seem to notice her embarrassment. 'I can drop in and let you know. I often pass this way.'

She's studying him, trying to work out why he's asking her out. He's wondering that himself.

'No. No, thank you.' She is polite but firm, the rebuff unmistakeable this time. 'Thank you again for the bicycle.'

Inside the house, she feels stronger, safer. He's younger than Jack. Less creased. Why had he kept on pressing her about the boat? It must have been obvious she wasn't interested. Bit creepy, she thinks. Bit desperate? And lonely. The collar isn't much of a come-on either.

I haven't been out in a boat for years, she thinks, remembering Richard's brief infatuation with yachts. He'd had lessons, chartering once a month and sailing in the bay. Cassie had loved the feeling of the boat pushing strongly through the water, powered by the wind.

But I was useless. Couldn't remember the terms. Couldn't think what I was supposed to do next.

'Get your legs out of the way of that rope!' he'd yell, to the great amusement of their friends. His friends. 'She's only here for decoration,' he told them. It was a joke. Naturally.

He'd been to Country Road and picked up some nautical-looking gear. They had photographs of him standing at the wheel in his cream wool sweater and blue peaked cap, his tanned face turned towards the sun. How I irritated him, she thinks. I won't go out in the fishing boat, but Kit might like to. It might be a new experience for him to write about.

Before nightfall, she goes out to close the garage door. The bicycle is propped against the wall on the right-hand side as usual. She examines it for signs of further wear and tear but it looks much the same.

Late in the evening, cosy in the firelight, she falls asleep on the sofa again with the television murmuring. She wakes half-frozen at four in the morning and gets up to go to bed, pausing to check through the curtains that the bin is still upright, the stone still in place on its lid.

When full daylight breaks, she sees what she'd missed earlier. The bin is upright and the stone is still in place on the lid, but rubbish has been scattered all over the garden again. It's a declaration of intent, she thinks, furious. To put the stone back on the lid. That is an act of war. A war of mean little tricks. Who is doing this? A sneaking, creeping opponent. What does he imagine I'm going to do? Roll over and die? I don't think so. Tricks. Schools are rife with them. Marriages are rife with them. Cassie knows all about tricks. She hears a weak voice, scarcely a whisper. *How can you do this to me? After all I've been through?* She ignores it.

I'm right, she thinks. Something weird is going on. She finds strength in the thought, an unexpected rush of exultation and the scent of battle.

'I'm going to find out who you are,' she says. 'I'm going to catch you out. You miserable little shit. You aren't going to drive me away.'

Whoever he is, he's picked the wrong woman, she thinks, with grim amusement. Try staring into the eyes of a child with leukaemia, mate. Try facing your husband of twenty-eight years when he tells you he's having a child with someone else. Try meeting despair with Valium in one hand, sleeping tablets in the other, and thinking why not? Try that, you creep. And never, ever, underestimate a woman who's been compared to a cabbage.

30

FOOL ON THE STOOL

'Grace? It's me, Cassie.'

'Who?'

'Cassie.'

'What's that rushing noise?'

'It's the wind. I'm up on the dunes. Hold on. Is that better?'

'Yes.'

'Grace, you know that man who sits in the corner of your shop reading? Simon Biddle?'

'The fool on the stool. What about him?'

'Is he all right?'

'All right? You mean all right in the head? Crazy?'

'Um, yes.'

'Why do you ask?'

'Well, the way he dresses, for one thing. You know, going round looking like a priest. That collar effect. Why does he do that?'

'He doesn't do it all the time. Perhaps it makes him feel better than he is. Perhaps it makes him feel braver, or stronger. I don't know. Why do people do anything?'

'But it's such an affectation!'

'It's only a white skivvy, Cassie,' says Grace mildly. 'No law against it. Whatever gets you through the night.'

'Has he always done it?'

'Listen to her! Only been in the town two minutes and wants all our stories.'

'I'm sorry. It's just . . . I just want to know, is he . . . is there any chance he's dangerous?'

'God, no. He can be a nuisance, hanging round places. Nobody's got much time for him. But dangerous? This is Shearwater, Cassie.'

There is a pause. Cassie wonders what he's done. What rules has he broken, that no one has time for him?

Grace says, 'Has anything happened, Cassie? Has something frightened you?'

Elizabeth Savage had warned Cassie. The town supports its eccentrics. She feels too constrained, too much the outsider, to expose her intruder theories to certain ridicule. She's given them all enough cause to gossip about her sanity.

'He asked me out,' she admits sheepishly. 'He offered to take me out in his boat.'

'You?'

Thanks a lot, Grace. 'Yes, me.' She's expecting some gentle ribbing, further questions.

But Grace is thoughtful. 'That's odd. I must tell Gudrun. That's a new development. Perhaps it's for the best, too. Are you going to go?'

'No, I . . . I told him I'm not a good sailor. He kept on asking. I said no. What do you mean, "a new development"?'

'He doesn't have a social life. Doesn't go out with women. Or men, for that matter. Doesn't drink. He's what you might call chaste.'

'But he must be –'

'Forty, I reckon, give or take a year. Mind you, my grandfather was a farmer and he always said you should never trust anything with balls. I never have.'

'Chaste,' Cassie repeats faintly, prudently withholding an opinion on the rural advice.

'Goes with the outfit, when you think about it. There must be something about you that's getting under his skin.'

'Great. That's all I need.'

'Don't worry. I'll have a word with Jack. Jack'll fix it.'

'Oh! Please don't say anything. There's nothing to fix.'

'Well then, let's keep it that way.'

Cassie thinks, I hope Kit's making plenty of notes about these people while he's here. He may never see the like again.

She asks, 'Have you got a copy of *Australian Seashores*, by Dakin, in stock? An old book, orange cover, gold sea-horse on the spine?'

'No, I don't think we have, but I can keep an eye open for you when we have a buy-in.'

'Yes, please.'

'You're settling in, aren't you?' Grace observes.

'I think I am.' The thought makes Cassie nervous with its implications of the future, but she knows the comment is kindly meant.

'You're getting to be more like one of us every day.'

Gee, thanks.

31

STORMS AND GEORGE CLOONEY

Mid-July, the wind turns and blows straight from Antarctica. Strong gusts pushing thick clouds across the sun, so there is intermittent glare and gloom. In the gloom, the awful solitude of the wild beach and grey waves. But in the sun glare, a sparkle of hope, a dancing optimism, bright and blue and shiny.

Cassie buys thermals – leggings and tops with purple and green stripes. She buys kid gloves and thick socks, and deliciously soft sheepskin slippers. She buys a purple beanie, pulls it down over her ears and looks at her reflection. Terrible.

One morning, she suspects that the photograph of herself and the children has been moved, but she can't be sure she hasn't nudged it during the dusting. Moving the sofa to vacuum beneath it, she finds a small black button. It's not one of hers. She's vacuumed under here before. Has it been planted there for her to find? Am I crazy, for thinking this? She checks the house for other signs and cannot convince herself. Has he or hasn't he been here?

Nothing else has happened. Not that she can be sure of. Perhaps he's given up. Maybe he's realised that she isn't going to be frightened away. She'd expected (hoped for?) further proof of her suspicions, even, perhaps, a confrontation. Life has become interesting, with more than a whiff of risk. How satisfying it would be, to take aim at an unequivocally deserving target.

After a week of gales and rain, the roof leaks in the spare bedroom. Water drips loudly into the pan Cassie has placed there. When she turns on the taps, the flow is brown, clearing after a few seconds. Rain hammering on the roof, blasting against the windows, reminds her of a movie she once saw about a storm at sea. She imagines the little cottage, isolated in the darkness, tossed on enormous waves, and where is George Clooney when you need him? She's glad Kit is under a sound roof at the pub and not braving this weather in his tent. It puzzles her, why he's still here in Shearwater. Perhaps he's writing? He hasn't visited her for almost two weeks, and she's grateful for his occasional company but tries not to anticipate it, or rely on it. She's sleeping badly at night because she's snoozing too much during the day, and the one time she tries to walk on the beach, she is quickly driven back indoors.

When the storms subside, the sea lies flat, discoloured by sediment washed down from the cliffs. An opaque grey with tints of pink and brown, and a thin line of deep blue-grey at the horizon. From the top of the dunes, rugged up in her new cold-weather gear, she can't discern a swell. There are no clear ribbons of light marking the flow of the currents. The sky is a pale washed blue with layers of thin ragged clouds. The air is fresh and exhilarating, and the beach offers up its treasures. On one walk, she finds a seal skull, and on another, three red plastic bait baskets that, surely, she will find a use for. And then she finds Jack Biddle.

She has to look twice, to be sure. He is wearing a dull green japara, the colour of the dune scrub. She waves. When he raises an arm in response, she decides to take it as an invitation and scrambles up the slope.

'Jack!' she says. 'How are you?'

'Good. You?'

'I'm getting fitter,' she tells him, choosing a spot to sit that seems least likely to send her slithering back down to the beach. 'That slope would have had me gasping a month ago.'

'Things okay at the cottage?'

Now why would he . . . has Grace been interfering or is he simply referring to its state of repair? She answers breezily.

'Yes, thank you. I feel like I'm beginning to settle in here.'

He gives her a look she cannot understand.

'See what I found,' she says and uncurls her fingers to reveal a small grey and white disk.

'Operculum,' he says. 'A little door. The sea creatures draw the disk in, to block the entrance to their shell. It keeps them from drying out.'

'Operculum,' she repeats, thinking of the small animal curled safe behind its door. She slips it into her pocket, sits hugging her knees, face turned up to the sun. He'd probably be happier alone. He's probably wishing I'd go away, she thinks. How does he know all these things? Books, I suppose. He absorbs facts. He chews them over and spits out particles of relevance, from some inner compulsion. Little spurts of pressure. Tidy, pre-digested packages. And behind all the facts, somewhere, is Jack.

She says, 'You remember the day you rescued me? You seemed to know your way around the cottage very well.' It comes out in a rush. It's been on her mind. 'Have you been there before? Inside the cottage?'

She doesn't look at him. He takes his time answering.

'Used to live there.'

'Oh.'

'I grew up in that house.'

Cassie can feel the tingle of a story. She wants to know more. Wants to draw him out. Thinks it might be like getting blood from a stone.

'Not a big house, for a family,' she ventures.

'No.' He makes an effort to lighten his tone. 'But we had the beach for our back garden.'

'And the ocean for your swimming pool.' She says the words without thinking, picking up on his cue. It is a mistake.

'That's no swimming pool,' he says.

'Oh, Jack, I'm sorry.'

After a moment, she asks gently, 'What was her name? Your daughter?'

A jolt runs though him. Heat and hurt and faintness, like it happened yesterday. Always, like it happened yesterday.

He is silent for so long that she thinks he isn't going to answer but he says, 'Susie. Her name is Susie. Short for Suzette.'

'I'm sorry,' she says again. Impossible to leave him in peace now. Impossible to simply get up and go after that blunder.

'I've been doing some work on the garden,' she says.

'I noticed.'

She tells him what she's done, what she's discovered. She explains how she hung the white seal skull under the branches of the old cypress tree. 'It suits the gloom of that tree, somehow.'

He'll think I'm mad, won't he? I don't care.

Amusement crinkles his eyes. She would like to invite him home for coffee, to talk to him and listen to the workings of his odd mind, but she hasn't the courage to ask. He might think I'm trying to lure him to my bed. An ageing predatory female. He'll be sure to misunderstand. That's all there is, really, when you think about it, degrees of misunderstanding. There's a lot to be said for sticking to facts.

She is melancholy again and feels a shiver of loneliness. Beware the pressure of pity, she warns herself. There are too many things that cannot be made better with a kiss. Too many times when it is better not to trust. You never know. She gets to her feet, brushes off the sand.

'What keeps you going, Jack? After something like that happens?'

She waits, looking down at him.

'Curiosity,' he says, eventually.

Fear, she guesses. Afraid to live, afraid to lose, afraid to die. Sitting on the fence, his heart sealed up tight behind a little door. Stuck on the threshold of the rest of his life. The very place she herself has chosen.

She has topped the dune and is stumbling down the other side when she thinks she hears him call out. Something about a ball. She stops to listen but hearing nothing else, goes back to the cottage.

Impossible to say what alerts her. From outside, everything looks as it usually does, but some sign reaches her, vibrating silently through the air. Hackles raised, she pushes open the back door, peers inside. On the kitchen table there is a pie. A large, white round pie dish. Is this Myrtle's doing? Chicken and mushroom, ready to pop into the oven? She walks around the table warily. There is no note. No card. She does not relax her guard but leans close and sniffs the pie. Odours of uncooked pastry and the sea. She prods it with one finger in the middle, feels it yield slightly. It has to be Myrtle. Who else would leave a pie for her?

And that's the question, isn't it?

She gets a knife, lifts the pastry from the edge of the dish. Sees something dark in there. Feathers? She eases the knife around the circumference of the dish and flips the pastry up and away. Inside, wings partially splayed and neck twisted cruelly to one side, is a dead shearwater.

Cassie leaps up and backwards, grasping the kitchen bench as blood drains from her face to her feet. Run! She forces herself to be still, to think. The bird doesn't smell. Shouldn't it stink? The thought that he's killed it, wrung that little neck with his bare hands and displayed the bird like this, oh! it makes her knees go weak. A closer look convinces her it's more likely that he's picked it up on the beach. One that didn't get away. She dons rubber gloves and lifts it from the dish. The bird is quite intact, mummified skin holding the skeleton together, feather-light, dried out by sun and wind, sand matted in its ruffled plumage. It has stiffened into the cruciform shape, head angled down. Poor little thing.

A nasty schoolboy trick. That's all this is.

'You deserve a better resting place,' she whispers.

She starts to wrap it in the pastry but, laying the bird there, bringing up the edges of the dough to tuck it in, makes her think of a pasty. She decides on a shroud of brown paper instead. Schoolboy rubbish, she thinks, smoothing earth over the little grave she's dug in the garden. What will it be next? Delivery of poo in a paper bag? She hopes not. Is grateful for the lack of a mailbox.

She scrubs the pie dish with disinfectant and hides it away with the box of oddments under the sink. She isn't sure what to do with the pastry. Doesn't want it in her garbage, inside or outside the house. Eventually she decides to take it to the river where she tears it into pieces and throws it all to the ducks, wondering, too late, if uncooked dough might give them digestive trouble. Visions of thirty dead ducks floating on their backs, thirty pairs of webbed feet pointing at the sky. You're more macabre than he is, she tells herself. But it's done. All traces removed. She makes a cup of tea then, and sips it slowly until she grows calm and the tremors in her hands cease.

32

TESTOSTERONE

There's a boy at school who'd do anything to get Lily to himself for a while. In the shower at home, he closes his eyes and dreams her hands, her mouth on his body, until his sister hammers at the bathroom door, shrieking that he'll make her late again. He's fit. Not a bad face. He knows there's no shortage of interest from elsewhere but It's Lily he wants. Lust chooses you. Lust gobbles you up and spits you out wet and dishevelled and wondering, when you finally come to your senses, *what was all that about?* His poor brain is fractured by the frequency of his offerings to the great god, Testosterone, and by the light in Lily's cold green eyes. Do you think he can get so much as a glance from her? Not a one. Till today.

Today, Lily has traded a kiss and a sweaty fumble at her breasts for a CD she knows Kit will like.

'I'll bring it back,' she lied. He knows the CD is lost to him, and doesn't care. Knows also with sad prescience that she won't notice him tomorrow. Wishes someone could tell him how to sit through double maths with an erection that won't go away. There ought to be something you can take, he thinks, gazing miserably at algebraic formula and seeing only Lily.

Lily skips media studies and gets home early. Kit has propped the old bicycle in the backyard at the pub. She smiles secretly when she sees it. Her first smile of the day. There had been another row at home that morning and the fury it raised carried Lily all through the long hours of school.

'You don't understand,' Hannah said, exasperated. Why does the girl wind her up at every possible opportunity? 'It's not right that you spend so much time at the aquarium with Simon. How often do I have to tell you?'

Till you squawk like a hen, Lily thought. Till your stupid voice gives up. Till you explain.

She screamed, 'What has he ever done to you? Nothing! Nothing!'

She knew it shamed her mother, to have others hear their quarrels, but Hannah left the room and Lily's words rang out with her own unacknowledged fear.

She plays the CD in her room, hoping Kit will hear. She plays it twice, until she's bored with it.

'Hiya,' she whispers to her reflection in the mirror. She loves the way he says that. Hiya. Not Hi, like everyone else. Hiya. It's funny. Just to think of it makes her feel shivery inside.

At the other end of the building, Kit and Hannah have finished redecorating for the day. Hannah peels off pink rubber gloves and pushes back a strand of hair. Kit is at the open window, puffing smoke outside. It's been a good afternoon's work, she thinks. He's been easy company today. Not so sulky. She stoops, gathering up paintbrushes and rollers, straightens, and is suddenly astonished by an impulse to hold him. It is so strong she doesn't dare move. Something emanating from her stillness reaches him. He turns, begins to raise an arm, the gesture a prelude to – what? A caress? A plea? But he has missed the moment.

She says, 'I'd better get cleaned up and start thinking about dinner, I suppose. Sounds like Lily's home.'

She's thinking, what madness was that? Must be the paint fumes. But she can't quite leave him. Not yet.

'Let's have a puff of your ciggy,' she says, unable to think of any other way to ease the mutual confusion she's caused.

'I didn't know you smoked.'

'I don't. I used to. A long time ago. Filthy habit. You ought to give it up. It'll kill you.' That's better. Sounding like a mother helps her to pin down who she is. For a while there, she'd forgotten.

'This isn't just tobacco,' he points out, but his eyes are continuing another conversation entirely. Fine eyes, she thinks. Wicked eyes. Just looking into them she can feel taut muscles wrapped around her. Testosterone's calling, and Hannah's right there saying, 'Come on down!'

Stop it.

She winks at him, plucks the spliff from his fingers. He's astonished. Good. She's satisfied that she's distracted him from other, more dangerous intentions.

It's the sound of their laughter that draws Lily out eventually. Murmuring and laughter. She listens for a while before pushing open the door of the guest room.

Two people standing at the window, very close to each other, their backs towards her, heads almost touching.

The earth opens beneath Lily's feet. She is falling so fast she has no time to be afraid. 'Kit?' she says.

Two heads turning from the window to face her.

Lily braces herself in the doorway, arms out to slow the descent. Seeing her, Kit tries to extricate himself quickly from the window frame without rubbing up against the softer parts of Hannah, who seems to be all soft parts. He bumps his head, hard, on the frame.

'Oh! Damn, that hurt. Hiya, Lily,' he says.

Hannah, uncharacteristically, blushes to the roots of her hair.

Lily says nothing.

Her mother stubs out a cigarette on the windowsill, blowing smoke outside. 'You caught me, Lil. Sneaking a ciggy with Kit. Don't tell Harry, will you?'

Lily says, very quietly, 'I'm not stupid. That's not a cigarette. You can smell it a mile away.'

'Can you?' Hannah is amazed.

Kit rushes to the rescue. 'It's one I had before that you can smell, Lily. That's all. Your mum just had a puff on an ordinary cigarette. Don't go getting the wrong idea.'

'Oh, I won't,' says Lily. Her voice sticky as treacle. 'You want to be careful, sharing things. Never know what you might catch.'

'That's enough, Lily. If you can't be pleasant, go to your room.' But the words are spoken without the energy of conviction, as though Hannah knows the balance has shifted. It's not what you do, or don't do, that counts, she thinks. It's what others believe. That's where the spells are conjured; that's where the die is cast. I might as well have kissed him.

Lily laughs and doesn't move. Kit looks from one to the other. Rubs his head.

'Let me look at that,' Hannah says, pulling his head low. 'You've got a bump coming. I'll get the witch-hazel.'

Lily edges from the doorway, eyes hardened with accusation and disgust, keeping her gaze on her mother. If they can lie about the dope, they can lie about anything. What else are they hiding?

Hannah returns quickly with the bottle and some cotton wool balls. 'Sit here, Kit, where I can get at you,' she says.

'Oooh, sit here, Kit, where I can get at you,' Lily mimics.

Kit ducks, waiting for the explosion, but Hannah laughs, her brief embarrassment apparently forgotten. And is there, in the slight lifting of the corner of her mouth, the pink flush of her cheeks, the buoyancy of her glance, a faint suggestion of satisfaction that Kit prefers her to her own daughter? She dabs lotion on his bruise, refusing to look at Lily who stands now with hands on her hips, issuing a dangerous, silent challenge.

How to protect this child who fights me every step of the

way? Why does she have to see me as the enemy? And the business with Simon . . . what good can come of that? Whatever I ask of her, she'll do the opposite. She knows too much and nothing at all. I can't tell her anything without telling her the whole of it, and I can't do that. I can't ever do that.

'Press down on that for a while,' she says to Kit, guiding his fingers to the soaked cotton wool. 'It'll keep the bruising down. In half an hour or so, you could give Harry a hand to get the beer up? That okay?'

'Fine,' says Kit, and flees, leaving the arena to mother and daughter.

33

TO BUILD AND TEND A GARDEN

To build and tend a garden is to stake a claim, to create the illusion of personal territory. It may or may not be an expression of personality but it is the statement of an inhabitant, not one who is merely passing through.

In her early twenties and studying for a graduate diploma in education, Cassie had lived alone in a small city flat. Many of her fellow students shared accommodation close to the university but Cassie couldn't do that. The thought of living with the idiosyncrasies of mere acquaintances was too alarming.

Set on the ground floor of a sturdy block of eight, built some time in the sixties, Cassie's flat had a private yard into which the sun crept for a couple of hours each day. She put a wooden chair in there, filled the space with white impatiens and red geraniums, sat sometimes with sunlight on her upturned face, ignoring the noise of the traffic from the freeway.

At Melaleuca Drive, the garden was large. Richard had

planned it as an extension of their architect-designed house. He insisted that a gardener came once a fortnight 'to keep things up to scratch'.

'I don't mind you doing the odd bit of weeding,' he said, 'but a gardener will keep it looking the way it's supposed to.'

Geometrically tidy garden beds and the deep gloss of camellia leaves. Heavy pink blossoms drooping over well-watered lawns. Two slender silver birch trees at the right-hand side of the house, a deep and shaded fernery on the left.

Cassie got the gardener on side and effected sabotage with scattered seeds and hidden bulbs that blazed into daisies and petunias, bluebells and snowdrops, daffodils and jonquils. Riots of colour. Richard protested. Cassie persisted, secretly. Richard replaced the gardener. Cassie gave up the struggle, smiled at the new gardener in passing, and always remembered to compliment him on his work with the camellias.

At the back of River Marsh Cottage there is no lawn and there are no plump pink buds or glossy green leaves, but bare fruit trees that appear to be dead or dying. A fig, she thinks. A bird plum. An apple tree with lichen-encrusted boughs. A rough wooden bench looks as though it has sprouted from the earth. Dandelions thrive amongst purple daisies, tangles of grasses and dead wood, native violets and rotting leaves. Silver-eyes visit and the New Holland honey-eaters with their cocky plumage of yellow, white and black. She often sees turtle doves, bright-eyed shrike thrushes, blackbirds, wattlebirds and blue wrens. Kookaburras, ruffled and fluffed against the wind, perch on her fence, watching for skinks, grubs, anything that moves. Next to the fence is a stand of twenty stems of ginger, their leaves fresh green. There is a gloomy corner of gnarled and stunted cypress where the seal skull hangs, and a small patch of bare earth where she buried the shearwater.

She discovers an ancient fuchsia, over two metres high with spidery arching branches that carry tiny clusters of leaves and small intense flowers of red and purple. Struggling upwards through the middle of a thicket of nandina, is an almond tree, barely alive. A few wizened dark-brown pouches hang like tiny bats from its branches.

As she clears and clips and weeds, filling large bags with debris, brown wrens gather, flitting over the disturbed earth, gathering the bounty her spade exposes. She has been working for several hours when Kit arrives. He hears her voice before he sees her, and peers around the corner, thinking he won't interrupt her if she has a visitor. She is alone, talking to herself. She laughs. A rich deep chuckle. Going out of her mind with loneliness, he thinks. I should have come sooner.

'Hiya.'

'Kit! Oh. I'd forgotten the time. Look. Look what I've found under the grass and sand.'

She shows him square slabs of bluestone, laid out to form ovals and rectangles. She's excited as an archaeologist with a major find. All he can see are a few old grey cobblestones.

'It might have been a herb garden, or perhaps vegetables, this close to the kitchen. Don't you think? I wonder how vegetables would like this salt wind.'

Beneath the sandy top layer, the soil is not as bad as she expected. Someone has worked this garden. All it needs is a good boost of organic material and she's got that in hand. The air is redolent with the scent of cow pats. A stack of them by the side of the garage, gathered from one of the river paddocks and drying nicely.

Kit asks, 'You coming to lunch?'

'I suppose so.' She looks at her dirty baggy trousers and loose shirt, and wipes the back of one hand across her forehead. 'Phew. It's tough work. I feel good.'

'You've got soil on your face.'

'I've been gardening. Soil on the face is obligatory.' She laughs. 'I'd forgotten about lunch. Sorry. I just got it into my head that I wanted to tidy up the garden.'

'Great idea.' It'll give her something to do.

'I found a lemon tree. A bit stunted. I think it's a Lisbon. Very big thorns.'

'Did you? Are you going to, um, tidy up a bit before we go?'

'Yes, I'd better.' She doesn't move.

'It's okay by me if you'd rather go another day.'

'It's just that there's a patch over there that's really quite interesting. Another old stone border. I might get some seedlings,' she says. Apprehension clouds her face as she feels the implication of such plans. There are no beginnings without endings.

Kit sees it's time to take charge. 'Why don't you get yourself cleaned up and we can have lunch at the garden centre outside Birandera? You can get your seedlings there at the same time.'

221

He is rewarded with an instant radiant smile that he hasn't seen before.

'You don't mind?' she says.

'Fine by me. What's in the bucket?'

'Urine. I won't be long. I'll just wash my face and hands and change out of my gardening clothes. Make yourself at home.'

Urine? Did she say urine?

She doesn't look much different when she comes out, though the smudge of soil is gone from her face. She hasn't bothered with make-up and she's rubbing white cream vigorously into her cheeks and forehead.

'Skin's peeling. All that wind on the beach.'

She takes a lipstick from her pocket and applies it without looking. The slash of colour is too red, too bold for her naked face. Looking up at him, she understands immediately what she sees in his eyes. She takes his arm and hustles him over to the car.

'You didn't lock up,' he says.

'No point,' she tells him.

He doesn't argue. Wrinkles his nose at the faint warm scent of cow manure that accompanies them all the way to lunch.

Must be the gardening that's making me feel so buoyant, she thinks. At the nursery, she flirts with the man selling bare-rooted roses and he flirts right back. Kit rolling his eyes in the background. Old people carrying on like they've got what it takes.

When they return, with a car full of bags and bottles and trays of plants, the first thing she does is examine the house for changes. Has he been here? Her intruder? She can detect nothing. Perhaps I should have fixed a hair to the door, she thinks. Then I'd know for sure.

Kit calls out. 'Where do you want this stuff?'

'Just pop it in the garage for me, please. Next to the bicycle.'

Ah, she's put the bicycle back. That's good. He stacks the heavy bags of potting mix and fertiliser against the back wall.

'Cass?'

'Yes? I'm here.'

'I'll be off now. Don't go trying to lift those bags on your own, will you? When you're ready for them, let me know. I've left one in the back garden for you to use now.'

'All right. Thank you.' So sweet. She knows perfectly well that she will drag the bags out herself when she needs them.

'Oh look,' she says. 'Now you're the one with a dirty mark on your face.' She drags out a handkerchief, licks a corner of it and rubs his cheek.

The shock is like a physical blow. Rigid with dignity, he waits for realisation to dawn.

'Oh! Oh, Kit! I'm so sorry. I forget, you know.' She's laughing at herself, at his horror-struck expression. Worlds colliding again, she thinks. Stuart in Kit's face. Her own mother, wetting a handkerchief in just that way. Cassie herself, cleaning a smudge from Ellie's chin, removing a hair from Richard's suit jacket, kissing a bruise on Tom's knee.

'Oh, Kit,' he mimics sourly to himself, escaping. If she'd laughed any more she'd have wet herself. He sighs, remembering the bucket. Something will have to be done about that. Something will also have to be done about the two unanswered phone messages from his mother. She'll probably have him listed as a missing person if he doesn't get back to her this week. On top of that, he's got Hannah mothering him and Cassie mothering him. Is there no getting away from the mothers?

He rides the bicycle back to town, parks it in the yard at the back of the pub and goes straight to his room to ring Richard.

'Hi. It's Kit. I think you should come down here.'

'Kit! You're still there? With Cassie? Is something wrong?'

'Things are getting a bit . . . weird.'

'Weird?'

'She talks to herself, and she's a bit, well, letting herself go, and . . .' She looks so old, you bastard, is what Kit wants to say, thinking of the vivid red slash of her lipstick.

'And what?' asks Richard.

And she's laughing a lot. Hard to say why that's a problem. Kit hasn't words to describe the pity that batters him when he looks at her. He doesn't understand the shame he feels, or the impulse to push her away with both hands and run. Her courage wounds him, her laughter pierces him through, and he can't help her. He can't make it right. He's nineteen years old. Cassie's over fifty and from a world he doesn't know. In the background, he can hear a baby's high wailing, a woman yelling something unintelligible.

He says, 'She was wandering about with a bucket of urine.'

'Urine? Did you say urine? Is there something wrong with the toilet?'

'No. I think you should come.'

'Dammit. It's really not . . . I mean, we've just had a baby for Christ's sake. I only got back from Queensland last night. I can't just . . . We're getting calls from her friends, you know. And from people at school. She hasn't explained anything to anyone. I don't know what I'm supposed to tell them. It's a ridiculous situation.'

'Why don't they ring her?'

'She said if I gave her mobile number out to anyone, she'd turn it off and leave it off. They haven't got the number. She only ever used the damn thing to call me when she got lost.' He takes a deep breath. 'Look, Kit, I'll see what I can do. Hang in there,' he says.

Once more, with feeling.

'Hang in there, buddy.'

Jeez! The guy's all heart, isn't he?

Richard does not check up on Cassie. Delegation being the key to good time management, he off-loads the responsibility to someone else.

Cassie jumps out of her skin when the phone rings. It's the middle of the night. Must be one of those moments when all the satellites are in conjunction or something, she thinks. The gods permitting me a signal. I didn't even know I'd left it switched on. Who would be calling her at this time? The question propels her out of bed in a flurry of blankets. America! It has to be Eleanor.

All she has to do is follow the sound until she finds the phone. Imbecile! Where has she put it? By the time she says hello, her daughter is already impatient.

'Mum! Do you actually know how to read messages on your phone? I mean, do you? People ring. People leave messages. You're supposed to check them and call back. That's how it works, you know.'

Cassie is so pleased that even exasperation touches her like tenderness.

'Ellie, oh, how lovely it is to hear your voice. How are you?'

'How am I? How are you, more to the point? Going off like that. Worrying everybody. Is everything all right?'

Is everything all right? What planet are you on, daughter of mine?

But Eleanor is asking, 'Do you need me to come home?'

She's developing an American accent. Cassie resists the urge to point this out. Need? Do I need her to come home? Dear Ellie, chickadee, I cannot begin to tell you how much I need you to fly to my side.

She says briskly, 'Of course not. Everything's fine. I'm sorry you've been worried about me. I didn't know how to tell you, Ellie. It was all a bit of a shock.' A slight wobble in her voice.

'What do you expect, Mum? You let yourself go. You know what men are like with their egos, especially when they get to Dad's age. I mean, it's all just so predictable. You didn't make any effort to look good for him. You never did anything with your hair, did you? And your weight. You don't take care of yourself. Still, it was bloody awful of him. A bloody awful thing to do.'

My weight? thinks Cassie numbly. My hair? Oh. That's why this has happened. I see. That explains everything. Eleanor has always been perceptive. Always been her father's girl.

'How is your father?' Cassie asks.

'Okay, I think. He seems to be spending a lot of time interstate right now.'

'Hasn't he –'

'Got a new baby. Yes, he has.'

Ellie sounds disgusted, admitting this. Well, well. So the baby has arrived. Some people change and some are doomed to repeat. Richard had spent a lot of time interstate just after Eleanor was born, too. His general approval of procreation had not extended to the chaotic state of his home during the infant months. Cassie had handled that alone.

'Mum? Mum? Are you still there.'

'Sorry, darling. You keep cutting out. It's very bad reception here. I usually have to climb to the top of the dunes to get a clear call. I'm fine, Ellie. I have a lovely cottage by the sea and I'm deciding what to do with my future. You mustn't worry. And Kit's here. Did Richard tell you? Kit has been marvellous. I wonder if he'll visit the States? You'd like him. He's turned into a very interesting boy. Well, he's not a boy really, is he? He's a young man now –'

'Mum! What are you waffling on about? I don't want to know about Kit. I want to know if you're all right.'

She wants to know *that* I'm all right, not if. But it is good of her to offer to come, even with the strains of reluctance in her voice. Good of her to call. She is a good girl. Despite all the pressure of her work and the fact that they have never understood each other at all, her daughter is doing the right thing. And she would come too. We'd fight, of course. And it would all be my fault. There are so many interesting and important things we could be talking about. Why can't we do that? What is it about me that irritates her so much? Or did she absorb the behaviour pattern from her father?

She says, 'I'd love to see you, Ellie, but not now. Perhaps when I'm more settled. When you're not so busy. I promise you, there's nothing to worry about. I'm getting on with my life. There's no need for you to drop everything and come rushing back. It's not as if I'm at death's door,' she says with a flush of guilt, and adds, 'I've survived worse.'

'So everything's fine, is it?'

'Of course it is.'

'Everything's hunky-dory.'

'Absolutely.'

'Well if everything's all right, why are you wandering around with buckets of urine, Mum?'

'Urine, darling? Did you say urine?' How extraordinary. Kit must have . . . and Richard . . . Oh dear. Cassie starts to laugh. How stories develop and spread. Right around the world in this case. A chain of people assessing her sanity. Reaching their own conclusions. She is tempted to help it along but doesn't want to be unfair to her daughter.

'Sorry, Ellie, it really is a bad line. I'll write to you. I promise. Everything is just fine. Lovely to talk. Are you taking care of yourself, darling? I–'

She cuts the phone off and laughs till her ribs ache, till she has to go hiccoughing into the kitchen for a glass of water, till she suspects she isn't laughing anymore but crying. Eleanor has such a long way to go. But you can't do it for them. She'll learn in her own way. Or not.

No chance of going back to sleep now. She opens a packet of chocolate biscuits, transferring them to a screw-top jar and absent-mindedly leaving a half dozen on a plate.

Fat and fifty-four, Cassie. Not a good look.

Not fat, she thinks. Sturdy. Stout might possibly be conceded. But not fat. And anyway, who's to see?

She eats a biscuit, thinking about her intruder. How would Ellie handle this situation? She'd have called the police as soon as the pie arrived. No – she'd have changed the locks after Myrtle left the chicken and mushroom casserole. I'd probably have done the same, in the real world.

Shall I leave a biscuit out for him, like we used to do for Santa Claus? Where is he, right now? Watching the cottage? Or staking out someone else's home? Does he do this with other places, other people? Or is it just this cottage? Just me? Does he want to frighten me? Does he want me to leave? Both?

She helps herself to another biscuit. Someone out there thinks he is pushing her to the edge. Ha! He doesn't realise she's been leaning over the edge for a long time. She pauses, mid-crunch, considering this, drawing strength from the thought, wondering how close to the waves she can fly.

34

WHATEVER YOU HOPE FOR

The water is the palest shimmering silver, broken by flecks and flat narrow bands of pewter increasing in number closer to the shore. No waves. No wind. A purling shore break on a lazy ebb tide.

A faint blue haze obscures the horizon and above it the sky is a dense smoky white. Midway between shore and the merging of sea and sky, a southern right whale breaches without warning, and disappears. She has come to calve and she is early. It's usually August when these enormous creatures arrive in Shearwater. That a scene of such tranquillity should hide her is miraculous to Jack. Where there's one, there may be others. Whales, that is. Miracles too, maybe. Don't hold your breath.

His knees creak when he gets to his feet. At the top of the dune he turns for a last look. There, out where the horizon should be, a darker stain is emerging, a blemish against the sea mist. He pauses, curious. It's a cloud formation. Isn't it? It's difficult to tell where the sky begins, in these conditions.

He crouches, arms loose on his knees, settles in for the wait. After an hour or so, the sea mist seems to be thinning and the dark stain is still visible, not moving or spreading. A tiny pulse of excitement begins to flicker in his throat. Could it be? Is it time?

He moves cautiously, aware that any change in perspective might dispel an illusion that he would prefer to hold onto for as long as possible. When he reaches the firm sand, it is still there. It's beginning to take on definite proportions, he thinks, straining to see dark cliffs, a flat-topped plateau. It is unbelievable and he is afraid.

Suddenly resolute, he bends to remove his boots, ready for the water, but when he looks up again, the south-westerly has caught one end of his island and spun it out in gossamer trails across the sky. Seems like whatever you hope for never happens. Not even this.

35

WHERE THERE'S LIFE

Three days later and Kit is back at the cottage. He's offered to lend a hand with some of the heavier gardening work, but Cassie has other things in mind. He calls out, not wanting to startle her as he wheels the bicycle around the side of the house. She has made her preparations. When he appears, she's brushing loose soil from a curved line of bluestones and the bucket stands not-so-innocently by the steps. She sits back on her heels. 'Hello.'

'Hiya, Cass.'

He's seen the bucket and walks past it without mentioning it, frowning.

'How are things?' she asks.

He kicks at a clod of earth, looking younger than his years. How like his father he is, she thinks. Even as a grown man, Stuart was capable of sulking for days if he didn't get his own way. Kit, she suspects, uses marijuana to insulate himself from whatever is beyond his control. Stuart had simply made life unbearable until the world gave in. She wonders if Annette has great powers of appeasement, or enough love to go around, or is she a martyr to the cause. All three maybe.

'Everything would be great if it wasn't for the women,' Kit grumbles. 'It's that girl.'

'Lily?'

'Yes.' It is so unfair, he thinks, and so totally cocked up, and how, just tell him how, Hannah can possibly be in love with a pillock like Fat Harry?

'She's very young,' says Cassie. 'Is she sweet on you?'

'Not anymore. She won't even speak to me.'

'That might be a little awkward, living at the pub.'

'Tell me about it.'

'Did something happen?'

'She saw me sharing a cigarette with Hannah, a while back. She went ballistic. I mean, honestly, where's the harm in it? She's crazy. I thought she'd forget about it but things are worse than ever. This morning, she walked straight past me like I wasn't there.'

Ah.

'What will you do?' she asks. Don't steer, Cassie. Don't direct, and whatever you do, don't advise.

'I don't know. I like living there. I don't want to move out.' He squats by the garage wall, studies his hands. He's still waiting for his chance with Hannah. Where there's life, there's hope, and he's too young to know what a time-waster that can be.

'Have you tried talking to her?' she ventures.

He frowns. 'I told you. She won't speak to me.'

He's impatient. She can see that he's already regretting the impulse to discuss it with her. If he moves out of the pub, there's a possibility he'll move out of the area, move on. He might even go home. The slight quickening of her pulse surprises her. I haven't been alone, she thinks. With Kit here, I haven't been alone.

'You've helped me, you know, Kit. I'll miss you, when you go. Poor Lily,' she adds.

'She hates her mother.'

'She'll grow out of that. Eleanor was a perfect harpie until she was seventeen.' Until she spread her wings wide enough to catch the slipstream of the earth's turning, and flew far, far away. I taught her to fear, she thinks. After Tom died, I needed Ellie to see the danger in everything, and stay safe. Is her life now ruled by a whole series of actions she barely recalls a reason for, except that something bad will happen if she doesn't do it that way? Is that why she stays away from me? Because I remind her to be afraid?

'Be kind,' she urges him, forgetting her caution about offering advice.

'That might be tricky. Kindness can be misinterpreted. Perhaps it's better if I leave her alone.' His glance moves to the bucket, veers away again.

She says, 'I'm sure you'll work something out. By the way, I bumped into Simon Biddle a couple of weeks ago. He offered to take me out in his fishing boat. I won't take him up on it but I thought you might be interested.' She decides not to mention the discarded bicycle. Seems like Kit has enough to worry about at the moment.

'Me? No way. He's weird.' Be more likely to throw me overboard than take me fishing, he thinks. 'I don't think you should see him, Aunt Cass. Why is he asking you out anyway?'

'I can't imagine. A decrepit old thing like me.'

Kit blushes. 'I didn't mean that.' He did.

'You've got to be careful with people,' he says. 'I've met all sorts, travelling around. Most of 'em are okay but some you need to stay away from, you know?'

'Yes, I know.' She is meek, deferring to this man of the world. How fragile they are.

'I saw the big redhead on the way here.'

'Grace?'

'She said to tell you she's got the Dakin in, if you want to pick it up.'

'That's good.' She'll be able to put it back in place on the coffee table.

Kit says thoughtfully, 'You know, you'd be better off in the city instead of stuck out here. You ought to meet people. Go out and have fun. It's tough on your own, Aunt Cassie,' he says seriously, with another averted glance at the bucket. 'It's tough.'

She pats his cheek. 'And so am I, Kit. Tough as they come.'

'Yeah, right.'

He doesn't believe me, she thinks. I wonder how long he'll be able to ignore the bucket?

Only ten minutes longer, as things turn out. They have to

walk past it to go into the kitchen for coffee. That does the trick.

'Er,' he says, 'is that urine again, Aunt Cass?'

'It is, Kit, and do call me Cass, please.'

'Why is it there? If it's not a rude question,' he adds hastily.

'Not rude at all. Urine is an infallible treatment for an ailing lemon tree. Not having access to that most useful appendage men have, I have to resort to a bucket, you see. Simple. Want to empty it under the tree for me?'

He declines her offer with a silent shake of his head, screwing up his eyes against the mental image of his aunt resorting to a bucket. Way too much information. He knows she's laughing at him.

She makes parmesan and chive omelettes for lunch with brown bread and butter. She listens with care to the subtext of his comments. Hannah this . . . Hannah that . . . She hopes the woman has enough sense not to encourage the boy. Will she know how to set him back in his expectations without crushing him? He has a tender heart.

'Look,' she says, when Kit pauses for breath. 'Come and look at my beach trophies.' She shows him the paper nautilus, perfect except for a short hairline crack. He sniffs dubiously at the partial skeleton of a bird, linked vertebrae and rib cage delicate as white coral lace.

'You should wash your hands when you touch things like that,' he says.

How conservative the young are. 'It's perfectly clean.'

'I doubt it. What is it?'

'Shearwater, I think.' She doesn't mention the other one, lying beneath the earth in her garden.

What's with all these bones? He's already horrified by the seal skull hanging from the cypress branch. Thought it was some kind of bird-feeder, till he was close enough to see the eye sockets. Wait till Richard sees that! Just my luck, he thinks. A gothic Australian aunt.

But he admires the beautiful intricacies of the paper nautilus. He studies the dimpled white surface, lighter than eggshell, turning it in his long brown fingers. Seeing his bitten fingernails, Cassie wants to hug him. Feels the empty ache of needing someone to protect.

'I'd really like to show this to Hannah,' he says. 'Can I borrow it?'

'No. It's too fragile. I'll have to varnish it. It won't last two minutes otherwise.' Her tone is sharper than she'd intended.

He looks up, surprised. Hadn't expected her to refuse.

Impossible for her to explain the feeling that it was a gift from the sea, from the universe, for Cassie Callinan, little mortal all alone on the beach. Award for bravery. Compensation. A small, endearing grace.

She shrugs. 'I like it. I don't want it broken.'

'That's okay,' he says. But she can see that it isn't.

Later he tells her, 'You should think about getting the phone connected here. It's not safe, with the mobile signal dropping in and out all the time. What if there's an emergency or something, and your mobile doesn't work?'

If I had the phone connected, she thinks, people wouldn't drop in. They could call me.

But you'd have to answer the phone.

Not if I don't want to. They could leave messages.

But if you don't get back to them, they'll come around to see if you're all right. With chicken casseroles. And mutton-bird pies?

Come out, come out wherever you are.

'I don't know,' she says. A landline telephone connection? It has an anchoring feel about it. Right now, she is neither here nor there but in between somewhere. No landfall, though she gets the scent of earth on the wind occasionally.

'Think about it,' he says. 'What if your friends want to call you?'

'It's easy enough to walk outside and get a signal if I want to talk to anyone.' End of discussion, her tone says.

When he's leaving, she kisses him on the cheek, feels stubble under her lips and smells the soap he's used.

Hannah, Hannah, Hannah, she thinks. Oh, Kit.

'Want to have dinner at the pub one night next week?' she asks, all innocence. It won't hurt to keep an eye on things.

'If you like. Oh, I nearly forgot. Have you picked up your mail recently? There's an invitation for you.'

'An invitation?' She hasn't been to the post office for days.

'Hold on, I've got mine here.' He shows her a buff-coloured card with gold lettering. It is an invitation to the Annual Shearwater Winter Ball at the end of August. Dress: Formal.

She smiles. 'I don't think so, Kit. I'm not much of a party girl.'

'I don't think refusal is an option. Not if you live here. Practically the whole town turns up. People come from miles around. There's food, drink and dancing at the pub, and a big bonfire with fireworks at Shearwater Point. It'll be great. It'll do you good to get out.'

'I do like fireworks,' she says. 'I might. I might come.'

Dress Formal? She thinks about her cocktail dresses, the silks and satins hanging in her wardrobe in a different space, in the other world that is Melaleuca Drive. She thinks about Jack Biddle, and immediately wishes she hadn't.

'What will you wear?' she asks, knowing his preference for ancient jeans.

'I'm working on it,' he says.

He sounds like he's looking forward to it. And why should that make her uneasy?

It might be fun to have Richard post off her party dresses. He'll wonder what's going on. Will it prickle his possessive streak? Will it cut a chink in that well-armoured conscience of his? Fat chance.

She scribbles a note later that day and posts it before she can change her mind. She describes the three dresses that she wants him to send as well as her dark-blue cashmere wrap. She'd pondered for a while, pen in her mouth, about some of the things she'd like to say to him, and said none of them.

It would be good to get a reaction from him after all this time.

A minimal acknowledgement of her ongoing existence. I won't hold my breath, she thinks, and wonders if she's been relegated to past tense at Melaleuca Drive. Cassie used to . . . Cassie had . . . It's more likely she's been consigned to the unmentionable closet, like a family skeleton but far less interesting. He won't want the new woman upset. Not with the baby. It might take him away from his work too much.

I'll buy a dress for the ball, she resolves. I won't wait for a reply. But after writing his name and allowing herself to dwell on these things, after sending a message skimming between their two worlds, it is not so easy to get Richard out of her mind.

Late in the afternoon, strolling on the beach, she is still thinking of him. His voice, his skin. His hands moving with practised, casual tenderness over her body. Against her best instincts, desire rises. Why now, she wonders?

Hormones, Cassie. Everything is hormones.

She allows herself to weep, without rancour and without self-pity, and by and by, she feels a little better.

It is almost dark when she gets back – she'd had to hurry, afraid she'd be stranded, left wandering the valleys of sand in complete darkness. There's a welcome glow from the cottage.

Hold on a minute.

I didn't put the light on. It wasn't dark when I left.

Well, the light is on.

Oh god . . .

She runs to the window at a crouch, mouth dry, pulse racing. She's eager now, for confirmation of her suspicions, eager for battle. Fearless and ready for the fray. Fingers gripping the window-ledge, she slowly raises her eyes to the level of the glass. Jack Biddle is sitting at her kitchen table, his head in his hands. He looks up when she hurls the door open. The exhaustion in his face is almost enough to cool her fury, but not quite.

'Can I help you?' It's a well-bred roar. Bred in the classroom. It booms. It bounces off the walls. All across the marshlands, startled birds topple from their roosts, furry marsupials freeze in their tracks, frogs enter a state of suspended animation and seven species of bat are obliged to fold their wings over their ears and so plummet from the skies. Jack is disconcerted, to say the least.

'I was hoping so,' he says mildly.

'And what exactly do you want?' She can't help herself. A vast reservoir of fear is fuelling her anger. Even as a part of her would like to utter soothing civilities and put the kettle on, another part, the part that has just received a very nasty shock, is yelling wild profanities, brandishing a dripping axe and holding up a severed head by its hair.

He gets to his feet, a hand out, palm up, placating. 'I'm sorry. I don't know what I thought. Coffee, or something? I . . . I'm sorry. I saw you down on the beach. I knew you wouldn't be long. I didn't think you'd mind if I waited. I'm sorry I've frightened you.'

He leaves.

Yes, you did, she thinks, looking restlessly around the empty kitchen in search of other prey. You did frighten me. Letting yourself into my house like that. What the hell is it with people round here?

But she has a strong feeling that she could have handled things better, a strong feeling that she's let someone down again, and on top of that, the axe is still dripping and she hasn't a clue what to do with it now.

36

CORE OF DARKNESS

As night draws in, the town beach is deserted, except for a lone wombat nosing amongst the debris at the high-tide line. Seaweed pops and sponges, fish eggs and fishing floats, smooth silky pieces of coloured glass, frayed rope and feathers, bones of fish, bird and mammal – even the larger mammals, the two-legged variety, if the stories hereabouts are to be believed.

Hannah sets a match to the wood that Kit has laid in the big hearth. Harry Oklow is bewitching a customer with stories. An out-of-season tourist. A short sallow man who grasps his beer like a lifeline as he leans in to hear Harry's words. Fair game.

'I remember the time some young bloke threatened suicide. He'd rung his girlfriend and told her he was going to jump from the cliff. Took the police hours to talk him out of it. They had the helicopter too. Amazing things, helicopters. It looked like it was hanging up there in the sky, you know. Not moving. All the stars behind it, the red light flashing, the searchlight sweeping the cliffs and then the water, back to the cliffs again, holding, holding. Poor bugger caught there like a roo in the headlights.'

Harry allows a few moments for the picture to form.

'And then, to top it all, as he was coming in, he slipped and fell. Despite all the commotion, and the helicopter, he got the job done anyway.'

'Might have been the light,' says the tourist, not knowing any better. 'Might have dazzled him.'

Harry ignores this, disliking impromptu embellishments from the audience. 'The last time they called out the helicopter, it was for that Asian fisherman. Remember, Hannah?' he calls. She nods, watching the flames.

Harry says, 'He went out on the rock platform west of Shearwater Point in waders. Waders on a rock platform. I ask you. You'd think people'd have more sense, wouldn't you?'

His audience has grown to five. All but the stranger know this story. They sip their beers, waiting, appreciating, assessing the gullibility of the newcomer.

'Two days, it took 'em, to find him. Two days!'

Harry shakes his head. His audience follow suit.

The man asks eagerly, 'What happened to him?'

Hooked.

'A big wave came up,' says Harry. 'Swept him off the rocks. Filled those waders up to the brim, it did. Took him right to the bottom. He never had a chance, poor bugger.'

'But they found the body?'

'Oh yes, they found the body. What was left of it.'

Lugubrious pause.

'Still had the waders on him, too. When they got them off, there was a big garfish inside each one. Nicely fattened up, they were.' Harry holds the man's eye with practised solemnity.

'Good god!'

'Terrible,' says Harry. 'More beer, gentlemen?'

'Must be Martin's shout,' says one of them. The others roar with laughter. It's always Martin's shout but he's never there when you need him.

'Martin wouldn't shout if a shark bit him,' Harry explains to the tourist, filling up his glass.

Cassie pauses outside the pub, steeling herself to open the door, already imagining the faces turned towards her, the conversations faltering. That woman from River Marsh Cottage. That woman who lives alone. That woman who has never before, in her entire life, walked into a pub on her own. But when she enters the warm bright room, no one seems to notice her. She looks round anxiously for Kit.

It had been a struggle, choosing her outfit, deciding what would be appropriate. She settled for black trousers and a fitted black top under her suede jacket. She'd put on her pearls, taken them off, put them back on again. A dusting of powder, a hint of blush, a soft lipstick. Not bad, she told her mirror, breathing in. Now her high heels are giving her a little dart of pain in the left knee but they boost her shaky confidence as she makes her way across the room and perches with some difficulty on a stool. She asks for a gin and tonic and tries to look nonchalant, but oh! she feels so conspicuous, up there at the bar, cast in profile like a figurehead on a prow. A group of men in a huddle at the other end. She returns a smile tentatively, then freezes. What if they get the wrong impression? Some old tart? Where are you, Kit? Do hurry.

Isn't that Jack Biddle standing by the fire with his back to her? She looks away quickly with a flush of embarrassment. Has he been watching her pantomime of Woman Accustomed to Drinking Alone in Pub? There's an unobtrusive empty table by the window. She decides to make a move.

There are several ways in which a plump woman may dismount from a bar stool. Cassie opts for straightening her rather short legs and sliding hopefully floorwards. A good strategy, had her heel not turned beneath her at the last minute, at a vital point of balance. Lovely, Cassie. Really well done. The carpet is gritty beneath her palms. She lifts her head, gazes up into Fat Harry's moon face peering over the bar at her.

'You lost something down there?' he says doubtfully.

'Earring,' she says quickly. 'And here it is!'

She stands up, fussing at some specks on her trousers, and shoots a look at Jack. It's all right. He's staring into the fire. The palms of her hands are stinging. Her left knee throbs. Her ankle – treacherous joint – seems unaffected.

She takes her drink over to the small square table. It's not so bad, she thinks. No one saw me fall, except for the big man behind the bar. And he didn't laugh. Could have happened to anyone. Couldn't it? She leans her arms on the top of the table but quickly removes them as her sleeve sticks to a cluster of rings from earlier drinks.

Hannah spots her and comes over.

'Hi, you must be Cassie. Kit won't be long. He's been gutting some fish for me and he's just gone to clean up. I'm Hannah. They're buggers, those stools, aren't they? I keep telling Harry we need something a bit more user friendly.'

Steps and a handrail wouldn't get me up there again, thinks Cassie, crestfallen. So this is Hannah. 'It's very nice in here,' she says. 'Friendly atmosphere.'

'It's the fire does that. Nothing like a big wood fire to bring them all in on a cold night. Want me to introduce you to anyone?' Hannah asks, watching her.

'No. No, thank you. I'll just wait here for Kit.' Cassie notices a generous cleavage. Lips painted rose-pink. The smile a precise offering, but it flashes warmly in eyes defined by a smear of bronze eye-shadow and grey liner. Hannah is not thin but the weight she carries is in all the right places. Her waist seems small by comparison and her thighs are long and slender in denim jeans. The belly is rounded but does not hang, as Cassie's does. Young *and* voluptuous, Cassie thinks enviously. Some women have it all, don't they?

Hannah says, 'I have to go and make a start on the meals. Things might get ugly if I don't get food into these boys, but we aren't expecting a rush tonight. I can join you later for a drink, if you like.'

'Please do. It's good to meet you. I ought to come in more

often,' she says, looking round vaguely. I look a sight, she thinks. I need a new bra. I need a red shirt just like hers. I ought to do sit-ups. Would grey eye-liner have that effect on my eyes?

'Why don't you find a warm spot by the fire?' Hannah suggests.

Cassie goes to buy another gin and tonic. When she looks over to the fire, Jack Biddle has gone.

'You look good,' Kit says.

She assumes it's a courtesy when in fact he's thinking she scrubbed up remarkably well. For a woman her age.

She wrinkles her nose, sniffs the air.

'Hey, I've been gutting fish. I did my best,' he says, laughing, holding out clean hands for her inspection.

The things we do for love.

Kit insists on paying for her dinner. She understands that the gesture is important to him. He tells her about the work he's been doing for Hannah – sanding back the old skirting boards and window frames, stripping wallpaper, painting the rooms. He's proud of himself. Kit the handyman.

'They look much better,' he says. 'Simple, bright and clean. That's all you need when you've got a good view.'

White paint flecks in his hair and under the rims of his fingernails. Heart on his sleeve.

After the meal, Hannah joins them with three glasses of port.

'On the house,' she says.

Cassie remembers, rummages in her handbag. 'I thought

you might like to have this,' she says, handing the framed photograph to Hannah. 'It was at the cottage when I moved in. It's your daughter, isn't it? Lily?'

Hannah is silent, looking at the image. 'No,' she says eventually. 'It's not Lily. It's me.'

'Hey! Cute,' says Kit, taking the opportunity to lean close to her to look.

Hannah puts the photograph face down on the table, with a brief, dismissive smile. Kit makes a grab for it but her hand is there first.

'No,' she says quietly. So quietly that he picks up the undercurrent of warning, and desists.

Cassie, watching the pair of them, thinks Hannah manages him with friendly authority. Despite the lively sparkle in Kit's eyes, she decides there is nothing to worry about. What would a woman like this want with a nineteen-year-old boy?

'I hope Kit's working hard for you, and earning his keep,' she says.

'Oh, he's a good boy,' says Hannah, patting his hand. There is a sureness and grace in the woman's movements, in the way her hands fly, small, fast and delicate, as she talks. When her fingers rest for a moment on Cassie's arm, they draw an old loneliness to the surface and stroke it with sharp pink fingernails.

Poor Kit, thinks Cassie. A good boy is the last thing he wants to be for Hannah. He'll get over it. And poor Lily, if she's got her heart set on this one.

'Where's Lily?' she asks.

'Probably up in her room,' says Hannah.

Cassie suggests to Kit, 'Why don't you ask her for a game of pool? I can watch you both and see how it's done.'

'He tried that,' says Hannah. 'She thrashed him.'

Kit grins at her. 'It was a pretty half-arsed attempt. I didn't have my mind on the game.'

'She's had lots of practice. She comes down here on her own and plays for hours. She's really good.'

Half-arsed, thinks Cassie. An excellent phrase. She tries it out silently and stores it away for future use. But what an odd and lonely image of a fourteen-year-old girl, playing pool on her own. Doesn't she have friends? Perhaps she doesn't have the knack for friendship. Never had much of a knack for it myself, Cassie thinks. At Lily's age, I was too uptight to be fun, too fearful to be treated without suspicion, and too quiet to be remembered. Then, one day, there was Richard. And one day, there was not.

Lily, emerging from her room where she has been reading about the lifecycle of the octopus, sees Kit smiling at her mother with desperate charm. Nothing new there. It's what they all do. But look at her. Isn't she sitting closer to him than she has to? She's practically pressed up against him. It's obscene.

'I thought you were different, Kit,' Lily whispers. She thinks of her octopus alone on the rocks in his tank. Loves me; loves me not. An octopus only lives for a year or two. All that intelligence, all that wonder. Such a short life. There is something wrong with the balance of everything. Unpredictable consequences, unrepentant predators. The chaos of the deep. There is something hidden here. A core of darkness she has always felt but never understood. She watches Cassie slip away from them all on a raft of private thought to a place where desolation shapes her face. It's a place Lily knows well.

'Seen Lily tonight?' asks Harry, a couple of hours later as he climbs into bed.

'No, I haven't. She's sulking as usual, I expect.' Hannah slips the photograph into her drawer without mentioning it to Harry.

'She didn't have any dinner. I wonder where she got to?'

'How the hell should I know? Stupid girl.'

Fact is, you can't make anybody happy, not even your own daughter. Not if they don't want to be.

Harry reaches for her but she moves away from him tonight, giving him a quick consoling kiss on his cheek. She has other things on her mind. The past is encroaching. The young girl in her red dress is calling to her, crying to her. Shush now, says Hannah silently to the child. Shhh . . . there, there. You're safe now.

Lily, out on the jetty, is standing alone under a spread of brilliant and surely auspicious stars. She is gazing at the light in the window she knows is Kit's, and wishing with all her heart. She's angry with him but she knows this will pass if only he'd come to his senses. If only he'd look at her the way he looks at Hannah. Then everything would be all right. In her arms is the octopus. Shivering a little, she kneels and, bending low as she can to the water, she releases him.

37

THE COAT STAND

Cassie has bought a coat stand. She hadn't set out to buy it. She has no definable need for a coat stand. It cannot be excused as a basic furnishing requirement. It will preclude a fast getaway, should she ever need one, because she loves it so much she cannot imagine ever leaving it behind.

She'd been racing back from the big supermarket, over an hour's drive from Shearwater. The car was full of groceries. She'd forgotten the esky and ice again. She can't get used to the idea that she needs an esky to go shopping. She knew that some of the frozen goods would be softening already, but there was the shop, set back from the highway, all manner of wind-chimes ringing from the eaves. She must have driven past it several times before without noticing, without hearing the call.

I shouldn't. I really shouldn't.

Inside, a rich chaos of colour and texture, with a hint of incense on the air. Shelves of thick alpaca sweaters and fringed shawls. Full skirts and loose embroidered shirts in bright cottons hung from brackets on the walls and floor racks. Jewellery shone from display cases. Silver and shells, amber and amethyst, turquoise and topaz. Hats dangled, tantalisingly adorned with ribbons, flowers and feathers. Around a dim corner, a long mirror framed with mother of pearl almost startled her into a greeting.

It is not, definitely not, Cassie's kind of shop. Touch me, said the bright cottons and soft, plump woollens. Try me, said the hats and shawls, sparkling necklaces and silver rings. It would be possible to completely transform yourself in a place like this, she thought, wandering in a fantasy of sensory delight, the groceries forgotten.

She bought a full-length skirt in a dark-blue fabric with exotic splashes of crimson flowers. A long-sleeved, cream silk shirt refused to be ignored. She spent a small fortune on a blue alpaca beaded shawl because when she swung its weight around her shoulders, it felt as though someone's arms had gently enfolded her. Intoxicated with possibilities, she looped glittering strands of gemstones around her neck and tried on bold rings with large square stones.

She had paid for her purchases and was waiting for them to be wrapped, already regretting some of them, already beginning to feel a little foolish, when she saw the coat stand. It was made from bleached branches of driftwood bound together with roughly twisted rope, the natural curves of the wood forming the feet at one end and the antlers at the other. She knew she couldn't leave the shop without it.

The woman named a price. Cassie grimaced, alarmed at the number of packages piling up on the counter. The price was promptly lowered and the deal struck. It took two of them to get it into the car. Wooden feet sticking out from the front passenger window and a flowering of antlers in the back. Groceries crammed into the boot. There's too much in there but a good slam of the lid takes care of that.

'Far to drive?' asked the woman.

'Yes. Quite a way.'

'Go carefully then,' she said, and raised a hand to wave as Cassie drove off. Best customer she's had in a year.

Oh! What a job she has, getting the coat stand out of the car. It seems to wrap itself around corners and cling wilfully to every protuberance. Sweating and struggling, she asks herself again and again. Why have I bought a coat stand? Where on earth am I going to put it?

She takes it into the house through the front door. She sets it down right inside the door and steps back to inspect it. The look of it there. She sees what it is. A symbol of habitation. A declaration of intent to stay. Yes! Quickly, she gathers up her thick blue winter scarf, a crimson silk scarf, a sun hat, her suede jacket and the red anorak that saved her life. She arranges these items on the coat stand, shuffling them around until they agree with the dictates of her personal sense of harmony. Indoor living design, Cassie-style. The room seems smaller but cosier. No one will be able to use the front door. The implication of the wide world at her back, tapping her on the shoulder when she's trying to relax, raising goosebumps of apprehension, has utterly vanished. Anyone coming through that door, anyone without invitation, for example, would get a hell of a shock.

She brings her new finery inside and tries it all on, slipping off her broad pink-gold wedding ring and replacing it with a large aquamarine set in silver. She walks around the cottage, twirling her new skirt, feeling exhilarated. She sits on the sofa as if posing, waiting for someone, or something to happen. Sees herself, waiting. Knows in that instant that hers has been a lifetime of waiting. Not asking for anything too much. A small miracle here and there. Nothing earth-shattering in the grand scheme of things. A husband's love. A daughter's understanding. A child's life. Rescue. All of these, any one of these, perhaps, might have been enough. And now? Now I shall have to be enough.

She takes off the outfit, folds it up and puts it away, re-inhabiting herself thoughtfully, as frozen peas and blueberries soften, leak and mingle their juices in the back of the silver Mercedes.

38

THE FISH

Light touches Cassie while she is still submerged. Light filters through and finds her and draws her up. An eye opens briefly. There is unexpected comfort in the air. It will not, she decides, be too much of a trial to get out of bed this morning. No frantic scrabble for dressing-gown and slippers to retain bed-warmth for a few more precious minutes. *It's positively balmy today. I've slept in.*

She lies still, listening. There is no wind, only the sound of waves breaking. She kicks away the quilt and draws back the curtains. Full, high cloud cover. A chill moves through the window glass, lifting the fine hairs on her arm and sending her scurrying for her dressing-gown after all.

As soon as she opens the bedroom door, she is buffeted by warm air. These are no smouldering embers from last night's fire. It's a full blaze, piled high with wood. She feels dazed.

Did I get up and light the fire earlier and then go back to bed?

Did I?

How could I not remember? I'm sure I didn't. Kit, she thinks. The boy is still trying to look after me.

'Kit? Kit, are you there?'

He is not. He must have dropped in and lit it so that she'd be warm when she got up. The fireguard is in place. It is thoughtful of him but very unsettling. I must speak to him about it, she thinks. I know I told him to take my key, but I simply cannot have people letting themselves in willy-nilly, however well-intentioned they are. Besides, it's too warm in here, and it can't be doing the fish any good at all.

The fish?

It slides into her consciousness like an object from Matisse. The biggest salmon she has ever seen is lying on the kitchen table. She walks around it, amazed. Kit again? She prods it. Firm and fresh. Real. Too big for the refrigerator. Too big for the oven. Damn! I'll have to cut it into three pieces, she thinks. Or four. She prods it again with one finger. The salmon seems to swell in response, and subside.

God! It's so fresh, it's still trying to breathe!

Part of the darkly silvered body rises, forming a slight hump, then relaxes again. She watches it, puzzled. Better put a knife between its eyes. Put it out of its misery. They suffocate, don't they, out of water? Cruel, to leave it a second longer. She sighs. All she wanted was a cup of tea and a piece of toast.

She picks up the kitchen knife and advances. The fish writhes. She retreats, alarmed, hovering with the knife. The fish squirms and heaves. Cassie gives a squeal of fright. Is it going to roll right off the table?

The fish gives a convulsive shudder, the black and silver skin rises to a point, impossibly taut. Cassie realises at precisely the same moment that the skin breaks: it isn't the fish that's struggling. It's something inside the fish!

What do salmon eat?

Oh, wrong question, Cassie. Totally wrong.

A large dark-brown rat bursts upwards, trailing gut and flesh. For one, two, three heartbeats, the rat seems to float on air above the fish, before it falls, scrabbling, races at nightmare speed across the table and disappears beneath the sink cupboards.

Cassie, screaming, runs outside, straight into the arms of Kit, who drops bags of eggs, milk and fresh baked bread to catch her.

'Salmon?' says Kit. 'Not me. I saw the smoke rising from the chimney and thought you might be ready for some company.'

He's studying the fish. 'This is where it came out?'

'Yes,' says Cassie from the doorway. She refuses to go back inside.

'You saw it burst out here? The rat made this hole?'

'Yes. For god's sake, Kit, let's get out of here.' She's going to stay at the pub, at least until someone can convince her that the rat has been irrevocably dealt with.

'This is amazing.'

'I could think of better words.'

'Are you okay?'

'Kit, I think someone has done this to frighten me.'

'What do you mean?'

'To frighten me away. Someone who doesn't want me here.'

'Who?'

'I don't know who!'

'Settle down,' he says, mildly. She needs to go back to town, he's thinking. She needs to be with people. She's losing it.

Cassie sees the thought pass across his face. But I'm entitled to shriek, she thinks. Who wouldn't? She says, 'It's just . . . it seems unnatural somehow. How could it happen?'

'Rats and fish go together pretty well. I can't imagine why anyone would do it deliberately. If they want you to leave, all they have to do is ask.'

'Well, yes, but . . .' Her voice is rising again.

'Okay, okay,' he says. 'We can sort this out later. Tell me what you need and I'll stick some things in a bag for you and drive you to Hannah's. I'll find Mr Biddle and he can deal with your rat.'

'Biddle?' she cries.

'Ralph Biddle. Newsagent and pest controller, apparently. And gardener and handyman. And fisherman. But everyone's a fisherman around here. Are you quite sure the rat didn't come out of a hole it had made before? On the way in, if you see what I mean?' He turns the fish over carefully and examines the other side before laying it back on the table. 'Champion fish.'

'Kit!'

'All right, I'm coming. I'll get your stuff. Here.' He throws her the red anorak and takes a last look at the fish. There is an exit wound, as they say in the police dramas, but where is the entry? How had the creature got inside the salmon? Would a rat crawl in through a salmon's mouth when the whole salmon was there for the eating? Cassie, yelling commands for clothes and toiletries, is making it hard for him to concentrate. It is a mystery. And not the only mystery today. The bicycle's gone again. What has she done with it? Must check it out when she's less hysterical. It's handy, having that bike to get around on.

High in the dunes, Jack Biddle relaxes his stance. He'd been about to rush down to the cottage, drawn on the line of Cassie's scream, but the boy is with her. He watches Cassie shrug her arms into the red coat and stamp the cold out of her feet. Remembers the day he saw that coat lying on the path. She's still here. Still fighting it. Still alive.

'Of course she can stay here!' says Hannah to Kit, enfolding a startled Cassie in a hug. Cassie pulls away. I don't hug, she thinks.

'I'll be off then,' says Kit. 'Okay if I take the Merc or shall I leave it for you?'

Nothing like taking advantage of the moment.

'Take it. I'll be fine. And, Kit, you make sure he doesn't use poison,' says Cassie over her shoulder as Hannah guides her towards the stairs. 'I don't want that thing crawling into a hole and rotting in my kitchen.'

'It's probably taken off already,' says Kit on his way out. 'That scream of yours was enough to terrify any self-respecting rodent. It terrified me.'

I don't scream either, thinks Cassie.

'Here.' Hannah pushes open a door with a proud flourish. 'The only guest bedroom with a private bathroom, and all newly-decorated! There's plenty of hot water too and . . . this might help.' She presses a small bottle into Cassie's hand. A miniature bottle of brandy. 'Ring down if you want anything, won't you?'

Brandy for lunch? 'You're very kind,' she says. 'I'm sorry. I'm a bit distracted.'

'Don't you worry about a thing. Kit will sort it all out. Why don't you have a lie down?'

Am I being soothed, like a fractious old woman? Why are they being so helpful? Did Ezekiel betray me after all? Do they all know I was going to kill myself?

'Strange business, a rat inside a fish,' says Hannah. 'Any idea where it came from?'

'Not a clue. It was lying on my table in the kitchen.' She shudders at the memory.

'Rats are clever creatures, you know. We'll have to find out who gave you the fish, won't we? It will be all right, I'm sure. But if it helps, you're welcome to stay here for as long as you like. We can come to an arrangement about the rent. How about if I bring up some tea and toast and a couple of soft-boiled eggs? Would you like that?'

'Oooh, it sounds like heaven. I haven't had breakfast. I was just going to make some toast when . . .' Her mind skitters away from the image of rat rising.

'We'll take good care of you. Kit has the room next door. You'll be able to bang on the wall if you want to talk to him. I'll go and get that food for you.'

Concern, Cassie thinks. They are concerned about me. He must have told them. Why else would they behave this way? She lies down on the bed with a long sigh. Remembers the fire. Someone lit her fire. Kit said he saw smoke rising from her chimney. It's still a matter of tricks. Nasty, sneaking tricks to frighten her. If the intruder was intent on rape or murder, he's had every opportunity. Somebody wants her out of that cottage.

Grace calls into the pub, mid-afternoon. 'Rat is deceased,' she informs them.

'How did he do it?' asks Hannah.

'Lured it out with a chunk of salmon and clobbered it with the spade.'

My spade! thinks Cassie, picturing gore.

'They've cleaned up,' Grace assures her. 'You wouldn't know it happened. Kit took the salmon down to the beach, threw it to the seagulls. Shameful waste of a good fish. Cottage is all ready for you, he says.'

'Oh, there's no rush,' says Hannah. 'Cassie's welcome to stay here. I'm sure I wouldn't be too eager to go back there, after something like this.'

Her voice, warm with reassurance, has the reverse effect on Cassie, who sits up straight and says firmly, 'No, I'd like to go back. I'm getting rather fond of the place. You should come and see the work I've done on the garden.' And she doesn't miss the quick glance the two women exchange, but she doesn't know what it means either.

Hannah offers to drive her. Cassie says she feels like a walk, and leaves them, with repeated thanks for the kindness. Across the room, she pauses, fumbles in her bag as though looking for keys. It gives her just enough time to hear Grace murmur a warning to Hannah.

'It might not have been deliberate, you know.'

At the cottage, Cassie finds a tidy pile of stringybark fire-eggs nestled in the corner by the back door. A smile lights her eyes at the sight of them but her mind warns, beware of gifts from strangers. She gathers them up, wary of leaping surprises, and takes them inside.

39

CONSOLATION

She's still here. She will not go! She puts away his belongings. Removes all traces of his gifts. She even replaces what he takes. And the garden. She is gardening! His misery is acute. He needs consolation and the reassurance of his little vice.

For several minutes he lies with his eyes closed, and not a muscle of his face betrays the conflict in his mind. Then, as though of its own volition, his hand creeps towards the white skivvy at his side. His eyes open and turn in supplication to his statue of the Holy Mother and Child. It's time, isn't it? Time to take another photograph.

Careful preparation is the key to success. He selects a stranger, always someone out of town. Never anyone on his own patch. He watches. He takes his research seriously. His power depends on it. When the time is right, it will lift him out of his little world and make a god of him, all-knowing and invisible and full of sadness. But there must be a sacrifice. Someone has to pay.

He's dressed warmly. Leaves the bicycle lying hidden in the long grass at the side of the road and steals over the gate. A moonless black night, but the tall bare poplar trees are silhouetted against the stars and he can hear the rustle of their breathing in the still air. He knows where the flat pastures run all the way to the river, seven kilometres south-east. He could make his way blindfolded, if he had to, to the single yellow rectangle of light at the end of the long driveway.

Closer, and light fans out from the window across a thick, springy lawn. The shape of the house emerges. Furrows in the green tin roof, pale mortar lines between clinker bricks and the shadowy holes of the other two windows on this side. A fox barks, high and insistent. Within the lighted room, an old man lifts his head to listen. The fox stops barking but the chained dogs have begun to howl, anxious to deal with the intruder. After a long time, they too settle down and everything grows quiet again.

He moves as the stars move, imperceptibly. One moment he is by the poplars, the next it seems, at the window, watching an old man pull a stained brown jumper over his head and toss it onto a chair. Underneath he wears a blue check shirt. Flannel for comfort, when there is little else for comfort, except the rasp of a dog's tongue against the grey stubble of your cheek.

On the cluttered table beside the bed stands a lamp with a dusty yellow shade, a folded newspaper and a pen, a small radio with its antenna slanting forwards, and a black and white, silver-framed photograph of a woman with a baby. She has dark curling hair, an old-fashioned look about her with that flowery, full-skirted dress and single strand of pearls. It looks like she's wearing her Sunday best. The shot might have been taken in the fifties. There she is, a perfect stranger, smiling down at the child in her arms with the air of a blissful Madonna.

Beneath the bed is a suitcase, so old that it is made of reinforced cardboard with leather corner pieces and leather straps. They don't make 'em like that anymore. The old man kneels with difficulty, pulls the case towards him and opens it. He throws a glance over his shoulder. Is anyone there? Anyone watching? He's had a feeling lately . . . You never know. He checks the contents. Look at the greed flickering from his profile, dancing and sparking along the line of his slumped shoulders. Reassured, he secures the straps again and pushes the case beneath the bed. Everyone needs a little something to help them through the night.

When the old one wakes in the morning, everything will seem normal. Gradually, an awareness will steal over him that there is a difference. The pattern has changed. How? He will try to shrug it off but the feeling of unease won't go away. Something is not as it was. His eyes will measure the shapes all around him. What? What is it? A growing panic. The suitcase!

No. Not the suitcase. Not the treasure you guard.

Only later, as he is spiralling down from the first peak of shock, will he notice that the photograph has gone.

40

SLIPPING THE JESSES

It has been a week since the fish-rat and Cassie can't decide if staying in the cottage is brave or foolhardy. She is discovering her capacity for obstinacy. And something else. She doesn't want to lose. It is not comfortable being here, waiting, watching, wondering. But to leave would be to lose, and Cassie has finally grown tired of giving in. She does consider moving the kitchen table up against the back door before she retires at night, but shies away from making her fear visible.

Bring it on, she thinks recklessly. Bring it on and let's see what you're made of.

But a little more company wouldn't hurt.

She calls on Elizabeth Savage to tell her about the leak in the roof. True, the roof leaked only once during a heavy downpour and there hasn't been a single drip since, but her landlady ought to be informed.

'I'll get Jack to take a look,' says Elizabeth, as Cassie had known she would.

The sofa is heaped with clothes. Satins and silks in purple, pink and blue, stiff yellow taffeta nudging lilac lace, gold lame and green net petticoats, turquoise brocade and silver polyester studded with pearls.

Cassie raises her eyebrows. 'What's all this?'

'For the ball,' says Elizabeth, holding up the biggest pair of trousers Cassie has ever seen. 'Most of the men wear the same things every year. Incredible as it may seem, Fat Harry's put on weight and I have to let more fabric into these. He thinks a red stripe down each side will do the trick.' She examines the black waistband critically. 'It's the women who like to make a splash with something different.'

'Are you making all the dresses?'

'Goodness, no. I'm altering them to fit.'

'Is it very grand?'

'People go to a lot of trouble.'

Cassie is mentally reviewing her own list of possible outfits and discarding them one by one.

Elizabeth says, 'The women start thinking about next year's outfit as soon as the ball is over.'

'It must cost a fortune.'

'Costs next to nothing. Op shops, usually. Clever adaptations. Though I say so myself. What are you going to wear?'

'I haven't decided yet.' I'll definitely have to buy something new, Cassie thinks. Hell, a tiara wouldn't be out of place with those dresses.

'Does everyone go?'

'Not everyone,' says Elizabeth.

'You'll miss it, won't you. Not being able to go outside.'

'I miss it every year, but I can see the bonfire and the fireworks from here. And I have the costumes.'

'Someone should record it for you.'

'Oh, no. People tend to put on performances for videos, don't you think? It ruins the spontaneity.'

'Photos, then?'

'There might be some. But what I like is to hear the stories afterwards.'

Stories?

Cassie is beginning to feel nervous about the event. Perhaps it would be better not to go.

Elizabeth says, 'Myrtle won't be there either. Every year on the night of the ball, Myrtle and Martin fill their house with other people's children. Babysitting.'

'I could do that,' says Cassie eagerly.

'Losing your nerve, dear? You have to go to the ball.' Elizabeth's smile is unexpectedly sweet, cajoling. 'And afterwards you can come and tell me all about it. It'll be nice to see it through fresh eyes.'

She puts down the trousers, picks up a dark-red dress in a soft, clinging fabric, holds it up. 'Lily has decided she is too old now to help with the babysitting. She's going to wear this dress. It's one of Hannah's.' Her gaze moves to the window and Cassie has the feeling she's been temporarily forgotten. She is relieved that Elizabeth hasn't asked her about the rat. It's like replaying a nightmare, to talk about it. Perhaps she hasn't heard. She examines the pile of fabrics on the sofa next to her. Moving one of the dresses, she dislodges a hat. She's seen it before. That scrap of green net and the three blue feathers held in place with a nappy pin. One of the feathers is slightly crushed. She smoothes it between finger and thumb. She's about to ask about the hat when a loud shout from the stairs makes them both jump.

Elizabeth says, hand on her chest, 'Goodness! It's Lily. That's why I didn't hear the doorbell.' She turns to Cassie, gestures at the heaped clothing. 'If you want my help with a costume, I'm afraid I can't promise I'll have anything ready for you in time.'

'That's all right. I'll think of something.'

Lily has stopped in the doorway. 'Hi,' she says, studying the floor as though suddenly shy.

She must have seen the car, Cassie thinks. She knew I was here. 'Hello, Lily. Excited about the ball, are you? I love your dress.'

'Yeah.' Spoken without a trace of excitement.

'Kit and I are going. We're looking forward to it. Our first Shearwater Winter Ball ever. I was just talking to Elizabeth about what I should wear. It'll be fun, won't it?'

Oh do stop prattling, Cassie. You know you can't hope to fill in all the gaps, all the silences, when there's a teenager around. You can't make it better for the girl and there's a good chance you'll make it worse. You can't ever be sure what's going on in their heads. It's a different kind of fear, a different kind of hope, a very different kind of anger. You have to be there. You have to inhabit that place, to know. Remember the lessons Eleanor taught. Remember how dismissive you were of your own mother for not having all the answers, for being vulnerable, not infallible, and sad. Poor Shona, who after all those years of Leonard's casual brutality, finally slipped the jesses one day and flew free beneath the peach tree. Sorry I didn't know how it was, Mother. Sorry I didn't understand. Sorry I wasn't old enough to have a clue about anyone's pain except my own.

Back at the cottage, she's just turned off the ignition when she hears her mobile phone ringing inside. Again? They must have put another tower up somewhere and improved the signal. Where has she put the phone? The house is so full of the sound that she can't decide which direction it's coming from. The ringing stops. She immediately finds the phone, behind a cushion on the sofa.

'Stupid thing.'

She throws it down in the same place.

Elizabeth Savage is kneeling on the floor with a mouth full of pins, altering the hem on the dark-red dress. Shuffle, pin, shuffle, pin. Her knees ache but she doesn't complain. Shuffle, pin, shuffle, pin. Nearly finished.

She looks up at Lily and notices with a shock the swelling curves of hips and breasts. It is as if, unprepared and dreaming through her days, she suddenly sees a vision of her younger self, and wakes to the certain knowledge of all that is lost. I'm sorry, she tells them all silently. Sorry, sorry, sorry.

'Ow! Watch it. You stabbed me!'

'Well keep still.'

Lily gives a theatrical sigh. 'How long is this going to take?'

'As long as it takes. Here. Give me your arm.' Elizabeth hauls herself to her feet.

'Hold your arms out like this.' She double-checks the waist, pinches the fabric under the arms, at the shoulder seams. 'No. It doesn't need taking in at all,' she says. 'You fill it out as well as Hannah does.'

'Really?' Lily, delighted, frees herself and twirls around the room. 'I'm going to put my hair up. Like this. What do you think?' She holds her hair up high with one hand.

Elizabeth watches the child vanish, the woman appear.

'Stop that! You'll have all those pins out. I'm not doing them again.'

Lily stops. It is essential that the skirt is shortened. Essential that he will have a good view of her legs.

'Just look at that cleavage,' Elizabeth mutters, disbelieving, doubting now, the wisdom of allowing Lily to wear this.

'Yup, just look at it!' Lily drops a curtsey, holding the skirt wide and letting her long hair fall forward, framing the deep cleft of her breasts, snug in the bodice of the red dress.

Elizabeth thinks, She's the image of her mother, before . . . .

41

HALF A CHANCE

'It's Saturday, Kit. Busy day. I can't just go off joyriding. Harry needs me here.'

'But there's no one in the place,' Kit protests, half-laughing, half-exasperated. Instinct warns him to keep it light, hide his desperation.

'There will be, soon enough.'

'Ah. The Shearwater lunch-time rush.'

Hannah smiles despite herself, and Kit leans on the bar, leans closer, trying to catch the moment's potential.

'Aw, come on. Take a little time out to enjoy yourself. Cassie's given me the keys specially.' He lowers his voice conspiratorially as Harry's bulk glimmers past the glass door.

She won't come. I'm being an idiot. It's hopeless. One last try . . .

'Bet you've never driven a Merc, have you?' He dangles the key from his index finger and holds his breath.

'Well . . .'

'I've got fresh bread rolls, brie, apples and – wait for it – chocolate doughnuts.'

'Chocolate doughnuts?'

'With sprinkles on top.'

'In that case, how could I refuse?'

She's humouring him, as you might take pity on a child who badgers for a treat. Kit doesn't care, as long as she comes with him. Just give me half a chance, he prays. Half a chance. Tucked in the back of the car is a bottle of cabernet merlot and two wine glasses. He has a thermos of coffee to keep out the cold but if things go according to plan, they won't need that to keep warm. He's got a little bud of marijuana to help things along too.

'A couple of hours,' she warns. 'No more.'

'Brilliant,' he says. 'Put your walking boots on.'

'Why? Where are we going?'

'It's a surprise.'

Ten minutes later, Harry, grazing on a platter of sardines, hears the Merc accelerate down the main street and lifts his head.

Hannah turns to Kit. 'Thought I was going to drive?'

'You get to drive on the way back,' he laughs. 'If you're good.'

She feels it then, a quiver, deep down inside where it shouldn't be happening. Not in this car. Not with Kit. She looks at his strong young hands on the steering wheel. A man's hands. She sees the shape of the muscles in his tanned forearms. Here it comes again, a throb of excitement that makes her cross her legs and look quickly, fixedly, out of the passenger window.

He is attracted to me, and that's okay. He's only a boy. He won't try anything. I can handle him.

But why are her fingernails leaving half-moon imprints on her palms? She applies lip balm to give her hands something to do, then clasps her fingers in her lap. The car swings smoothly around a bend and a great vista of white-flecked blue ocean opens up before them.

'Gorgeous,' says Kit, grinning broadly.

Hannah realises she's got one foot outside the magic circle. Tempting, is it? A good idea? One little push can make a world of difference. One little push over the line.

Lily finds Cassie coming down the street with the papers under one arm and a sourdough loaf under the other. Balancing her bicycle, she calls out, 'Is Kit at your place?'

'No. No, he's not, Lily. He's taken the car. He said something about going up to Genbar Crater Lake today, to have a look around.'

Lily looks at Cassie. Cassie returns the look. Both of them suddenly understand that Kit has not gone to Genbar Lake alone. How does this happen? How does suspicion in one mind become a certainty in two? How many stories start this way? All the juicy ones.

Lily pauses for only a second to check that the street is clear and then she swings the bike around and pedals inland faster and faster until she has no breath left for breathing and a great stitch in her heart. She cuts across country, using every short cut she knows, to the ridge that will give her the best view of Genbar Lake.

Cassie is almost at the cottage when she hears a car engine roaring behind her, the urgency of a rattling acceleration. She side-steps onto the grass, begins to hurry without knowing why. A country back road, no one else in sight . . . It sounds as if the vehicle is coming straight for her. She turns to confront it. A dusty blue ute barrelling down the middle of the road. Brakes slammed on. Jack leans across and pushes open the passenger door. A glimpse of scattered gravel, sand, empty bottles, newspaper, frayed rope and scrunched brown-paper bags.

'Get in. Quick.'

She flings herself inside.

'What is it?' Sits on a packet of potato chips and goodness knows what else, nervously strapping her seatbelt on, thinking of accidents, heart attacks, shipwrecks.

'Whales,' he says, swinging vigorously on the steering wheel. 'Off the Point.'

Whales!

She abandons her shopping to grip the seat as he accelerates back the way he came.

There are three of them. Southern right whales, he tells her. Lolling dark, huge and sleek, only twelve metres off-shore. So close that she can see the white barnacle-like encrustations on their heads.

Jack produces a can of lemonade from the debris in the ute and sets it down on the bonnet.

'You sat on my chips,' he says, holding up the flattened packet.

She can't take her eyes off the whales. The size of their flukes as they roll and dive, the great circle of fizzing white water they leave behind. She feels unexpected tears on her cheeks. Hands shaking too much to hold the binoculars he's given her. She wipes her face with cold fingers.

'Oh!' she says. 'Oh! Oh, Jack.'

He's looking at her. A frown creasing his brow as the words in his head go scuttling and clattering like crays at the bottom of a basket. How to extract them without injury? It takes courage. It takes some doing.

She's laughing, embarrassed. Can't stop the tears.

'This your first time?' he asks at last, tender as a lover, and proffers an enormous handkerchief.

42

DECLAN

The phone rings from beneath the cushion on the sofa. It's Richard. He's talking in a rush, without preamble, without greeting her. Richard in a panic? How odd. How nice. Cassie lets the newspaper fall to the floor, curls up her legs and listens.

'She wants to sell the house, Cass. She says it smells of you. Ridiculous. Says she doesn't like living with all your things around her. Well, I can understand that much. I've packed some of your stuff away. Most of it. It isn't as though I'm not prepared to be accommodating. It isn't as though I can't compromise, is it?'

Cassie holds the phone in front of her face, looks at it in astonishment, shakes it, returns it to her ear.

'. . . pictures, ornaments, clothes. I had to move your clothes to make room for hers. Yours are in the garage, in boxes. I'm sorry, Cass, but I've no idea which box the evening dresses are in. I can't fit your car in. It has to sit out in the driveway with hers. How's the Merc, by the way? But the house, Cass. She says we should buy a new place, without memories, and furnish it from scratch.'

Cassie interrupts. 'My clothes are in boxes?'

'What? Yes. I can't let this happen. This house has always been a haven for me, you know that.'

The man has absolutely no sense of irony. She says, 'I'm surprised you didn't spend more time there, if that's the case.'

'It's precisely because I have so little time that I need this place. There has to be something in life you can take for granted, draw your comfort from. It's the old story, Cass. You don't always grasp the importance of things, till you realise you might lose them forever.'

Ah. But wait. No. He isn't talking about her.

And now she is unable to extract a single comprehensible sentence from the mass of outrage, resentment and yearning that is clamouring and jostling for position in her mind.

'We're getting calls too. It's not helping, Cass.'

'Calls?'

'About you. People are starting to wonder where you are. Sheila what's-her-name even called at the house. I'm sure she thinks I've got you buried in the backyard.'

'How awkward,' Cassie murmurs.

'Dammit, Cass. It's not funny.'

'You haven't given my number out?'

'No, but –'

'I'll be in touch with people when I'm ready. Not before.'

A door slams in that other world. She can actually see the

door with its elegant leadlight inserts that she designed herself. A voice calls out. A woman's voice. The fretful cry of a hungry baby. All at once, Cassie is deathly tired. The phone has grown so heavy she can barely hold it.

She says, 'I doubt the dresses will fit me now anyway.'

'What?'

'The dresses. It doesn't matter. I've just realised, they won't fit me now. I've lost a lot of weight.' She is reluctant to utter words, any words, into the atmosphere where the other woman stands. She thinks, I can make do with my long black skirt, my old magenta top. It doesn't really matter, does it?

'Cassie, if you want to come and sort out what you'd like to keep, I can arrange things. I mean, I can arrange things so you'll have some time by yourself here. Or we could talk. We've known each other for a long time. I'd like to think we can come through this as friends.'

Talk? *Now* he wants to talk?

Is she still there? The other woman. Is she listening to this with Richard's child at her swollen breast? Is she frowning? No need to frown. Simply enter his field of vision with the babe in your arms. Intimations of comfort, sensuality and immortality all in one. You can't lose. Not yet, anyway.

'I think it's a good idea, to sell the house,' she says brightly, surprised to find that she means it. The crying of the baby reaches her again. Richard can't hear what she's saying.

'Sorry?'

'I said I think it's a good idea to sell the house.'

'But I don't want to. I'm used to it. I – Christ! This is impossible. Can't you do something about that noise? I'm trying to have a conversation!'

Perhaps she hasn't got a mother's touch, his new woman. Perhaps she wanted Richard more than she wanted a child. Has Richard, too, got more than he bargained for? He's caught. She can hear it in his voice. He isn't capable of stating, as he would doubtless have stated to Cassie, that he doesn't want to sell the house, end of story. He has something to lose, now. Something he treasures. Not something he can take for granted. He's already lost that.

There is muffled sound. He's put his hand over the phone. He's talking to the other woman. Neither Richard nor Kit has once mentioned her name to Cassie, who in any case feels safer with an anonymous, archetypal target but wonders what she looks like, and how young? How young? Has Richard made her cry, shouting like that? How easy it is to cry when you have a warm and milky baby heavy in your arms, endlessly in your arms, all your emotions brimming at the surface, and the only thing you want is for someone to be nice to you, to reassure you, to be there. It was all such a long time ago. She pictures him in the study, standing by his big desk of flame mahogany with the lamp at one side and the etched crystal rose bowl at the other. She sees light fall from the bay window, thick cream curtains caught back to allow full view of his precious camellias.

'Domestic bliss?' she asks, when he can hear her again.

'Declan suffers from colic,' he sighs.

Declan? Her husband has a new baby called Declan. Not a name he would have chosen, she's sure of that. Her husband has a son. A second son. Reality attack. With cool detachment, she watches her hand begin to shake, sees the tremor pass to her arm. The phone falls to the floor, emits a kind of strangled squawking, as though something inside there is dying.

43

THE LAST STRAW

'She is mocking me.'

Simon's voice is a breathy whine. His fear has been building for weeks and is now tight and sore as a great boil. Nothing has worked. When you are afraid, seek out the mother. He is kneeling at her feet, waiting not for intercession or forgiveness but for inspiration. He bows his head, eyes closed, and allows her gentle voice to fill him. The plan is bold but if the thing is discovered, it will link him to the deed. It is dangerous.

'Never in Shearwater,' he whispers, shaking his head, thrilled and alarmed. If they found him with it, no one would be able to look the other way. Not anymore.

I could destroy it.

But you won't.

No.

He has done this many times, but not here. This is a pleasure he's always taken a long way from home, riding the bicycle through the night, silently, urgently.

'It's supposed to be a baby,' he whispers. 'Mother and baby. You know. It won't fit the pattern.'

And this is personal. Not a stranger. The woman, Cassie, taunting him with her lack of response, her ongoing, infuriating, inescapable presence at the place of comfort.

'It won't look like the others,' he protests, querulous now, and nervous. 'It won't be the same.'

But he listens. She is right. This will work, when nothing else has. This single action will rid him of Cassie Callinan and clear the way for his dreams.

Take it, says the Virgin.

'Take it,' he agrees.

Take it. Take it. Take it. Take it. Take it.

He opens his eyes, sees a host of Madonnas swim before him. He is transported by gratitude; his breathing grows ragged and fast. She has come through for him, given him the answer. His ardour swells and burns. He turns his shining face up to her and is flooded with love.

For several days after Richard's call, Cassie walks and walks and speaks to no one. She follows bush trails and beach tracks. She sees the sun set through forest canopies and from cliff-top perches. She doesn't lose her way. She doesn't lose her mind. She doesn't lose herself. In the evenings, when she feels a need for oblivion, she helps herself to whisky, toasting the firelight with wry patience and falling asleep, as she so often has, on the sofa.

One such night, she wakes in the early hours and doesn't know what has disturbed her. She lies still, listening to the boom of the surf, imagining it crashing white, foaming under starlight. There is no other sound that she can distinguish. She drags herself to the bathroom, mutters to her reflection, 'You look like the wreck of the Hesperus, Cass, old girl.' And staggers into bed.

He waits, invisible, silent. Waits for peace to envelop the cottage. Waits until the night breathes easily and she is deeply asleep. Soon, there will be no more waiting. Soon, she will be gone.

Task accomplished, he slides from the building but does not leave immediately. He creeps close, low and close to her window, listening. Tempted to wake her. To have her see it now, to hear her cry out. He resists. Tomorrow will be soon enough to enjoy the results. Heaviness weighs sweetly on one side of his jacket. It is a solid thing. It is the last straw. He knows it.

When Cassie wakes for the second time, the sun is up. She immediately feels a disturbance in her consciousness. Something has slipped out of alignment, here, in the bedroom. What? The room is cold, bereft, the scent of hostility faint upon the air. She has a fluttering of panic. What is it? The dregs of a nightmare? Why do I feel so afraid?

On the table, where the sea-green glass vase absorbs and transforms the morning light, where the Valium and sleeping tablets still offer ultimate closure, the silver photograph of Cassie with her children has vanished.

She only deludes herself for a short time, checking down the back of the table, searching the floor, under the bed. She rushes from room to room looking for other signs but she knows he has only taken the photograph. There is no need for him to do anything else. No need at all. With this acknowledgement, she sits on the edge of the bed, overwhelmed by the utter futility of the fight. She knows what he is telling her.

I am right here. I am right beside you when you sleep. I am breathing in the air you breathe out. I can touch what is most precious to you. I can take it away from you.

How very clever, she thinks. There isn't a damn thing she can do about it. Inside her mind, she can hear her own voice wailing. *After all I've been through. How can this happen to me, after all I've been through?* There is no answer. There is never an answer. When is the world going to make amends? She folds a wing over her head and in the darkness hears the pulse of her heart and the waves beckoning.

After an age, her chin comes up. Her eyes regain their focus. I'll have to go, she decides. I'll start again, a long way from here and a long way from Richard, who will have to sell the house. I will go somewhere warmer with kinder winds. I will go, knowing that nowhere is safe and you just have to get on with it. I'll go back to teaching. She sees the face of a little girl in her Grade 5 class, Emily with the home haircut who startled at the slightest thing, and the thin sly boy in Grade 2 who stole his lunch from other children and never had any of his own. She thinks of Tom, when they gave him the lumbar puncture, and her thoughts do not veer away from his puzzled, pain-filled brown eyes. Some things are worth the fight, right to the end, no matter what they tell you. But not this.

Whoever it is can have the damn cottage. I'll take Kit's advice and live in a city again. I'll get a small flat with a garden. I'll have all sorts of shops close by and I won't ever have to put an esky in the car when I go shopping. I'll have cafes and markets and life all around me again. I'll step back into the world.

Much later, it occurs to her that for someone to take such a risk, for someone to choose with such a delicate certainty of causing pain, he must be waiting, eagerly waiting, for a sign of her fear. There is one more move to be made. One last satisfaction she can deny him. She won't mention the loss of the photograph to anyone. I won't behave any differently, she thinks. When I'm ready, I'll slip away as quietly as I came. I'll just pack up the car and drive north. Or maybe west. This is how her thoughts are running. What to take. What to jettison. What, indeed, will she need for ballast? But she is stronger now. Flying headlong into uncertain winds every day develops some unexpected muscle. Beneath her thoughts, she can hear the pure song of her anger, untrammelled by grief or guilt.

If he thinks I haven't noticed, it might make him crazy. He could make a mistake. I could find out who has done this.

And then?

She can feel the weight of the axe in her hand, and it is good.

After lunch, Cassie drives up to see Elizabeth Savage with an overdue rent cheque. This much, she had planned. What she hadn't planned was to park outside the front door and toot the horn. It appears that Cassie Callinan has had enough of looking in the wrong direction, listening to the wrong sound. She's been wondering about Elizabeth Savage since she spotted the feathered hat on her sofa during the last visit. Elizabeth, who never leaves the house . . .

Elizabeth hovers in the doorway. 'Won't you come up for a minute?'

Cassie calls through the driver's window, 'No, thank you. I have so much to do before the Ball tonight. I'm a bit rushed. Sorry the cheque is late. I meant to drop it off last time I saw you but I was distracted by all those lovely dresses. I've been carrying it around in my wallet ever since.'

'You could have left it at the store with Myrtle.'

'I wanted to explain in person.' Will she come out?

'Cassie . . . is there a problem? Anything I can help with? You seem a little anxious.'

'Me? No. Everything's fine. I'm looking forward to the fireworks.'

She holds out the cheque. Elizabeth doesn't move, offers a bewildered, wrinkled smile. Cassie realises she's going to have to get out of the car and hand the cheque over. She'd thought this was one mystery she might be able to force to a conclusion, but she can't bring herself to do it.

'Did you get the red dress finished for Lily?' she asks, settling herself behind the steering wheel again, offering the question as a last courtesy and diversion.

'Yes. She looks very beautiful in it. Very grown up.'

'I have no doubt Lily Oklow will be the belle of the ball.'

Cassie makes sure to smile as she drives away. Anxious? Me?

'Not Lily Oklow,' says Elizabeth to herself, watching the silver Mercedes depart. 'Lily Biddle.'

44

THE BALL

The mirror reflects a woman dressed in understated but impeccable attire for a formal social function. Looking like this, Cassie feels the loss of Richard so keenly that it affects her balance, like an imperceptible limp. It's no good. I can't go, she thinks. But Grace had threatened to come and find her if she chickens out. Besides, everyone Cassie knows here in Shearwater is involved in the Ball. Does she really want to sit alone all night, wondering if she's being watched, listening for sounds that will tell her he is here?

Somehow, the outfit isn't striking the right note. Is it the shoes? Does she need higher heels? She studies her reflection glumly. I look like the Queen Mother on a bad day at Ascot, she thinks. It isn't the shoes she needs to change, it's herself. In a flash, she is hunting through the wardrobe, knowing exactly what she needs to wear.

Shoulders back, chin up, Cass. You can do it.

A cheerful noise, a blend of bass beat and raised voices, already emanates from the pub. The bright glow from inside is an open invitation. Cassie is halfway back to her car when Grace raps loudly on a window and rushes out.

'Come on,' she says, grabbing Cassie's arm so there is no chance of escape. 'There'll be lots of familiar faces once you're inside.' She nods in the direction of the Mercedes. 'That'll still be there in the morning.'

'Oh, no,' says Cassie, horrified. 'I won't be drinking a lot. I probably won't even stay long.' She is trying hard not to stare.

Grace is wearing a vast purple gown with turquoise beading around the neckline. Five long turquoise feathers, pinned to her strawberry curls with a diamante daisy, hang in a drooping arc that ends at the level of her enormous cone-shaped breasts. Wide silver bracelets studded with turquoise adorn each wrist. A dull-eyed fox draped around her immense shoulders looks as stupefied as Cassie.

'You like?' Grace says, striking a pose.

Cassie nods, speechless. She'd been worried that she might have overdone her own colour and glitter. Not a chance.

Poor thing, thinks Grace, looking Cassie up and down. No idea how to dress for a ball.

Inside, Cassie gasps. It is a carnival of costumes and colour, put together with wit and mischief. The men are for the most part in black, but even they have devised some little twist to pervert the formality – a top hat with plastic flowers, a bow-tie worn sideways on a bare neck, black waistcoat over a hairy chest, a cummerbund of coloured ribbons . . . But the women!

Gudrun approaches unsteadily, the image of a tiny princess in full-skirted ivory satin complete with, to Cassie's amazement, a sparkling tiara.

'Do you like it?' She twirls vigorously, one little hand holding the tiara in place. They catch her as she staggers to the left of them. Grace hisses to Cassie, 'She's only had a thimbleful. She'll be asleep before the bonfire. Same every year.'

'It was a wedding dress,' says Gudrun. 'Grace found it in the op shop at Werong, the clever darling.' Her face is flushed and her dark eyes are sparkling. She looks closer to sixteen than sixty. Cassie wonders what was in the thimbleful.

'You look so beautiful, Cassie.' Gudrun strokes the blue alpaca shawl, fingers the bright new necklace. 'Doesn't she look beautiful, Grace?'

Grace studies Cassie from head to toe, feathers bobbing. Looks at her blue skirt with its crimson flowers. At her pink cheeks and short, neat hair. Looks into her steady grey eyes, sees a flicker of something fierce there, and grins.

'Needs a little something,' is her verdict.

'Needs a stiff gin,' says Cassie, whose mouth keeps falling open as she glimpses new creations swirling past.

'And the Mercedes?' Grace cocks an eyebrow.

'Will be there in the morning.' Why fight it?

The large main room has been cleared for dancing, tables and chairs pushed to the walls. A live band – The Jazz

Rockers — have set up in one corner. Cassie feels the beat moving through her hips, unlocking her knees, thinks, yes, I might dance. Remembers the parties she went to with Richard. Ending up alone in some corner, back to the wall, clutching a drink. *Christ! Can't you look a bit happier?* She'd been so relieved when the need to accompany him to social events had diminished. It hadn't occurred to her that someone had taken her place. Maybe his new partner knows how to have a good time without drinking too much because she's bored to tears. Maybe she isn't afraid of being judged and found wanting, of clever-clever conversations with clever-clever people, those arch and impenetrable comments that left Cassie numb. Perhaps his new partner is One of Them. *What was I doing at all those ghastly gatherings?* Paying the price for Richard.

She scans the room for any sign of Kit. Where the hell is he? He was supposed to meet her here. Fat Harry's got help behind the bar. A cheerful rosy-faced woman in her forties with a come-hither smile and starched white apron over blue lace. Simon Biddle, standing with his back to the wall, hasn't made any concessions to dress requirements. All in black with his white collar. What a fraud. She despises him suddenly. A little bubble of rage finding an outlet. Careful, Cassie. It could be him. It could be any one of them. Or none of them.

The loss of the photograph is like an aching bruise inside her chest. All the things the intruder might have stolen. Her watch, gold jewellery, her wallet. But he didn't. It's a sickness, she realises. Quite beyond tricks.

'She won't come out of her room,' says Hannah over her shoulder to Kit, as they come through the door bearing aloft platters of spring rolls and dipping sauce.

'Duck!' she calls enthusiastically to Cassie who, bewildered, bobs her head.

'The spring rolls,' murmurs Kit. 'Duck spring rolls.'

'Oh.'

Hannah is in a bright red dress, cut very low over her breasts, body-hugging but flaring into frills and flounces. She has pinned red gerberas into the coiled mass of her hair. Kit is in a black suit, with a fitted red shirt, and a red bandana tied around his head. Oooh! Cassie thinks. They look like a couple, in co-ordinated costumes. That's a bit risky. Cheeky. I mean cheeky. Why did I think risky?

'I won't be long. Just got to get the food out,' Kit tells her, and hurries after Hannah.

'I told her she'll miss all the fun,' Hannah says to him, 'but she won't open her door. She hasn't spoken to me for days. Have you had a chance to talk to her? You haven't said anything about . . .'

'Me? No! Of course I haven't. Look, stop worrying. I expect she's getting ready. Probably wants to make an entrance. She'll be down later, you'll see.'

'I don't know. I think something's really wrong this time. It's almost like she knows.'

'What's to know?' he says sourly.

'Kit.' She gives his arm a gentle squeeze. What can she say? She should never have agreed to go with him. That kind of fun is best left to dreaming. Dreams, like Harry, are safe. Out there, no one is safe. Only within the circle that Harry creates can Hannah be the woman she was always meant to be. And now she's hurt Kit and he won't let it go.

'Hannah,' he says, taking advantage of the noise level to brush her ear with his lips, 'we need to talk.'

Why can't he just sulk? Why does he have to be so mature in some ways and so very young in others? But that's partly where the attraction lies.

'There's nothing to discuss, Kit. It isn't going to happen again. It was a mistake. It was my fault. I'm sorry.'

'I don't understand!' He is frantic.

'No,' she says gently, 'you couldn't possibly understand. There are things . . . I'm sorry.'

'Try me. At least give me a chance. Talk to me.'

She shakes her head sadly and moves away from him through the press of people.

Cassie sees the rebuff and her heart goes out to Kit but she is relieved and grateful to Hannah. She wonders, not for the first time, at her choice of partner. Fat Harry, round and glistening behind the bar. A big age difference, but they seem happy. Whatever the deal is, conscious or unconscious, it appears to be working.

An hour later, Jack sidles through the door wearing faded black denim jeans, a white shirt and a black tail coat. Where had he found that? And what is he using for a tie? It looks like . . . it is. A stiff spray of black seaweed. He sees her, gives her a nod but doesn't approach. Cassie isn't sure whether to feel relieved or not. How ridiculous, how incomprehensible, that she should feel so pleased to see him, and so nervous. The flush of awareness that his presence lends to the moment, as though everything in the room, including Cassie, is shining a little more brightly.

'Let me get you another one of those.'

Simon Biddle is at her elbow.

'Oh! Hello. How are you? No, thanks very much. I'll stick with this one for a while. Great night, isn't it?'

'You like bonfires, do you? Fireworks and all that?'

He is watching her closely, standing in her shadow. It puts her on edge. There's nothing more off-putting than someone else's loneliness.

'Doesn't everyone?' she says. 'When do they light it?'

'Ten-thirty.'

'So late? It'll make it a late night for the children, won't it?'

'It's not a children's bonfire,' he says with what she can only suppose is his version of a leer, though there's an odd hint of anger behind it. Is he cross because she declined his boat trip? How very uncomfortable. Perhaps he sees this in her eyes because he drifts away towards the buffet table. Immediately, she feels a tug of remorse and wishes she'd been kinder. He is quite as solitary as his brother, though more eccentric. Everyone in the crowded room is moving in their own little orbits, glancing off others and dancing around, the pull, the spin, the space. To her eyes, each one of them is utterly alone. Pity those who think they are not.

She remembers Elizabeth alone in her house on the hill. She

thinks about River Marsh Cottage, the thief who comes and goes as he pleases, and she is briefly comforted to be amongst people who know her name. I don't want to leave, she realises. I don't want to go. Perhaps I'm developing a taste for adventure after all. Better late than never. Being lost is not without its merits. To believe that you know where you're going is the true absurdity. China-walkers, she thinks. China-walkers, everywhere you look.

There's Jack, sitting with Hannah, heads close as they talk, very much at ease in each other's company. Cassie goes to the bar for a refill. Fat Harry, sweating over his unhurried labours, tells her, 'You look beaut.'

'Who? Me?' She laughs disbelievingly.

'You make a fine couple,' he adds with a wink, confusing her until she sees Jack at her side.

She blushes immediately. Harry tips her another wink, moves off to serve someone else.

Jack's eyes play over the crowd. 'Look at them,' he nods. 'That's the thing about the Winter Ball. You can be anything you want to be for just one night.'

Even in his quaintly formal coat, there is something earthy and distracted, something windblown about him. He would never look the part, as Richard had.

She takes a big gulp of her drink. 'And who are you?' she asks, flippantly. Stalker? Burglar? Thief in the night? She's not convinced.

'Fred Astaire.' He flips the tail of his frock coat, gives the seaweed a flick and kicks up a poor semblance of a soft-shoe shuffle.

She laughs.

'Care to dance?' he asks.

The words sound like a plea for forgiveness, but what is there to forgive? She looks across at Hannah, who sends her an unmistakeable nod of warm encouragement.

Why the hell not?

45
LILY'S PLAN

Lily, mutinous and silent in her bedroom, has come up with a plan that she's pretty sure will drive Hannah crazy. A two-part plan. A double-edged thrust. How is it that her mother gets whatever she wants? How had she managed to get Kit? No prizes for guessing that one. Lily knows Hannah's tricks. *If she thinks she can tell me what to do, she'd better think again. Things are going to change around here, very, very soon.*

'Ugly,' she whispers to her reflection. 'Stupid, fat, ugly. Why would he look at you?' But he will. She'll make him. She creeps from her room and sits at the top of the stairs looking for Kit, sees her mother making a show of herself.

Hannah's hair has come loose, rippling around her bare shoulders, one limp red flower still clinging to her ear. She's dancing with Fat Harry, eyes closed, arms above her head, hips swaying. Harry barely moves his feet, just rumbles quietly from the chest down. To Kit, Hannah looks like she's dancing alone, like she's spinning out the music from the ends of her long hair, like all the rhythm in the room is shuddering out of her body. When the music stops, Hannah opens her eyes and looks straight at Kit without seeing him, and Kit cannot hear anything but the soft moan she made when he kissed her, and cannot see anything but her. All his hopes are pinned on the slim chance that he'll be able to get her alone later, with a few drinks inside her to soften her resolve.

From where she's sitting, Lily can't see Kit but she knows he's there, knows he's watching her mother, knows her mother is dancing for him. The music reaches her in wave after battering wave. When it stops, she is so full of hate she can hardly breathe. If hate could move mortar, she'd bring the whole roof crashing down on them. But she's going to show them. She's got a win-win situation all worked out. A win for Lily and . . . another win for Lily.

There is a loud whoop! from Hannah as her heel skids, slips on the wet floor and the arms of three men instantly support her. Lily wants to throw up. Look at them. They're all besotted. Panting for her like dogs with their big wet tongues hanging out. Her mother, all smiles. Well, two can play at that game.

At 10.15, Harry clangs the big brass bell behind the bar and the whole giggling, weaving mass of them moves out onto the street in a bizarre parade. Women tottering and squealing as uncertain heels encounter uneven surfaces. Men carrying bottles and boxes. Hannah is arm in arm with Jack. Kit is escorting Cassie. Old Ralph Biddle carries his top hat in his arms, long tubes of plastic glasses spraying out from it in a strange bouquet.

The members of the band pack up their gear and join the procession to the beach, where their sound will be increased, if not enhanced, by two more guitarists – Rod and Belle from the caravan park. Also, Nick, a cray fisherman and wannabe drummer, Errol, a trumpet player from the Salvos, and an ex-nun (whom everyone still calls Sister Mary, even though it's been twenty years since she gave up the habit) with a treble recorder.

Harry takes off his white apron, big as a bedsheet, checks that the fireguard is in place, upends a sealed bottle of port into each of his jacket pockets and reaches up for a bottle of malt whisky from the top shelf. The night will not want for merriment. Not if Harry has anything to do with it. He'd asked Martin to light the bonfire at ten, so a cheerful blaze will welcome the revellers when they arrive at the beach, where several crates of beer and bubbles also await.

But what's Lily up to? He can't remember seeing her all evening. She must have been here, he reasons. Wasn't there some chatter from Hannah about a red dress for Lily to wear to the ball? It's been a busy night. Plenty of people he didn't see, no doubt. Lily wouldn't miss the fun, would she? She wouldn't miss the fireworks because of a fit of the sulks? He hesitates. Should he go up and see if she's there? And get his head bitten off, likely as not. He stands at the foot of the stairs, a hand on the banisters, and calls to her.

'Lily? Lily, are you there, girl?'

There's no answer. She's probably down at the beach with everyone else. A last look around and he leaves, locking the front door behind him, not from fear of burglars but to avoid falling over recumbent bodies in the morning.

The first part of Lily's plan involves finding Simon. He'll be at the bonfire, if he can handle the crowd. Otherwise he'll be in the shack alone. She's going to move into the aquarium, live there until she can get a job and earn some real money. No way is she staying here at the pub after what's happened. She needs Simon to agree to this but he will want to know why. And he won't want to upset her mother. It's not going to be easy to persuade him but if he won't allow it, she will tell them all that she'll run away and live on the streets and they'll never see her again.

Will she tell Simon what she saw? Their bodies lying close, the wine bottle tipped on its side. Kit leaning over to kiss her mother. She screws her eyes tight, fleeing from the image as she had fled the certainty of what was about to happen that day at Genbar Lake. A part of her is snarling at her mother's shame; she wants everyone to know. Another part is weeping, shocked and hurt, putting out a hand in the darkness and finding nothing there. Through her confusion, a voice warns of Harry's grief. Somehow, that must be avoided. This is no game. She holds the key to disaster. One turn, and all the patterns dissolve. All the certainties disappear. She has to be careful. It's a question of getting the balance right. How much will she have to reveal, to achieve what she needs?

And Kit? Part two of the plan. First the deed, and then the telling.

'I don't mind playing second fiddle,' she says softly, speaking aloud because the sound of her voice makes her feel braver, and what she is about to do will be irrevocable. But oh how sweet it will feel when Hannah finds out. And Hannah will find out. She'll make sure of that.

She hears Fat Harry call her name and she waits in silence till he locks up. That means everyone has gone. She puts on the crimson dress and runs downstairs to fill an empty water bottle with vodka. In the main bedroom, she takes her mother's black stiletto shoes from the wardrobe and slips them onto her feet. The height they give her. This dress. In the long mirror, she sees herself transformed. She can smell Hannah's perfume on the air, and her heart quickens to the thrill and fear of trespass.

Sitting defiantly at the dressing-table, she watches her reflection take a slug of the vodka. Better make it quick, in case someone comes back. She sprays herself with Hannah's perfume and applies Hannah's lipstick, eye-liner and mascara. She takes another drink of vodka and doesn't notice that the eye-liner isn't straight, that the mascara has smudged under her left eye.

I'm coming, Kit. I'm on my way.

All she has to do is confuse him – that shouldn't be too difficult tonight – and then they'll both get what they want. What's that noise? Has someone come back? No, it's just the roof creaking as the night air grows colder. Another sip, to calm herself. Her breath is coming hard, as if she's been running a race. In the mirror, she looks like somebody else. She looks like somebody.

Kit will have had plenty to drink by now. A flash of terror as she thinks of her mother getting to him first. Her mother, lying back, her arms reaching up and pulling Kit's face down to her own, his body moving to cover hers. No! Even Hannah couldn't manage to have Kit with Fat Harry on the scene.

She lets her hair out from its bun. It swings in dark waves past her shoulders. She allows it to fall forward, and tosses it back the way Hannah does, watching the movement, taking courage from it. Her eyes are shining beneath the make-up. You're on your way, Lily. Making something happen.

But what?

Anything. Anything will do. Anything at all.

46

MIRTH AND SOLACE

You can't get drunk when you want to. It's one of those rules, isn't it? Like Murphy's Law, or Paddy's Law, or whatever. Kit would give his right arm for a spliff tonight but he won't risk that. Doesn't want to be out of it, in case he gets a chance to be with Hannah. He knows he didn't imagine her body's response to him, the hungry excitement that she controlled with a visible effort. So he's waiting.

The fireworks spectacle had thrilled everyone and, as always, they were over too soon. The air still holds the scent of cordite and the flat, expectant tension that is all you have left when magic departs. The bonfire is burning well. Its roaring flames push back the night borders, lighting the eyes and smiles of ordinary Shearwater people with more than a hint of bacchanalian possibility. Miserably, Kit watches all the fun and carousing from a high, quiet vantage point. Every now and then, he sees someone stumble by below, either to take a leak in the bushes or hand in hand with someone else. They cannot see him, and he draws a sour satisfaction from the thought. Straining his eyes against the darkness, he prays for a glimpse of Hannah. He moved too fast, at Genbar Lake. Frightened her off. Softly, softly, next time. If there is a next time. Oh please, there has to be a next time.

Is that Aunt Cass, dancing in bare feet, waving a bottle in the air? Good luck to her, he thinks. She'll have a hell of a hangover in the morning. Jack Biddle, throwing his arms about, long thin body gyrating. What a crap dancer. They all look different tonight, as though they've let go of something. Jack catches hold of Cassie and deftly relieves her of the bottle. He stays close. So close, in fact, that Kit wonders if he's planning to make a move on her. Oh, bad pictures. Very bad pictures. But there at last is Hannah, in the thick of it. When is he ever going to find her alone? Does she think he isn't aware of the consequences? Does she think he's irresponsible? If only she'll let me talk to her. I can make her understand. I know I can.

It's the port that's caused all the trouble.

Of course it is.

Cassie lies back on the sand, exhausted, exhilarated and feeling a little sick. My gorgeous skirt will be ruined, she thinks, and giggles. The port bottle is empty. Many bottles are empty and lie scattered on the sand. She can see Jack sitting some distance away, knees drawn up, head resting on them. Has he gone to sleep? No wonder, after all that dancing. Who would have thought Jack could move like that? And the ex-nun was lively company, once Jack had persuaded her to stop playing warbling versions of Johnny Cash songs and put down the treble recorder. The band finished up ages ago but four CD players were produced, fingers synchronised on the Play buttons to run the same CDs. It seemed like a good idea at the time. Fat Harry had danced with Cassie too, and Grace had made a lunge for her and swung her around for a while. Poor Gudrun had been put to bed at nine-thirty, smiling blissfully, utterly comatose. Cassie feels like she's been dancing for hours. In all my life to this moment, she thinks, I'll bet I haven't danced as much as I have tonight. It's wonderful. She pulls her discarded shawl closer, bunches it under her head. Oh, bed. Sleep. Bed. Lovely.

The dark bulk of an elephant seal trumpets and snores on the lower reaches of a grassy slope behind her. Cassie crawls over cautiously to investigate. She prods the inert mass with an insistent finger. It's Grace.

'Wha.. wha.. whassa matter? Stop it. Stop that! Who is it? Cassie, is that you? Cut it out.' She lifts her head. Her eyes roll as she tries to focus on her tormentor.

'It's the port, Grace,' says Cassie solemnly.

'It's always the damn port,' says Grace, allowing her head to fall back onto her arms.

'I've lost my shoes, Grace.'

'I've lost my fox.'

'Poor fox. What am I going to do, Grace?'

'Eh? What? Find yourself a good woman. That's what you need.'

Cassie giggles. 'I don't think so.'

'S'true. A good woman. Someone to love you. Really love you. Know what I mean?' She rouses herself, raises her head to wink, and collapses again.

Cassie sighs, confides, 'I've never been much good at that sort of thing. Sex, I mean. I'm tense. I'm unco-ordinated. I say the wrong thing, do the wrong thing, and I always laugh at the wrong moment.'

Grace, touched by this excess of alcohol and candour throws an arm over Cassie and mumbles, 'How do you know?'

'Oh, I've been told,' says Cassie sadly, snuggling down beside her. 'But I like it. I really do like it. I miss it.'

'Then find someone to tell you otherwise.'

Out of the mouths of babes and drunken, giant, red-haired women . . .

Cassie allows Grace to go back to sleep but the snoring is too terrible to bear at close quarters. How does Gudrun stand it? Love must be deaf as well as blind, she concludes, crawling back to her shawl. She can see Hannah on the other side of the fire with two women Cassie doesn't know. Harry is sharing stories with some of his drinking pals. What has happened to Kit? She hasn't seen him for ages. At least he's not hanging around Hannah. And where's young Lily? I haven't seen her all night. She sits up abruptly. There's far too much spinning going on. The fire is warm on her face but she can feel the cold at her back. The urge to lie down again is overwhelming. Good grief! Am I going to be sick? How on earth am I going to get home? And where are my shoes?

'Getting cold?' It's Jack.

'Mmm, a bit. Time to go home, I think. Somehow.'

He crouches beside her. 'Hannah will put you up at the pub, if you like. Might only be a sofa, but she'll find you something. No problem.'

'I . . . oh, oh dear, I feel terrible all of a sudden.'

'It's because you've stopped dancing. The alcohol is catching up with you.'

She looks up at him, a mute and shameless plea for solace. He tilts her chin with one finger and kisses her, very gently.

Is this curiosity, she wonders, or something nicer?

Her body moves towards him, she curls her legs closer, snakes her arms around him, topples him onto the sand.

Cassie?

I could have him right now, she thinks, keeping her eyes shut so as not to look too closely at what she's doing. Probably. Maybe. I could have him right here.

'I like kissing,' she mumbles, some time later. 'Haven't done a lot of it. Haven't done it for years. Think I'm a little bit drunk.'

She opens one eye and shuts it quickly because he's laughing at her. She remembers the bleak sadness in his eyes the first time she saw him. It made her feel that anything else appearing in them would be only a courtesy, a kindness, a reflection. She reaches for his hand in the dark, holds it firmly.

'You going to stay here, Cassie? In Shearwater?'

A great log collapses into the embers of the bonfire, sending up a shower of sparks. Am I? Am I going to stay here? She's forgotten all about her pledge to leave.

She says, 'I didn't come here to live.'

'No. I remember that.'

They are quiet for a while, not moving, drawing comfort from proximity. From the darkness comes the brief mournful wail of the treble recorder, then silence.

'Banshee,' says Jack. 'They're terrible at this time of year.'

'What about you, Jack? Are you going to stay here?'

'Ah well, you know what they say. To everything there is a season,' he says, and looks at her. 'Probably not.'

No. That's what I thought.

She believes she knows now, how much and how little she can do for him.

He pulls at a blanket that someone's left lying on the sand and wraps it around them both. Cassie shivers inside the hard curve of his arm, as if he is not lending her warmth, but sharing the essence of his sadness. As if with bodies touching, he is trying to tell her what it means to be Jack Biddle. Trying to help her understand why not.

She stirs herself. I can kiss it better.

You know better than that, Cassie.

'Can I have another one, Jack?'

'Another what?'

'Another kiss.'

He sighs, hugs her close. 'It's no good, Cassie. Not with me. There'll be tears before bedtime.'

'I don't care, Jack. I'm not going to sleep tonight.'

Here comes Lily, tottering in her high heels, hurrying because she'd drunk too much vodka and fallen asleep on the bed and by now anything might have happened. There's no knowing how many opportunities she's missed. No time to waste. She's shivering as she slips quietly through the back door. She wishes she had her jacket but a jacket would spoil the effect, and the effect is all important tonight.

I'll show them, she thinks, and sets off at a brisk walk, heels ringing out on the pavement, goosebumps on her arms, nipples straining at the thin fabric of the red dress.

47

WOMAN OF YOUR DREAMS

The party is over. Amost everyone has gone home. The bonfire is a pile of embers, the sky a scattering of stars. Lily is stumbling around in the dark, stubbing her toes on bottles, tripping over party remnants and the odd body. She's looked everywhere but she can't find Simon or Kit. She's cursing the fact that she fell asleep when she should have been keeping an eye on them, waiting for her chance. And she's freezing to death, even under the jacket she grabbed from Fat Harry as he half-carried Hannah back to the pub an hour ago.

'Lily!' he cried, tongue confounded by the l's. 'Where've you been? Where are you off to?'

She smiled and shook her head at him. Don't ask, fat man.

He had his hands full with Hannah. It was all he could do to stay on his feet, but he hesitated.

'I'm fine,' she told him. It was what he wanted to know.

She's just so sad about everything. Nothing works out the way she wants it to. Might as well give up and go home, she's thinking, when she sees a figure at the far end of the jetty. He's sitting in a space between the lights. How typical of Kit, out there on his own in the dark, sulking. Suspicion flares, warming her, pushing back the edges of her tiredness. Is he sulking or is he waiting for Hannah? Have they arranged to meet? What a pity that Hannah won't be able to make it. Mustn't disappoint him.

She's been carrying around her mother's shoes for the last hour. Now she bends down and slips them on. She throws off the jacket, shakes her hair forward, pushes her breasts up and puts a sway into her hips. She knows what he will see. She knows what he will think. That's the idea.

Look up, look up, Kit.

The woman of your dreams is coming.

'Martin? Martin? What are you doing? Are you coming to bed or getting up? What time is it? Oooh! It's so cold. Martin? Won't you come and warm my feet for me? Are you there? You wake any of those children and you'll be sorry. Don't put the light on. I'll never get back to sleep if you do that. What's the time? It's four in the morning! You're not taking the boat out, are you? Tonight? You'll freeze to death. I don't know why I bother. You never listen to a word I say. Martin. Martin! It's four o'clock in the morning. Martin! Oh, I'm too old for this, I am. And you're daft in the head. Make sure you put those long johns on. And that special singlet I got you last winter. The one you always forget about. You know? The one from the catalogue. The one with the space-shuttle technology fibre. That'll keep you warm. There's no wind, is there? It'll be still as a mill pond out there and the sky full of stars. Is there a moon? Is there a haze around it? I wouldn't be surprised if there's a frost tonight. I can feel it in my bones.

'Martin? Are you there? Have you put your hat on? Seventy-five per cent of the body's heat is lost through the top of the head, you know. And you haven't even got hair to keep it in. Martin? Martin! You've left the door open. Oh, that man will be the death of me. Never there when you need him.'

Up on the grass, Kit stays very still, concentrating, then with a sudden movement he pinches himself hard on the arm. Shit! He's not hallucinating. It *is* Hannah down by the jetty. And she's alone. The last time he looked, he couldn't see her anywhere. She must have gone home with Harry and now she's come back. He can think of only one reason for that. She knows what she's missing and she's come to get it. Perhaps the whole thing had been an act, this evening. Perhaps she's been waiting all night for a safe opportunity to tell him she's realised how much she needs him. He'd given up on her. He'd lost faith. The only reason he's still sitting up here is because he couldn't bear the agony of lying under her roof tonight, not having her. And now look! You never know your luck, do you? His body, cramped and cold, is roused to miraculous life. He leaps to his feet.

The woman crosses a pool of silver-white beneath the jetty light. It is Hannah. Isn't it? She passes into darkness then emerges under the next light. Kit starts down the slope, not taking his eyes from her. There's something about the walk. What is it? He stops, focusing on the figure below him.

Is it? Is it?

Who else can it be?

Uh-oh . . .

She hasn't even noticed the photograph is gone. He is nothing to her – a flea, a mosquito buzzing around her would get more reaction. He wants her to be afraid, as she should be, as the others are afraid, of the one who comes and goes and leaves no trace and takes only what pleases him. He wants her to go. Why won't she go? What now?

Footsteps on the jetty. He turns sharply and the empty whisky bottle falls from his fingers and slips into the water unnoticed. A second bottle beside him is half-empty. Sharp heels tapping on the wooden boards. Who? Who is it?

He cannot believe it. He cannot believe that such prayers are answered. That she has come for him. The blinding movement of her body as she walks towards him. He struggles to his feet, sees her smile, warm and welcoming, so different tonight from the face that spurns him, from the eyes that mistrust and despise him.

Here my love. My dream. Come here, into my arms. Don't struggle. There, there. No need to struggle. It's all good. You're safe now. Everything is going to be all right.

He inhales the perfume of her hair and her body writhes against him. He holds her closer and warms her and stops her cries with his own mouth.

Kit hears the scream tear through the night as the two figures merge, and he's racing towards the jetty but – oh! – he is so far away. Who is it? Who's got her?

Halfway down the slope, tripping and stumbling and swearing his frustration, he sees a third figure rise into the light, moving quickly towards the struggling couple. He reaches the firm boards of the jetty, running faster than he's ever run. He is close enough to hear Lily's desperate cry, 'Uncle Simon!' when the three figures meet, fly apart and the man is sent flying with one sweep of a powerful arm, straight into the dark water. There is a loud splash, then nothing.

Grace! She has her arm around the frightened girl. She's murmuring words of comfort.

Lily's saying, 'But why? Oh Gracie, why would he? I only wanted to talk to him.'

Grace kicks at the whisky bottle without letting go of Lily. 'That, for one thing, and for another, you look the image of your mother. Hush now, hush,' she says, for Lily is crying hard again.

Kit stands close, watching them, wishing he'd got there sooner. Wishing there was someone he could punch, or someone he could hold and comfort. He feels like a spare part.

'Ah, Grace?'

'What do you want?' she snaps. Men, the cause of all problems. Men, hurting lovely young Lily. Men after one thing and one thing only, and not even kin to be trusted. She tightens her hold on Lily.

Kit's voice has a wobble in it. 'I . . . he went in, Grace. Simon Biddle. He went in the water. I saw him.'

'Bloody good riddance,' she says.

Lily screams, 'Oh no! He can't swim, Grace. He can't. I know. He told me. Oh god.'

Shit. Grace hurls Lily into Kit's arms and runs to release the lifebuoy. She calls out to Simon but there is no answering voice.

'I've got my mobile here. Should I call someone?' Kit, an arm awkwardly around Lily, is doing his best to be of some use.

'Try 000 for starters,' says Grace. 'And then ring 7835 and get Ralph Biddle to find Jack.' They'll all be out cold after the party, she thinks. No one will be any help at all. Christ. What a mess.

'And Kit, when you've done that, you wait here till they come. You saw it all. You can tell them. I'm going to get this girl home. And try not to panic. He's probably crawled out further down the beach. He's probably home already.'

They all look towards the shack where Simon lives. No lights.

'Call them,' she says, tersely.

And then they leave him alone with the night and the water and the bobbing red and white circle of the lifebuoy.

48

THE THINGS WE SURVIVE

'I didn't mean to drown him,' Grace confides, over coffee with Gudrun and Cassie the following week. 'I only wanted to get him away from Lily.'

'You certainly did that,' says Gudrun.

'And somebody fished him out of the water?' Cassie can't get a grip on this story. Keeps feeling that she's missing the point somehow.

'Myrtle said Martin found him. The current carried the bastard out to sea and brought him back in towards the other side of Shearwater Point but he was half-dead from the cold and the whisky by then. Martin was out after crays when he felt something big bump against the tinny. Gave him a real shock, she said, because he's been dreaming about those giant squids lately. He hauled the bugger over the side and nearly lost the both of them in the process. Should have left him in there.'

'Grace!' says Gudrun, horrified, but Grace is unrepentant.

'Better not show his face around here again, that's all I can say.'

'It was a mistake,' Gudrun points out.

'And how does that improve the situation? Pervert. What are we supposed to do? Sit around and wait for him to make another mistake? He ought to be locked up.'

'There won't be any charges laid, you know that,' says Gudrun.

'But . . .' Cassie is bewildered.

Gudrun explains, 'He was drunk. First time in years he's had a drink. You have to wonder what tipped him over the edge, why he needed it, that particular night.'

'Is Lily all right?' Cassie is appalled that Gudrun is showing any sympathy for Simon Biddle.

'She's fine,' says Grace. 'Poor little love, all that make-up smeared on her face and crying so hard she could barely speak. He didn't do any physical harm to her but it was a terrible shock. Someone she's trusted, you know. She was clinging to me like she was the one drowning, not him. I would have got there sooner but I didn't have my glasses with me. I saw her go by but I thought it was Hannah, till I heard her scream.'

Cassie asks, 'Does he . . . you know, go after young girls?'

'Not that we know,' says Gudrun quickly, before Grace can speak.

'Well, I think they should arrest him,' says Cassie. 'Why won't they lay charges? You don't want people like him wandering the streets.'

'My dear, it's not so simple. You see she was wearing Hannah's clothes and Hannah's perfume. He thought it was Hannah coming towards him.'

Simon and Hannah? And poor Lily, all dressed up. She was looking for Kit, Cassie thinks. Kit has moved into her spare room and is booked on a flight to England next week. 'Enough,' he said. 'It's all seriously stuffed. Time to go home.' She didn't try to talk him out of it. She could see in his face that it was time. And though she doesn't believe it's a case of a broken heart, she feels like pinning his name and address onto his sleeve, he seems so lost.

Grace remarks that it will be even more difficult to get a newspaper now that old Ralph Biddle has gone. 'Good riddance to him too,' she adds. 'You can never trust a man who baits his cray pots with penguin.'

Penguin?

'He always said you had less trouble with the sea lice, using penguin. Not that that excuses it,' says Gudrun. 'He's gone to Tasmania, with Simon. They've got a place in the south-west somewhere. They'll be no trouble to anyone there. Very isolated. It's not as if we knew what was happening. Not really.'

Cassie is still bewildered. 'What about all those photos Simon had on his wall? Mothers and babies. Where did they come from? What will they do with them all?'

She has seen the photographs. Half the town found one reason or another to visit the shack and see the photographs. Cassie has told no one about her own stolen photograph. She went there, desperately hoping to find it, and came away puzzled but very relieved that she and her children were not a part of that strange sad collection of faces.

'They're being packed up with some of Ralph's stuff. Going to a second-hand dealer, according to Myrtle. You'd never be able to track where they all came from. Nearly thirty of them. All stolen,' says Grace, shaking her head. 'No way of knowing how long it's been going on for. People have negatives. People have copies of photographs, don't they?'

Sometimes. Somewhere.

Gudrun says, 'Lily's staying with her grandmother for the time being. She didn't want to go home, naturally.'

'Why?' asks Cassie. 'Why didn't she want to go home? I would have thought home was where she'd feel safest. With her mother and Fat Harry.'

'There's a lot to explain,' says Gudrun.

'And when all's said and done, it's Elizabeth's responsibility,' Grace adds. 'She's the one who ought to explain, if anyone's going to.'

This is too much for Cassie. She looks from one to the other. 'Elizabeth?'

'Elizabeth Savage. Lily's grandmother.'

'Elizabeth Savage is Lily Oklow's grandmother?'

'Not Lily Oklow,' says Gudrun. 'Lily Biddle. Daughter of Hannah Biddle.'

'And Simon Biddle,' adds Grace.

'No!'

'Grace! We don't know that.'

'Well, you have to admit, it's starting to look that way. Some say it was Ralph, some say Simon. Hannah wouldn't ever tell. But Simon's always been crazy for his sister. That's why he never married. Hannah can't bear the sight of him. It's not something we talk about. For Lily's sake.'

'Of course.' Cassie's head is reeling. 'But Elizabeth . . .'

'Goodness, woman! Haven't you been listening to anything I've said? Elizabeth Savage was married to Ralph Biddle. She had three children. Jack, Simon, and then much later, Hannah. Savage is her maiden name.

'When Hannah became pregnant, she was only fourteen. Elizabeth's reaction was to move out of the house – the house you're living in – and run away from her family. She shut herself up in the house on the hill. She rented it at first – it'd been empty since old Matt Jessop died – but she bought it as soon as she could. Washed her hands of the whole business. Walled it all up inside her heart. It wasn't until Jack's daughter died that Elizabeth re-established contact with any of them.'

'What a terrible thing for a mother to do.'

Gudrun covers Cassie's hand with her own. 'Listen, I've thought a great deal about this,' she says. 'Elizabeth believed she was living a certain life, in a world that was completely familiar, completely known to her. She probably felt, as we all do, that she had a measure of control over things. When she found out that it was all a sham, rotten at the core, it broke her. Some of us break more easily than others. I'm sure, in her own way, she watches over them. We do what we can, my dear, not always what we ought to.'

'But what about Hannah?'

'Hannah stayed,' says Grace. 'Had her baby. Things would have been different if Jack had been there, but he was long gone. He's almost twenty years older than Hannah. She wasn't even born when he left home. He was away for years and when he did come back, he had a wife and child with him.

'Ralph Biddle eventually took over the newsagency and moved in there. Simon stayed on at the cottage. It was Simon who looked after Hannah and the baby.'

'But if Simon was the one who stayed by her and looked after her, why won't she have anything to do with him now?'

'Who knows. Maybe he crossed the line. Maybe he got to thinking it was his own little family. His own little wife. Hannah threw him out. Wouldn't ever talk about it. That was enough of a crucifixion in its own way. People didn't know for sure what he'd done but we all had our suspicions. Like father, like son.

'Years later, when Elizabeth got the cottage as part of the divorce settlement, she refused to let any of them live there. She wanted permanent tenants. Strangers. But we think Simon kept driving people away. He's got the little shack by the jetty but he was forever hanging around the cottage. Remembering the good old days, perhaps.' It was said without a trace of irony.

'The rat,' says Cassie.

'Cassie, my dear . . .' It's Gudrun, reproving her.

'No, I mean the rat in the salmon.'

'We couldn't be certain.' Grace is embarrassed, her cheeks almost as red as her hair.

Cassie asks, 'And Harry?'

'Harry is Hannah's white knight,' says Gudrun. 'Worships the ground she walks on. Harry's never going to let anyone hurt Hannah ever again.'

'Hannah's never going to let anyone hurt Hannah ever again,' says Grace.

Cassie's thinking about Simon Biddle, losing his first family and then his second. Which madonna did he yearn for? Elizabeth, with the baby Hannah, or Hannah, with her baby, Lily? Hannah, the beautiful laughing girl in the photograph Cassie had found at the cottage.

'How do you know?' she asks. 'How do you know all this? How do you know it's true?' The motivations, she's thinking. How can anyone truly know why?

'You hear things,' says Grace. 'Everybody knows everything about everybody else round here. Good and bad. And terrible. Stuff happens. You get on with your life. You look out for each other as best you can for as long as you can. That's what living is all about, isn't it? That's the whole point. The things we survive,' she says thoughtfully. 'Sometimes, you wonder how. You really do.'

49

WALKING A LITTLE FASTER

Cassie hasn't seen Jack since the night of the Ball. He'd driven her home in the old blue ute and she has a vague memory of hearing voices when he left, much later. But perhaps she dreamed it.

In cold daylight, she can hardly believe the things they did together. Mid-gasp, she had looked at him in astonishment and he laughed shyly, proudly, and told her, 'It's the only thing I've ever been any good at. Bit out of practice.'

She saw something then, shutters raised, a spark of light behind his eyes, gone so quickly she might have missed it if she hadn't been vibrating on exactly the same wavelength. Bit out of practice? Practise on me, Jack. Oh, please, practise on me. She has forgotten nothing. There is no mercy. When night falls, all she can think of is that, one day, before she dies, if the gods are kind, she might get the chance to do it again.

She waits to hear. He has a lot on his plate, with all the worry about Lily and Simon. Every day she thinks to herself, he'll drop in. He'll come knocking for a cup of coffee. When she goes out, she finds herself hurrying back in case he's sitting at her kitchen table. At the sink washing pots, in the garden pulling up grass, at the store with a loaf of brown bread in her hand, she is startled by the vision of his pale naked body above her, the raised muscles of his abdomen, his penis emerging and sinking into her, emerging, sinking, scooping up sanity and sense until she is breathless and weightless, loose and lost to joy. She hesitates over the soap suds, lays down the torn grass, pauses, loaf in hand, listening, looking around, unsure if reliving that moment, she has cried out.

On the beach, she walks a little faster than usual, eyes not on the water but on the dunes. Occasionally she has the feeling she is being watched, hopes she is being watched. It was a kindness, she thinks. An itch relieved. A drunken coming-together. A yielding. It was the port. It was nothing. It was wonderful.

I have no right to expect one night to change anything. But it has changed her. It has opened up a pain that is not of his making, and when she wakes in the mornings now, her pillow is sometimes damp with tears. When she makes her breakfast, looking out over the garden where trees are delicately frilled with white and pink blossoms, she feels the uncurling of their new green leaves, tenderly, beneath her own skin.

'Coo-ee! Hello? Anybody there?'

It's Myrtle, already coming through the door.

'Oh, there you are, Cassie. I was just going to leave this on your kitchen table. It's from Lily. She asked if you'd mind forwarding it to Kit in England. It's only a scrap of paper, no envelope. I told her you'd be writing to him. I said you could pop it in with one of yours. All right?'

'Of course I will. I'll be glad to. I'll send it this week. He hasn't been home for long. I'm sure he'll be glad to hear from her. How is she?'

'She's good. They're very resilient at that age. Just as well, I suppose, or we'd all be extinct. She's home again now. Your garden's looking a treat. I must tell Elizabeth. Have you seen her? She's a bit low. Not surprising. You'll call in, in a week or so, will you? She's opened the curtains now so it's all right. Look at the blossom on that tree. You wouldn't credit it, would you? Jack been around, has he? Have to dash. I've left Martin minding the shop but he's likely to forget about it and wander off somewhere. Never there when you need him, that man. See you soon. Bye!'

Cassie takes the sheet of paper covered with Lily's careful round handwriting. She is reading the letter before she can think to stop herself.

Dear Kit, a lot has happened here in the last few weeks. I am going to stay with Harry's sister and her family, in America! Everyone thinks it will do me good to get away from here for a while. After that, I'm going back to school and I'll try to get into university here. I want to be a marine biologist. What do you think of that? Bet you're laughing. I've never told anyone before. I might even turn up on your doorstep one day. You never know your luck. I think about you a lot. I hope you are happy. Don't be a stranger.

Love, Lily.

PS You can write to me at the pub, if you want to. Mum will make sure I get your letter. Everybody's being really nice to me, like I'm sick or something. It's great! Please write to me, Kit. Please.

He won't write, Cassie thinks. He'll mean to, but he'll keep putting it off. He's shaken us all out of his hair in his hurry to get home. He'll think about us now and again, until new experiences replace us, and in time we will fade like old photographs that seem closer to dreams than reality. Lily will go to America and forget all about him.

She fills the kettle with water and turns it on. Measures tea by the spoonful. One for me, one for the pot.

Kit has stopped smoking (both kinds of smoke). He has signed up to study geology, a field in which he will excel. Stuart doubts the wisdom of this, tells his son it's a narrowing of his career prospects. Kit returned is not the Kit who went away. His mother mourns the once tender boy who now displays such firmness of purpose and impatience.

But Kit will grow tender again. He is not the kind of man for whom armour is a daily necessity. Right now, he is avoiding relationships, regards love as too dangerous an adventure, but in his third year at university, he will meet Christine, a brisk New

Zealander, and in time, he will fall in love and marry her. They will buy a house in Auckland, New Zealand, and there, he will watch islands grow.

Now and again, something reminds him that he meant to write a book one day, but with three children, two boys, Nicholas and James, and then a daughter, there is never time. His wife decides she wants to call the baby Lilian, after her own grandmother, and for a moment Kit will remember the octopus and Shearwater and tell her, 'I once knew a girl called Lily.'

In America, Lily falls in love, but only briefly. She breaks a heart. Not hers. It is not the last time this will happen. She comes home to Shearwater and works hard to get the results she needs to study marine science at university.

In years to come, she will gain international recognition for her research papers on species, habitats and irreversible degradation of the Great Barrier Reef in Queensland.

When she grows older, too old for the rigours of diving, she will accept the lucrative position of consultant to a large and very popular tropical aquarium. And in retirement, she will write a series of bestselling picture story-books to help children understand the creatures of the sea.

She will never lose her love of the octopus. She will never marry. She doesn't forget.

50

STANDING IN THE MIDDLE OF IT

Cassie wakes, startled, certain that someone has just called her name. Hard white daylight is another shock. She'd fallen asleep a little warily last night, deliberately leaving the curtains open, watching the stars, waking at intervals and seeing the pattern changed. She lies still, listening. No one has called out. No one is here.

Yesterday, Gudrun and Grace came to pick her up. The birds were coming home. Thousands of shearwaters returning on schedule. Cassie had wrapped her crimson silk scarf about her neck as she left, for courage.

The sea was a ruffled amethyst, the sky pale at the horizon, merging into a broad layer of rose, reaching up to a line of bright scallop clouds, and right over their heads, a cold, clear blue. The call had gone up, and the first speck appeared. The women stood in silence beneath the ghostly circling birds. When the shearwaters began to come in, wings whirring, when they landed and made their way with such admirable, heart-wrenching certainty to their own burrows, something inside Cassie Callinan finally dissolved.

Gudrun thought she was overcome by the beauty of the spectacle. Grace suspected it had more to do with Jack Biddle, and offered a cotton handkerchief. Cassie, mopping up, wondered where all the tears were coming from.

Grace stood with her hood thrown back recklessly. ''Bout time somebody had some luck round here,' she said.

It was all a question of perspective, Cassie thought. The way things are might be the luckiest outcome of all. You can't tell which way is up, when you're standing in the middle of it.

She couldn't stop herself from glancing round at the gathered figures. Jack wouldn't miss the birds, would he? Once, she thought she caught a whiff of a cigarette above the scent of brine and seaweed, and she turned with a glad heart but there was no one behind her.

It wasn't until torch beams began to play over the shrubs and the night crowded in, hiding her face, that she managed to say, quite casually, 'I thought Jack would be here tonight.'

'Poor Jack,' said Gudrun. 'So much to organise. Everything splintering, flying apart like that. We thought Elizabeth was going to have a nervous breakdown. When Lily went home, Elizabeth drew the curtains for a week and refused to talk to anyone except Jack. But now she seems just the same as usual. A bit thinner, perhaps. Another layer of sadness to carry.'

Grace said, 'I heard that Hannah was on the happy tablets for a while, and Jack was all for it. He said it was the only way to stop her cutting off Simon's balls. That, and Bass Strait lying between the two of them.'

'Anger can be a wonderful restorative,' said Gudrun equably.

As the three women made their way back to the car, Cassie thought about the shearwaters, defined by the wind, confined only by the stratosphere. The risk, the freedom, the warm sandy burrows they seek out and fly back to.

Back at River Marsh Cottage, Gudrun accepted a cup of tea while Grace and Cassie had a large whisky apiece to keep out the cold.

Grace asked her, 'Will you stay on here?'

Cassie had been wondering about that herself. 'I'm not sure. I don't think I can stay, after everything that's happened.'

'You're not leaving us? Perish the thought, woman! We're only just starting to get used to you.'

Cassie laughed. 'I meant the cottage. I thought, after I divorce Richard, maybe I could buy a small place. Somewhere quiet, close to the river. Here in Shearwater.'

'That's more like it. You could run the newsagent's, now that Ralph's gone. Time somebody did. Come on, get your skates on, Gudrun. It's way past your bedtime. Where's your hat?'

'It's here, darling. Cassie, my dear, I heard that Pollonbeck Primary School needs a relief teacher. Mary Kennedy is going overseas for a year. Do you know Pollonbeck? It's about fifteen kilometres north-west of here. An easy drive.'

Cassie, propped on her pillows, smiles, remembering this.

The lovers want her to stay. The birds are back. The season is turning. People make mistakes. People give their hearts, all the time, to others they don't know, to others who have no idea what is being offered, or how precious it is, to others who receive the gift of someone else's trust and measure it in terms of what they can achieve with it, how far it will get them, how it might be put to use. All the time, there is this giving and taking, certain and ceaseless as the tides. And then there are those who know what it is that they hold, and because of this, are afraid. If she lives to be a hundred years old, if she doesn't ever see him again, she will not regret what she shared with Jack Biddle. Patterns are eclipsed, renewed, begun. There's a time to hold on tight, and a time to let the wind take you.

The air in the room is still cold. She reaches out to flick on the heater at her bedside and pulls the heavy quilt up to her chin. Feels like there was a frost last night.

Jack, eyes fixed on a brilliance of white mist and silver water, wonders at what point eccentricity becomes insanity. When does need become obsession and tip over into psychosis? He wishes there was someone who could explain this to him. It's keeping him awake at nights, seeing his brother lying in the room of the photographs with dreams of Hannah curdling his heart.

Despite everything, despite the certainty he should somehow have prevented it all, it is the photographs he can't get out of his mind. An entire wall of framed photographs, each one a mother with a baby in her arms. Different people, different places, different decades, by the look of them. Why had Simon done this? Why did he need them? Where had they all come from? Some of the images were old, black and white. A couple of them were sepia. Frames of wood, silver, pewter, plastic, even one of bakelite. Others unframed, stuck onto the bare plaster. Joyful images. And so sad. Then he'd seen one that didn't fit the pattern. No baby. He looked closer and understood at last how his brother had come by these pictures.

They'd got Simon onto his own bed by the time Jack arrived. The ambulance was on its way. Simon, who had uttered no words since Martin dragged him into the boat, lay white-faced, staring at Jack as though he was a beacon of safety. Jack, seeing the darkness of deep water behind his eyes, understood that his brother was still drowning. He sat on the bed and took Simon's hand in his own.

'It's all right,' he said. 'It's going to be all right.' He didn't know how.

Jack talked and talked. He spewed out facts about the manta ray and the octopus, about granite and amber, about how beer is made and the effects of a stone liver, about the admirable qualities of glass and the curious shape of raindrops. He talked about stars and boats and birds and trees and anything at all that came to mind, anything that might lead his brother up out of the dark waters that held him down. When he finished, Simon was sleeping peacefully and Jack felt utterly drained of facts. And all the time, there was the photograph on the wall, right in front of Jack's face. Stolen, he understood now, like all the others.

When the paramedics arrived, Jack had to prise Simon's fingers from his hand. Saw his eyes open. Saw the fear return to them.

'Jack,' he said, his voice barely a whisper, 'Jack, I didn't touch her. Didn't lay a finger on her. It wasn't me.'

Jack shook his head sadly. He knew Grace had to pull them apart. Was about to say, *you held her, you kissed her*, when he realised. Simon wasn't talking about Lily.

'I am not our father. Understand me. Please, Jack. I am not our father.'

'I know,' said Jack, thinking, who am I to forgive or absolve anyone of anything? But he laid a hand briefly on his brother's forehead as they carried him out. Then he slipped the photograph of Cassie Callinan with her young son and daughter into his pocket and left.

The sharp white light and cold air make his eyes sting and water. He wipes the back of his hand across his cheek, tastes salt tears on his lips.

It's eight in the morning. All around him, a heavy dew lies on the grass, spangling leaves and cobwebs. He thinks, yes, it was cold enough for a frost last night.

51

GOING HOME

By nine o'clock a dead white light still hangs over the ocean and thick swathes of mist lie in the gullies of the far headlands. No birds call, no insects, just the muted shush of the waves.

Jack, looking for the place where the sea joins the sky, can find no horizon in the haze. Minute by minute, the light is growing stronger and the water dazzles as the mist begins to recede. Somewhere behind him, a skylark trills sharply and falls silent again. A long narrow bank of grey cloud appears.

The horizon becomes keen-edged as the sun rises but the dark cloud does not move or change shape. It sits out there, at the meeting point of sea and sky, a soft blur that looks for all the world like a flat-topped island, and it does not disappear.

Cassie emerges, groping for sheepskin slippers and dressing-gown, makes her way sleepily into the kitchen for a cup of tea. As she stirs in a spoonful of sugar, a shrike thrush calls a series of pure notes from the stringybark tree. A feeling of peace and contentment steals over her. No need to burnish the armour and man the battlements now. No more intruder, no more unsettling occurrences in the cottage, no more Kit to worry about, and even Richard has slipped away to a less urgent, less painful place in her thoughts.

She carries the cup of tea back to bed, snuggles down under the quilt. It might be time. It might be possible to make some decisions about life. She has begun to feel curious about her future. A desire to have a hand in the shaping of it is slowly growing, sure as daylight. Warm and safe, she falls asleep again. Her tea grows cold on the bedside table.

An hour later, the first thing she sees is a narrow dazzling beam of light shooting a white diagonal across the room. The sun, shining on her dressing-table. The sun, shining on a rectangle of glass. It's the photograph.

When the sun has burned away the mist and high swirls of cirrus are beginning to streak across the blue sky, Jack feels the breeze strengthen. The swell is rising, as though the sea too, with its lazy never-failing heartbeat, is waking now and shrugging off the still, white dreams of the night. He hears Hannah's voice: *You'll keep an eye on things, Jack, will you?* Jack will fix it. Jack will sort it. Jack will save you. But I've never been able to save anyone at all, he thinks.

He studies the waves, sees where the rip curves out, away from the tethering beaches, away from the shadowing cliffs, away from the tangles of stories, the people who bind and fasten you with their hopes and expectations, their love and their pain.

It isn't a trick of the light. The photograph is definitely there, on her dressing-table. But . . . ?

Someone has been here, inside her bedroom. Someone has been here while she slept. When? I should be afraid, she thinks, but she is not.

Jack. She is certain of it.

She sits up in bed, clutching a pillow to her breasts with both arms, staring at the photograph, willing herself motionless, as though any movement stronger than a heartbeat might cause her children to vanish again.

Out and away the rip curves, under the bright sun, cutting its smooth sure path through the water, pointing the way to the island cloud. Jack gets to his feet, grunts at the stiffness in his knees. He raises a hand to his eyes. Squints. Is it a trick of the light?

He's anxious now, slipping in the soft sand, almost turning an ankle in his haste to reach the beach. Will it vanish from his line of sight? Or will it vanish?

Cassie gets out of bed and goes over to the photograph. Her hand moves uncertainly towards the frame, then grasps it firmly. She lifts it, turns it. No sign of damage. No sign that anyone has touched it, or that it has ever been anywhere else but here with her. It seems nothing short of a miracle. She looks at her own younger smiling face, arms round her children. She raises the frame to her lips and presses a kiss on the cool glass.

At the water's edge, scallops of pearly foam creep up and back, up and back, leaving opalescent bubbles on the sand. The waves wash over his boots, enter and fill his boots. He glances back, sees his footprints fill with water, clear as glass. Further up the beach, his trail is plain, coming from the dunes. He goes back, takes off his boots and places them side by side, well above the high tide line, so someone will know.

He thinks of Cassie Callinan, her warm whisper tickling his ear: *I should warn you, I've been told I make love like a cabbage.* Could she really have said that? He doesn't understand the comparison but knows it's enough to break your heart.

She wants someone to save, doesn't she, Jack?

Not me, he thinks.

Having someone, having her, so close and so vulnerable . . . it confused him. Skewed the perspective and shone light into corners that were better, much better, left dark. How could he have done that? He knows she'll be expecting to see him. He's been avoiding her. She has a future. You can see it in her face. She has strength enough for that. It was arousal. It was illusion. It had the shape of something remembered, but different. Some snug harbour. It was nothing. He shuts out any thought of the sadness he'll cause, shuts out, too, the memory of her arms around him, her surprised delighted laughter, and concentrates on the water.

Walking out into the ocean, out and out and farther out, the cold is nothing he has not known before and the water is his ally. A slender shape, tall and a little hunched against the chill, is forming and reforming, beckoning. A kiss of ice on his cheek as a wave splashes high. For as long as he is able, he keeps his eyes on the island, willing it closer, faster, sooner. And then he dives into the curl of the wave and through the wave.

Now he can feel the pull of the rip and allows it to take him, easy, easy, and the water that erases everything is carrying Jack away. Already, from the shore, he might be a piece of bull kelp rising on the swell or the dark shape of a seal. But it is Jack. Only Jack. Going home at last.

52

LITTLE DOOR

She sees on the kitchen table what she should have noticed the first time, when she came in to make her cup of tea. How could she have missed it? A square of white paper weighted with a small white disc. A flat spiral etched on the disc. Operculum. Little door. She picks it up. It is cool and smooth as marble.

Jack.

She smiles. She picks up the paper but there's only one thing written on it. His name. The other side is blank. An elusive man, she thinks, happy that he's made contact. He's simply letting her know he's the one who's returned the photograph. That's it, isn't it? He's telling her not to be afraid. But she has no need to be afraid of intruders now, and who else performs miracles around here, except Jack?

She puts the note back exactly where it had lain and replaces the operculum on top. She looks at it. Jack, she reads, and makes the connection. *Something poignant and beautiful and clean. Something that will be remembered for a little while.*

Suddenly, she has no doubt at all what he is telling her.

She grabs her phone that has been sitting in the recharger, turned on and waiting for his call since the night of the Winter Ball. She runs across the garden, hopping, tugging her boots on, red anorak flying out behind her, and soon she is flying too, up and over the sand-hills at a speed she wouldn't have believed possible. She tears along the ridge, scanning the waters for a sign, any sign at all.

'More chance of spotting him from up here,' she mutters.

What if I've got it wrong? What if I'm being really stupid?

She wants to call for helicopters. She wants them out there, circling, searching for him. Finding him. How can she ring the emergency number when all she has to go on is a feeling of dread and a piece of paper with his name written on it? That's why he's done it this way, she realises. To give himself time. By the time she's convinced them there is an emergency, that she isn't a madwoman . . .

You could be wrong, Cassie. You might be panicking about nothing.

Oh, yes, let me be wrong!

But she knows she isn't.

She is panting and hurting but she doesn't slacken her pace and his name leaves her lips over and over again as she exhales, half-breath, half-sob. Jack.

53

PINK FLOATS

A dark huddled shape on the rock platform. It isn't a pile of seaweed. It isn't a boulder.

Cassie is terrified now of what she might find. Unconsciously, she slows her pace. When she's close enough to see that he's soaked and shivering from head to foot, she stops. She hasn't made a sound but she sees a movement of his head, as if he's trying to lift it. She flings herself at him.

Hands. Fingers at his throat. Someone rolls him over. Someone shaking him. Shaking him? He opens an eye, sees her. Oh fuck. Wrath personified. He warms himself on the surge of her anger.

How do you address someone who's just tried to commit suicide? *How are you?* seems a tad redundant. *Better luck next time*, might cover it. She's in the grip of a strong compulsion to hit out, to slap and punch and yell, and restrains herself with difficulty.

'Jesus! Haven't I got enough problems, Jack?'

She's thinking, why is he still here? Perhaps the conditions were wrong and he's waiting for the right moment, the right current to take him away again? Maybe I'm an unwelcome interruption. Maybe there's no point stripping the wet jumper off him and wrapping him tightly in the quilted red anorak, bullying his arms into the sleeves, zipping him into it, pulling the hood close. No point at all in clasping him tightly in an attempt to stop his shivering with her own body. But she is satisfied when he begins to loosen and uncurl.

'Been for a swim?' she says, eventually.

He coughs, laughs weakly. 'Bloody water's too cold.'

'You going to try again?'

He looks at her wordlessly. Who can say?

'Nice note,' she says. From the corner of her eye, she thinks she sees him grin. How can he grin? She might have been holding that note when they brought his body in. The image doesn't bring a tear to her eye; she wants to strangle him.

As soon as he is able to stand, they move slowly away from the water. He has no choice but to allow her to support much of his weight. At the foot of the dunes, they rest and he tells her where he left his boots, some way down the beach.

'Don't sit down yet,' she warns him. 'Stay standing. Keep your feet moving up and down, or take little steps if you can.' She has no idea if this is the right thing for him to be doing but it sounds sensible and she feels less inclined to shriek when she's issuing orders.

She finds the boots, kneels irritably to wrestle his wet feet into them. There's a round hole in the heel of one of his grey socks. Beneath her fingers, his cold skin and a gritty layer of sand. His hand rests heavily on her shoulder. He lifts one foot obediently, then the other. He looks back. From this perspective, the island is only a cloud. Hard to imagine how it could have appeared otherwise, unless you very much wanted it to.

Ahead of him, the slope has never looked so long, nor so steep. He climbs like an old man, stopping often, but she can see the shivering has stopped.

'My heart feels like it's going to burst out of my chest,' he pants.

'You're alive then.'

She won't offer sympathy. She hasn't looked him in the eye once since she found him. She's waiting for a sign from him. She wants to know she isn't wasting her time.

They sit for a while.

He says, 'The Huon pine is capable of growing for more than three thousand years. It's unique to Tasmania.'

'Stop that,' she says sharply.

'That's where Dad's taken Simon.'

'I know.'

'Perhaps it's for the best.'

'Perhaps.'

He says, looking at the ocean, 'When you're out there, fishing for weeks on end, it's the colour you miss. It's all blue and grey and white, out there. People don't realise. You get to the point you'd give anything to see colours.'

She doesn't respond. He isn't sure if he's said the words aloud or only in his head. He clears his throat, tries again. 'Those pink floats really hit you on a dull day.'

'I can't save you,' she says, thinking, yes, we could all do with a pink float now and again. She gets to her feet, brushing sand from her clothes. 'You have to want to save yourself.'

He makes no comment.

Furious but hiding it, she holds out a hand and hauls him to his feet. 'It was a pretty half-arsed attempt, if you ask me.' Had a better shot at it than I did, she thinks.

He agrees, but not aloud. He believed that peace was the only aim and that, at the right time, the water would bring him absolution. All that forgiveness, lapping at his chest, splashing in his face, closing over his head as the rip gave out. Every stroke, and his clothes sodden and weighing him down, and the certainty, the rightness of it, yelling louder and louder, screaming inside his head, and the shame opening up inside him, shame gushing warm and deep, red as sea anemones, and yet . . .

And yet there it was. A single pinpoint of light, insistent as a star on a clear, frosty night, or a baby's cry, or a woman's voice, breathing his name over and over. And suddenly, every stroke was taking him further from the conviction that he was doing what had to be done. Somewhere between the fade-out of the rip and the tantalising prospect of his island, Jack became aware, for the first time in seven years, of an alternative destination. He didn't want to be cold and wet. He didn't want to be alone at night. Great timing, Jack. Now what? He was almost there, but he had turned around and begun the long haul back to shore, without any clear idea of anything anymore.

She's leading the way up the slope. If he falls too far behind, he'll get a mouthful of the sand flung out from her boots. She's muttering, breathing heavily, spitting out words sideways at him, throwing them back over her shoulder.

'You have to want nothing.' She's trying to explain, seriously, as though he might not understand. 'To do that. You have to want nothing with all your heart. Because that's what you'll get. Not heaven. Not hell. Not reunion with loved ones. Not peace. You get nothing. Is that it? Is that what you want?'

He doesn't answer.

What a pair we are, she thinks. And here am I, lecturing him when he's probably in shock. Hypothermic. This isn't the right time. But when will it be? How do you know if you have time, to say what you need to say?

He's busy catching his breath, watching where he puts his feet, trying to control the spasms of weakness in his arms and legs, trying to understand why a core of light inside him is persisting.

At the top they rest again. A few trails of mist still float above the marshes and the river. They look out over the pale gold of the reed beds, out across the flatlands to where black-faced sheep graze the smooth hills, and even farther out to the blue and ghostly peaks of two extinct volcanoes.

'Isn't it odd?' she says, carefully keeping her tone light, testing the air. 'Sometimes, those marshes are absolutely full of birds.

I've seen black swans and moorhens there. Cormorants, ibis and plovers. I've seen goshawks and grebes . . . and ducks of course. Lots of ducks. But look at it today. It's deserted. I can only see one duck.'

She waits.

He clears his throat. He can't look at her because suddenly, idiotically, he's happy, and he knows if he catches her eye, he's going to laugh out loud and frighten the life out of her. So he keeps his gaze on the marshes and does his best to explain.

'Shelduck,' he says.

Her head comes up at the change in his voice.

'The chestnut-breasted shelduck, also known as the mountain duck. Very fond of marshes.'

She glares at him, but she's not sure.

'Why leave me a note? If you wanted to kill yourself, why leave me a note?'

'It was for the photograph. I didn't want you to be afraid. I didn't want you to think he'd come back.'

'You mean it wasn't . . . you didn't . . .'

She isn't sure if she believes that.

She says, pouring scorn into the question 'You can see from here, what kind of duck it is?'

'I can see from here,' he assures her. 'And sometimes, you know, one duck is all it takes. One little duck.'

He slips his fingers into hers.

With the utter unpredictability of memory, she is given an image of herself. Three, four years old? Walking on a beach, not here. A gentle beach, a Sunday picnic beach, in mild sunshine. The child knows of the white froth of waves at the edge of her vision but she is concentrating. Knows too that the low cliffs rise up on her right-hand side and that the sea has left behind smooth silver-blue stretches of water, mirror flat on the wide landscape of sand. The breeze teases loose her white hair-ribbon so that one long strand whips this way and that around her head with its gathered blonde curls. She walks steadily, just beyond reach of the water, a small frown puckering her forehead. One after another, her white sandals come into view, decorated with tiny eyelet holes and fastened across the instep with a dainty strap. Her steps are carefully in time with the song she is singing under her breath. She is creating solitude, though she doesn't know this. Sea to the left, cliffs to the right, sand straight ahead and the soft crooning syllables falling from her lips over and over again. The strangeness of it is a cool wave encroaching. She makes her voice a little louder to strengthen her sense of herself in the presence of infinity. The sea has untethered her so that, young as she is, and still with an eye for an audience, she bumps along, white dress full and fluttering around her plump knees, performing her small soul's dance. She knows she is brave, and special. She imagines how they, the grown-ups, will say, 'Look at her', fondly, proudly, shaking their heads over these little oddities in their daughter. She has some sense of this, and feels something else uncurl inside her too. Something unnameable. Joy is too wide a word for this tiny, spiky feeling; glee is too small, yet there are touches of glee. Exultation is altogether too grand . . . and yet it is grand. She lifts her head briefly to take in the forever horizon of the sea. The things that define her are out of sight. Anything might happen. Anything at all.

ACKNOWLEDGEMENTS

I want to thank the people of beautiful Aireys Inlet in Victoria, who offered me their friendship, hospitality and employment. My thanks also to Ann Acton, a wonderful teacher; to Ali Watts at Penguin for giving me this opportunity to tell Cassie's story, and for sharing the fun once again; to Belinda Byrne, my editor, for her generous support, sound advice and extraordinary grace; to Nan McNab for her warm encouragement; to Carole Bloomer for general hilarity and insights on hand-line fishing; to Sue Wilson, who kept various drafts safe from bushfires; to Rob Wilcock for the stringybark trick; to Ed Featherston for his kindness; to Angus Brooksby for generosity in the nick of time; and last but most importantly, to my son, Ben Walt, without whom I would never have found the courage to begin.